THE
WHITEWASHED
TOMBS

Books by the author

The Inspector Darko Dawson Mysteries
Wife of the Gods
Children of the Street
Murder at Cape Three Points
Gold of Our Fathers
Death by His Grace

The Emma Djan Mysteries
The Missing American
Sleep Well, My Lady
Last Seen in Lapaz
The Whitewashed Tombs

Other Books
Death at the Voyager Hotel
Kamila

THE WHITEWASHED TOMBS

KWEI QUARTEY

Published by
Soho Press, Inc.
227 W 17th Street
New York, NY 10011

Library of Congress Cataloging-in-Publication Data

Names: Quartey, Kwei, author.
Title: The whitewashed tombs / Kwei Quartey.
Description: New York, NY : Soho Crime, 2024.
Series: Emma Djan mysteries ; 4
Identifiers: LCCN 2024007525

ISBN 978-1-64129-588-8
eISBN 978-1-64129-589-5

Subjects: LCSH: Women private investigators—Ghana—Fiction. | Sexual
minorities—Crimes against—Fiction. | Murder—Investigation—Fiction. |
LCGFT: Queer fiction. | Detective and mystery fiction. |
Thrillers (Fiction) | Novels.
Classification: LCC PS3617.U37 W48 2024 |
DDC 813'.6—dc23/eng/20240301
LC record available at https://lccn.loc.gov/2024007525

Interior design by Janine Agro, Soho Press, Inc.

10 9 8 7 6 5 4 3 2 1

To human rights activists everywhere

. . . Hypocrites! You are like whitewashed tombs. They look beautiful on the outside. But inside they are full of dead bones and all kinds of filth. —Matthew 23:27

AUTHOR'S NOTE

As I present *The Whitewashed Tombs* to you, dear reader, it's imperative to frame this narrative within the contemporary sociopolitical climate of Ghana, where love and identity are under threat. *The Whitewashed Tombs* isn't just a work of fiction; it's a deeply personal narrative in a way that none of my other novels have been, delving into the harrowing realities of LGBTQ+ murders and human rights violations in Ghana. At the time of writing this, Ghana's parliament has enacted a bill that marks a grave regression in equality and human rights. This legislation, now before the president for signature, criminalizes LGBTQ+ relationships, a stance that contradicts the foundational tenets of Ghana's constitution and the Universal Declaration of Human Rights. This story is, therefore, a reflection of my heritage and identity as a queer Ghanaian-American writer, my personal advocacy, and, indeed, quite some pain over the Human Sexual Rights and Ghanaian Family Values Bill.

The push for this bill is not solely a domestic affair. Right-wing factions from the United States have seeped into and inflamed the local discourse. This external meddling has bolstered the baseless assertion that homosexuality is an alien concept to African societies. Yet, as revealed in the comprehensive book, *Boy-Wives and Female Husbands* by Stephen O. Murray and Will Roscoe, the historical record provides irrefutable evidence of same-sex relationships in African cultures long before the advent of colonialism.

It is with a heavy heart that I note *The Whitewashed Tombs* explores themes of violence directed at LGBTQ+ individuals, a reflection of the current, stark realities that such draconian laws could further intensify. This novel, therefore, might be a trigger for some, and I urge readers to approach it with caution and mindfulness.

In weaving this murder mystery set in the heart of Ghana, where I grew up, my aim is to engross and intrigue and cast a light on the shadowed corners of society where injustice and prejudice lie in wait. This book is an invitation to peer beyond the surface, question and understand the complex layers of human rights, cultural heritage, and the enduring power of love and identity in the face of adversity. May it inspire empathy and a call to action to protect and celebrate diversity in all its forms.

Kwei Quartey, February 2024

CAST OF CHARACTERS

Amoah: police officer in Weija

Madam Abigail Nartey: Ghana's first lady

Abraham Quao: worked at Ego's with Marcelo

Addo and Adjei Adamah: macho brothers

Akosua Djan: Emma's mother

Beverly: Yemo Sowah's administrative assistant at Sowah Agency

Boateng, Detective Chief Inspector: CID homicide detective

Christopher (Chris) Cortland: Leader of ICF

Courage: Emma's boyfriend

Diana Cortland: Christopher's wife

Ebenezer: works at Ego's

Emma Djan: protagonist and private investigator at Sowah Agency

Festus: works at Ego's

Flora Ansah: wife of Peter Ansah

Florence: friend of Henrietta and Georgina

George Mason: works for ICF

Georgina: Henrietta's mother

Gertrude (Gerty) Cortland: Christopher's sister; helps run ICF

Gideon: tech guru at Sowah Agency

Godfrey Tetteh: Marcelo's father

Gus Seeza: talk show host

Henrietta Blay: famous Ghanaian singer who is openly trans

JB Timothy: pastor

Jeremiah Boseman: police inspector

Jojo Ayitey: private investigator at Sowah Agency

Julius Heman-Ackah: company lawyer for Sowah Agency

Kwabena Mamfe: works for ICF; Paloma's boyfriend

Marcelo Tetteh: famous LGBTQ+ rights activist

Maude: Dr. Mamattah's assistant

Newlove Mamattah: doctor famous for treating LGBTQ patients

Nii Lante II: chief of the township of La

Ofori: Jojo's friend

Commissioner Ohene: Director-General of CID

Paloma Smith-Hughes: Kwabena's girlfriend

Peter Ansah: Minister of Tourism, Arts, and Culture in Ghana

Richie: Henrietta's uncle and Georgina's brother

Rosa Jauregui: forensic pathologist

Ruby Mensah: Emma's undercover identity

Simon Thomas: president of the Africa West area of the Church of Jesus Christ of LDS

Walter Manu: private investigator at Sowah Agency

Yemo Sowah: founder and owner of the Sowah Agency

CHAPTER ONE

Accra

DIANA CORTLAND, IN ALL her luminous blondness, burst onstage in a sparkling scarlet gown. A white orb over a sea of black faces, she floated to the podium amid thunderous applause. With a capacity of seven hundred, Mövenpick Hotel's main ballroom was large enough to host the two-day event. It was an auspicious setting with twinkling chandeliers, recessed lighting, wood-paneled walls, and plush carpeting.

Diana looked around the auditorium and anointed the audience with her brilliant smile and perfect teeth. "Ladies and gentlemen!" she said into the mic, "I want to welcome you all to this gathering! Isn't this just such a beautiful hotel? Let's express our gratitude to our wonderful Mövenpick hosts!"

Diana led the audience in applause.

"I am Diana Cortland," she continued, "and I'm *so* excited to open the second annual International Congress of Families Conference. It's just wonderful to see every one of you here. I know how dedicated you all are to God and family, and I want you to give yourselves and each other a round of applause."

The room clapped enthusiastically.

"Now, before we go on," Diana said, lowering her voice, "let's bow our heads in prayer. Heavenly Father, we come before you in your name to seek your blessings and wisdom.

As we prepare to receive the message that you've placed within the heart of your servant, my husband, we ask that you anoint his words to reflect your truth and love. Lord, let this congregation be a tapestry of your grace, each thread woven with your compassion and mercy. May we be united in spirit, bonded by our faith, and strengthened by our fellowship. Open our ears to hear, our eyes to see, and our hearts to understand the depth of your teachings. In Jesus's name, we pray. Amen."

"Amen!" came the response. Diana looked up, her eyes twinkling and moist. "And now," she said, her voice winding up to a crescendo, "let's get to what we've all been waiting for!"

As she glided away to stage right, a startling fanfare of trumpets blasted out of the sound system, and smoke from a fog machine began to swirl up from stage left. The audience leaned forward with delicious anticipation. Like a phantom, a man in black appeared backlit against the smoke as a deep male voice boomed over the sound system, "Lllladies and gentlemen! *Please* give it up for the International Congress of Families CEO, our leader and man of God: Christopherrr Cort-land!"

The audience leaped to their feet, clapping and screaming, "Chris! Chris! Chris!"

He strutted to the front of the stage. "Good *eeeeevening*, Accraaaa!"

That educed a renewed, exuberant response from the attendees. Hooked up to a lavalier mic, Cortland paced across the stage, then pirouetted and strode back in the opposite direction with his arms raised triumphantly as a catchy Christian rock song played from the loudspeakers. Christopher repeatedly thanked the audience for their marvelous welcome while allowing the jubilation to continue before asking his admirers to take their seats. They settled down.

Illuminated by overhead stage lights, Christopher was quite a sight. His striking red hair had turned bright copper in the Ghanaian sun, creating a shocking contrast with his pale, translucent white skin.

Diana took her place onstage to her husband's right and settled in a sun-yellow armchair the hotel had provided at her request. The contrast with her scarlet gown, which offered a tantalizing glimpse of her demurely crossed legs, was mesmerizing. That she might distract the audience didn't bother Christopher. The crowd got the hang of it within minutes: Diana cued them when they should clap, cheer, or stand to applaud Christopher.

"God bless you all, and thank you, once again," he said. "I'm overjoyed to be back in your beautiful country, which I call my second home. *Ete sen?*"

Christopher's delivery of this Twi greeting, "How are you?" in a halfway-decent Ghanaian accent had the crowd rolling, but not in derision. His attempt to speak Ghana's most widely spoken indigenous language was a delightful gesture.

They followed Diana's lead as she threw her head back in good-natured laughter, giving a playful flap of her hand and winking conspiratorially at Christopher's animated fans.

Standing away from the podium, Christopher continued: "You know, Diana, my wife, and I are so inspired to see wonderful people like you who have chosen a godly life and turned away from sin by asking the Lord Jesus Christ to come into their hearts. When you do this, you become a new person altogether. Can I get an 'amen'?"

"*Amen!*"

"Jesus died on the cross for our sins," Christopher

continued. "Those who brought their Bibles, hold them up
so we can see." Christopher looked around the room with
approval as copies of the holy book popped up throughout
the audience. He walked to the lectern. "I want you to turn
to the book of Peter 2:24, where it says, 'He himself bore our
sins in his body on the tree, that we might die to sin and
live to righteousness. By his wounds'—listen carefully—'by his
wounds you have healed.' In other words, Jesus shed blood
for us.

"We learn this in Isaiah 53:5, where it tells us Jesus was
'pierced for our transgressions; he was crushed for our
iniquities; upon him was the chastisement that brought us
peace.'"

Christopher became still, as did Diana, who waited in
rapt attention. "All have sinned, my brothers and sisters," he
continued, "but God and his beloved son offer us a lifeline,
a way to return to the path of righteousness. Acts 4:12 reads,
'For there is salvation in no one else, for there is no other
name under heaven given among men by which we must be
saved.'"

Christopher left his well-worn Bible on the lectern and
paced a few steps while resting his gaze on randomly chosen
faces in the audience.

"Now, let's go to Genesis 18:19."

Christopher returned to the lectern amid the rustle of
pages from the Bible-wielding audience. "Genesis 18:19. Are
you all with me?"

Yes, they were.

"So, God says, 'For I have known him, to the end that
he may command his children and his household after
him, that they may keep the way of the Lord, to do justice
and judgment; to the end that the Lord may bring upon
Abraham that which he hath spoken of him.' Here, God

is describing two things in the context of Abraham and the people of Sodom: first, a man's role as the head of his household, and second, that within this family structure, a man should not only lead but instruct his family in the ways of our Lord *and* do what is righteous and just.

"But the Lord also has more to say about a man's relationship with women. In Matthew 19:5, he tells us, 'For this cause shall a man leave father and mother, and shall cleave to his wife: and they twain shall be one flesh.' You see, the Pharisees were trying to trick Jesus into saying something against the law of Moses. Their thinking about marriage was tarnished and confused by their earthly desires. And Jesus replied, 'Wait a minute, haven't you read the account of the creation, which has the very first instance of marriage?' Anything different from that would be wrong. So, when a man cleaves to his wife, meaning to join with his wife, and he does it in the sight of the Lord, this is the very best for us. My friends, make no mistake, holy matrimony prepares us to enter the kingdom of heaven, and in turn, the state of marriage must be entered with much prayer and solemnity. And yes, my brothers and sisters, God has blessed me and my wife, this lovely lady right here"—he turned to look at her—"with two beautiful children. Ladies and gentlemen, my right hand, my beautiful and faithful wife, Diana."

She rose and came to his side, kissing him on the cheek. This drove the audience into rapturous madness as they jumped up and down, screaming their approbation. Diana bowed to them and returned to her seat.

"Therefore, I say to you," Christopher continued, "that any attempt to destroy the holy union of a man and woman goes against the word of God. We must not allow this to happen." Christopher's jaw tightened, and his voice hardened. "Trying to make same-sex marriage equivalent to true marriage between a man and woman is not acceptable. It is a sin. No homosexual can enter the kingdom of God."

A rustle of unrest passed through the audience as a man close to the aisle stood up. He was in his late twenties and lanky, with hair styled in box braids. Shouting in a voice loud enough to hear without a microphone, he addressed Christopher. "Are gay people not human beings? Weren't we also created in God's image? Do you believe in human rights? Do you think God loves you any more than he loves me, a gay man?"

The crowd exploded into hisses and cries of outrage. Two audience members lunged at the rabble-rouser, chairs scattering as they attempted to bring him down. Somehow, he wriggled away and ran down the aisle toward the stage yelling at Christopher, "Do you want us to be murdered in the streets?"

Two security guards reached him and tackled him. But the miscreant had supporters who materialized from the crowd to jump the guards and pull them off. The response was swift. As enemies in the audience were identified, a brawl caught fire and spread quickly.

"Please, take your seats," Christopher said, attempting to raise his voice above the ruckus, but his attempt was futile. A hotel security officer bounded up the stage steps to his lectern and yelled, "Sir, we have to evacuate. It's not safe for you to be here."

"Yes, yes," he said nervously, turning to where Diana had been sitting. She was gone. "My wife—" he stammered.

"Sir," the guard said urgently. "*Please*, come with me now."

CHAPTER TWO

As the mayhem unfolded, Diana stood up, uncertain about what to do next. As if out of nowhere, a man appeared at her side and said, "Come with me, madam."

Dressed in dark slacks, a white shirt, and a *kente* tunic, he grabbed Diana by the arm and swept her into the wings so quickly she gasped and broke into a run to keep up with his long stride.

"Where . . ." she stammered. What was happening?

The man didn't answer. Still holding on to Diana, he zigzagged into the bowels of the wings until they reached a small, dim, and musty storage space, where he stopped to look down at her. "Are you okay?"

"I think so," she said, placing her hand over her heart. "My husband—"

"He'll be fine with the guards," the man said, "but I chose to bring you this way instead because it's safer—so you wouldn't get hurt."

"Oh, thank you. I'm sorry, I—"

"My name is Kwabena Mamfe. I'm one of the ICF-Ghana senior officers."

"Yes, I think Christopher—my husband—mentioned you. I'm Diana."

He smiled. "I know."

"Where were you?" she asked nervously. "You appeared out of the blue."

"I was backstage, madam—not too far from where you were sitting."

Had he been watching her? Their eyes met fleetingly. His were dark pools, deep and soft under a heavy brow. In his late twenties, he had coal-black skin that possessed a sheen in the gloom.

"Should we go back?" Diana said. "Not to the stage, of course—"

"The restaurant," Kwabena said. "That's where we'll hold the reception, but wait for me to check all is clear."

He disappeared around the corner. Diana shivered, even though it was sultry without air-conditioning.

Kwabena returned. "All is well. There's extra security at the restaurant too."

"Good," Diana said, relieved.

"I'll escort you there, madam. Come with me, please."

Kwabena switched on his flashlight and aimed the beam at the floor so Diana could see where she was treading. She fell into step with him as they rounded a corner to a flight of five steps.

"Be careful," Kwabena said. "It's a bit steep. I'll go first."

At the bottom, he turned to give her his hand as she held up her dress slightly to avoid tripping as she descended. His palm was large and calloused.

"Thank you," she said with a small laugh.

"Just I was worried about the high heels, madam."

She shrugged that off with a smile and a flick of the head. "You know—years of practice. The name was Kwabena, right?"

"Yes please," he said. "We can go now."

He led her to a door a few feet away and pushed it open. "Here we are."

They emerged into the Mövenpick Hotel's imposing lobby. The rich sienna ceramic floor reflected the gold-tinted illumination from the high ceiling. A large plant arrangement adorned the center of the floor. The conference hall had been cleared and closed up, but security was still urging stragglers out.

"There's your husband," Kwabena said, pointing.

Not far from the reception desk, a fretful Christopher was in urgent conversation with a white man in a gray suit and a Ghanaian speaking into a walkie-talkie.

"Christopher!" Diana called out as she and Kwabena approached the three men.

He spun around at the sound of her voice, his anxiety transforming to relief. He rushed up to embrace his wife. "My God. I was so worried. Are you okay?"

All Diana's composure was back as she smiled sweetly. "I'm fine, honey. Kwabena here was my hero. He got me quickly backstage to safety."

"Thank you," Christopher said to him. "We're both very grateful."

The other two men, manager and assistant respectively, came up to Diana to apologize profusely for the disturbance. What had transpired was a bad look for the hotel, and the worst aspect was that several people on the sidelines had filmed the whole catastrophe. By now, the video would already be spreading on social media.

"But the situation is secure now," the manager said, "and they're ready for your reception in the restaurant."

"I will escort them," Kwabena said reassuringly.

Diana walked between him and Christopher across the lobby. It wasn't so much her husband that made her feel safe as it was Kwabena. His height, broad shoulders, and easy stride were packed with power.

"Here it is," Kwabena said as they arrived at the One2One restaurant.

"Fabulouus," Diana murmured as they entered. She took in the espresso-colored floor and white marble pillars. Tan, low-profile seats were arranged four to a table, and high chairs lined the bar, where the mixologists had begun concocting drinks.

Christopher's sister, Gertrude, joined them from just inside the entrance, where she had been standing. "Did you guys survive the riot?"

Angular and bony, she always appeared awkward and uncomfortable.

"Yeah," Diana said. "Thanks to Kwabena." She smiled at him.

"Thank God I was at the back of the room," Gertrude said. "I got out fast."

"Smart," Christopher said. He admired his sister. Anyone could see that from the way he looked at her.

"Do you know who that man was?" Christopher asked Kwabena. "The guy who started all the trouble?"

"His name is Marcelo," Kwabena responded. "Don't mind him. He's a gay—always organizing marches and protests with his friend Abraham Quao, who works at that club for gays."

"In other words, a pair of troublemakers," Christopher said in an attempt at being wry. But no one else was laughing. Gertrude was seething. She planned these events meticulously for her brother, and she didn't like it when things were amiss in any way.

The Honorable Peter Ansah, Minister of Tourism, Arts, and Culture, arguably the most important guest at the reception, had witnessed the catastrophe in the conference hall. Ansah, who had met Christopher on the American's first visit to Accra the previous year, welcomed him.

"Good to see you again, Chris," he said, smiling broadly and shaking hands with his meaty paw.

"And you as well!" Christopher said.

Ansah was large in every sense—big head, big body, big voice, but his most prominent feature was his albinism, which gave him ginger hair, freckled, pastel-brown skin, and astonishing, translucent, sepia-colored eyes. After Christopher and Diana, Ansah was the palest person present.

"I want to sincerely apologize for the disturbance during your speech. This should never have happened. I've lodged a formal complaint with the management."

"That's okay, Peter. Things go wrong. So, who is this Marcelo guy?"

"Marcelo Tetteh. He's a very vocal LGBTQ activist; an example of the type of person we will silence with the passing of the anti-gay bill."

"How far along is it?"

"Winding its way through multiple parliament stages before it gets to the president's desk for assent."

"Do you have some time? Let's sit and chat awhile," Christopher said.

They found an empty table and Ansah beckoned to one of the waiters, who trotted over to take their orders. Ansah wanted red wine, Christopher white.

"First, Chris," Ansah said, "I want to express my deep gratitude for your donations to my campaign and all your help drawing up the bill."

"Of course, my friend. We're behind you all the way. Do you have any new thoughts on strategy?"

Ansah steepled his fingers. "You see, the more influence we exert on respected institutions, the more pressure there'll be to push the bill through. That means we need buy-in from the chiefs, church leaders, and the medical profession."

The waiter returned with the wine, poured it, and left.

"Good stuff," Christopher said with an approving sip.

"How would you influence Ghana's religious establishment?"

"From several angles," Ansah said. "For example, we have the traditional churches like the Anglican and Roman Catholic, and then the most powerful, the Charismatic Church, a good example being JB Timothy's International Church of Divine Deliverance. All of these stand against LGBTQ practices, but we need to keep in touch with them and encourage their vocal opposition with gifts and so on.

"I've also devised a way to link religious institutions with the local chiefs. Simon Thomas, the president of the Africa West area of the Church of Jesus Christ of LDS, is open to collaborating with the chiefs to alert their subjects to the gays infiltrating society and converting children to the homosexual lifestyle. I suggest the ICF and LDS sponsor a municipal project like a school or public toilet facilities. In return, we win solid support from the Council of Chiefs, who are highly respected. How do you like my idea?"

"We'd be thrilled to sponsor something like that."

"Good. I have Nii Lante II in mind. He's chief of the township of La, not too far from here. It has a high profile in the news."

"What about the medical establishment?" Christopher asked.

"That's the trickiest one. We want to empower doctors to refuse to treat these homosexuals with STIs resulting from their practices."

"That might be more difficult, no?" Christopher said, staring into his wine glass. "The Hippocratic Oath and all that?"

"Not only that. The Ghana Medical Association is set to elect a doctor called Newlove Mamattah as their president. He sides with the LGBTQ people. He's written a lot of articles sympathizing with so-called gay rights, not to mention being out there on radio and TV defending gays."

"I've never heard of him," Christopher said. "Is he gay?"

Ansah shook his head. "He is not, but he is a formidable opponent who is well respected. All members of the Ghana Medical Association will fall in line if he bans them from denying treatment to gay people."

"That means doctors, including Mamattah, could go to prison for disobeying the law, surely," Christopher said.

Ansah grunted and shook his head. "Imprisoning doctors would be a PR nightmare. Ministers will be besieged with angry constituents." Ansah shook his head. "The GMA wields too much power, and the organization is well lawyered-up. I'm a lawyer myself. I attended the same elite schools that Ghanaian doctors did, and we hang out in the same circles, attend the same parties, and so on. Trust me. No doctor in Ghana is going to prison for treating a gay person."

"Is there another physician we could . . . I mean, perhaps a doctor we could, um, incentivize to oppose him?"

"Short answer? No."

Christopher nodded. "Got it. We must choose our battles, and Mamattah isn't one of them."

CHAPTER THREE

Two weeks later

THE DAILY BRIEFING WAS always at eight o'clock. Yemo Sowah, founder and CEO of the eponymous private investigator agency, was never late. Manu, the most senior detective, was on time for a change, joining Emma and their two other colleagues, Jojo and Gideon.

Sowah, a trim man who wore his age well and enjoyed a good game of tennis, sat at the apex of the semicircle formed by the investigators' stations. Invariably well-dressed and seldom without a tie, he was as professorial as avuncular. The only anomaly in his turnout today was a loosely fitting sandal on his right foot, as he was suffering through one of his rare but painful gout attacks. Nevertheless, Sowah showed up to work, dismissing his employees' urges to rest at home.

"Morning, all," he said with a smile.

They chorused their reply. Manu was sporting a new salt-and-pepper goatee and noticeably putting on a bit of weight. His diametric opposite was Jojo, who was slight and smooth at thirty-three but could pass for twenty-three. The resident IT expert, Gideon, was a little older and more solidly built than Jojo. Added to the meetings now was Beverly, Sowah's faithful assistant for years. She took notes at every morning briefing, something Sowah hadn't established in the past but now realized was invaluable.

The whiteboard was at its usual central spot. Normally,

Sowah would stand beside it to scribble critical points on an ongoing case. Now, though, he was restricted to sitting down and propping up his aggrieved foot.

"After you'd all gone home yesterday, a Godfrey Tetteh came to see me as I was locking up for the day. Someone murdered his son, Marcelo, on Friday night, the nineteenth. A couple of boys spotted the body Saturday morning behind the old Trade Fair site dumped in an old, discarded minivan, of all things. The police report said Marcelo had been butchered to death, probably with a machete. Marcelo was a vocal gay activist, so it could have been a hate crime."

Silence fell over the group for a while.

Manu cleared his throat. "So Mr. Tetteh wants us to find who killed his son?"

"Right," Sowah said. "He's worried that because Marcelo was gay, the police might not give the case high priority."

He's probably right, Emma thought. Some murders mattered more than others. Gay people and sex workers were at the bottom of the list.

Manu grunted. "If it's a hate crime and it happened at night behind the Trade Fair with no witnesses, no suspects . . . that's a tough one, sir."

"I didn't say there were no suspects," Sowah said with a half-smile.

"Oh," Manu said sheepishly. "Sorry, sir."

"Mr. Tetteh has reason to believe there were people after his son's life," Sowah said. "Marcelo and the trans entertainer Henrietta Blay are the most high-profile activists in the country. Peter Ansah, Minister of Tourism, Arts, and Culture, has publicly denounced them and set them up as targets. On a TV program, he said, 'Everybody, remember what these two people look like. If you see them in the streets, you know what to do.'"

Emma nodded. "Yes, I saw that. A couple of weeks ago."

"That's wicked," Gideon said.

Emma stole a glance at Jojo. His head was down. She was the only person in the room who knew he was gay. "So," she said, "Mr. Tetteh thinks Minister Ansah hated Marcelo so much that he killed him or had him killed?"

"Hmm," Gideon said. "Just because Ansah made this threat doesn't mean he had something to do with the murder."

"Well," Sowah said, "Mr. Tetteh thinks there's a good reason Minister Ansah could be directly tied to it. The rumor is that Ansah himself is a closeted homosexual and that Marcelo knew that."

"Ah," Emma said. Now they were getting somewhere. "And so, Marcelo could have been blackmailing Ansah or threatening to expose him."

Sowah dabbed his forefinger at her. "Correct."

"Okay, I could see that," Manu agreed.

"That isn't all," Sowah continued. "There's an American man called Christopher Cortland, the CEO of the religious organization International Congress of Families—ICF for short. It dedicates itself to what they call traditional marriages between a man and a woman. According to them, anything outside of that is against God's will. They've had an ongoing crusade against LGBTQ rights in Africa and successfully helped create anti-gay laws in places like Uganda and Nigeria. Now they're working on Ghana.

"This month on the sixth, the ICF held a big event in Accra at the Mövenpick. Cortland was making his welcome speech when Marcelo confronted him from the audience. A fight broke out when Marcelo's supporters attacked the security officers."

Manu snorted. "Mr. Tetteh seriously believes this

American guy would even worry about someone like Marcelo?"

"Maybe not Cortland himself," Sowah said, "but someone in the organization.

"Sure, the American and his wife can always jet back to the US, but Marcelo remained a nuisance for the ICF branch in Accra. Don't underestimate the power of hatred toward LGBTQ people."

"Did Mr. Tetteh name anyone else of concern besides Mr. Cortland?" Emma asked.

Sowah shook his head. "He doesn't know of anyone there."

"Sir," Gideon piped up, "apart from the activism, did Marcelo work? Maybe he had some enemies at work?"

"He organized gay get-togethers at a nightclub called Ego's here in Accra," Sowah said, "which had some kind of payment arrangement with him. Mr. Tetteh told me Marcelo had a coworker who was his boyfriend. Mr. Tetteh went to Ego's asking after everyone yesterday afternoon, and it seems one of Marcelo's coworkers has disappeared. This man, Quao, never reported for work and couldn't be reached. Could he have had a role in Marcelo's death? Or is he also a victim of foul play, his body somewhere undiscovered? We don't know."

"Is Quao his first or last name, sir?" Emma asked.

"His first name is Abraham, if I recall. Obviously, we need to find him because he might know something. So, that's what we have to work with thus far."

"I must say, it isn't much," Manu muttered.

"I agree," Sowah conceded. "But there could be more pieces to the puzzle. That's for us to find out."

With that comment, Emma thought of her mother, Akosua, who loved jigsaw and word puzzles. Emma had once compared Akosua's passion to police work—moving pieces around to find if and how they fit together. But her mother's retort was, "Jigsaws are a lot safer." Not much disagreement there, but in truth, plodding desk work was *most* of what Emma and her colleagues did at the agency—background checks for employers, infidelity cases, missing persons, company theft and fraud, and so on. In fact, this Marcelo Tetteh case was the first promising investigation in months.

"Manu and Jojo, I want you on the case."

Manu looked uncomfortable. "I still have that big one, sir. If possible, can someone else take it?"

"I can do it," Emma said, jumping in quickly. She liked working with Jojo.

"All right, then," Sowah agreed, as Manu's face showed relief. Emma wondered if it was more his unease over homosexuality than how busy he was.

"Your first stop, I think," Sowah said, "should be the club Ego's. Talk to the manager or whoever is in charge and find out where this Abraham Quao has run off."

"Got it," Emma said. She was eager to get going.

CHAPTER FOUR

AFTER THE MORNING BRIEFING, Jojo approached Emma. "Come with me," he said in a low voice. "I need to get something to eat."

Emma smiled. "Sure, why not?"

Jojo's appetite was legendary. He didn't so much eat to live as live to eat.

Outside on the street, drivers blared their horns as if it would make any difference to the jammed traffic, and hardened pedestrians weaved between vehicles while crossing the street with nary a cough or splutter against the smoky exhaust from battered *tro-tros*.

Emma and Jojo rounded the corner of the building, where it was a little quieter.

"To be honest," he said to Emma, "the real reason I wanted you to come with me is that I have something to tell you."

"Ah, I see," Emma said. "What's up?"

They stopped momentarily as Jojo leaned against the wall to face Emma. "There's a problem," he said. "I knew Marcelo Tetteh well. In fact, I was dating him for a while."

"Oh," Emma said. This was unexpected.

"But I stopped," Jojo continued, "not because of a quarrel or anything like that, but because he was so out there, if you understand me. I thought it might jeopardize my work. You know, as private investigators, we have to be out of the public eye as much as possible."

Emma nodded. "Yes, you're right."

"The thing is, I'm worried my previous relationship with him will affect how I work on the case. I mean, I won't exactly be a neutral party—or what do you think?"

"Hm," Emma said. "I see what you mean."

"So, I was wondering if I have to back out."

"Oh, no," Emma said in heavy disappointment. "Really? But we work so well together."

"I know. I feel the same way, but what if, at some point, the boss discovers I was involved with Marcelo, and I didn't tell him? That would look bad. Are you getting me?"

"For sure."

"At the same time," Jojo said, his brow creasing, "I feel scared to tell the boss the reason I'm going off the case—that I was Marcelo's boyfriend and that I'm gay. I mean, I don't know how he feels about gays. What if he sacks me?"

Emma shook her head. "He won't do that."

"You sure? You don't know what it's like to be gay in Ghana."

"I don't know *exactly*," Emma conceded, "but I can imagine it's very tough. Still, the boss is a fair-minded person, and he values you a lot."

Jojo chewed his bottom lip. "What if I make up another excuse?"

Emma chuckled. "That won't work with Yemo; you know that. He's too smart for that, and you don't want to be caught in a lie."

"You're right. Boss Sowah is the father I hardly knew."

"Yes." Emma knew that Jojo's father had been mostly absent from Jojo's life.

"So that's why it feels funny telling Mr. Sowah I'm gay. Cuz I never told my dad."

"I understand." Emma met Jojo's gaze. "So what should we do? The final decision is yours, but you know I'll support you no matter what."

"I appreciate that." Jojo smiled, and his expression softened. "You're very good to me."

Emma playfully pinched his cheek. He had marvelous skin. "If you decide to tell the boss, I can go with you for moral support."

"Thanks." Jojo grinned. "I think I should face the music alone, though."

"I know you can do it. And you know what? I think Mr. Sowah will admire you even more for being so truthful with him."

"Do you really think he admires me?" Jojo said, sounding surprised.

"Absolutely," Emma said fiercely.

"That's a relief to hear."

"Did you doubt it?"

Jojo cocked his head. "Well, you know how it is. Sometimes I don't have enough confidence in myself."

Emma nodded. "I have that problem, too."

"Thanks for listening."

"You're welcome. I'm always here for you, Jojo. Anyway, who could resist that adorable face?"

Jojo laughed and put his arm around Emma's shoulders. "Come on, let's get back to work."

"No food?"

"Actually, I've had breakfast, so I'm good for a couple of hours."

"Until your tapeworm starts to cry," Emma joked, walking alongside him.

"Yeah," Jojo said with a giggle. "Jojo Junior. High maintenance."

SEVERAL TIMES THAT morning, Jojo wavered, his mind swinging back and forth like a pendulum as he wrestled with whether to come clean with Sowah. Nevertheless, at nine-thirty, Jojo tapped on Sowah's open door. "Sir?"

"Yes, Jojo," he said, looking up. "Come in."

"Please, may I shut the door?"

"Of course. Have a seat." Sowah put his papers aside. "What's up?"

Facing the boss, Jojo squirmed in his chair. "Please, I don't think I should be on the new case."

Sowah looked concerned. "Why, what's going on?"

"Um . . . it's because I knew Marcelo well."

"Really? In what context?"

"Well, he was my close friend."

"Aha," Sowah said, waiting for more. "As in . . ."

"I mean . . ." Jojo gulped and then rushed through the rest. "I mean romantically."

"Oh, okay, okay," Sowah said, nodding. "I get you now. You were dating him?"

Jojo was stunned by the boss's matter-of-fact tone. *No disapproval?* "Yes," Jojo said nervously. "For about six months, up until last Christmas. He was an activist and very good at what he did—that's why so many people hated him—but at the same time, I worried my association with him might draw attention to me, which wouldn't be good for my undercover work. So I decided to part ways."

"How did he receive that?"

"Well, he was angry. Said I betrayed him."

"Did you remain in touch after that?"

"It was one of those things where we both played it cool. Sometimes he texted me to say he missed me, or to check how I was doing."

"How did *you* feel about terminating the relationship?" Sowah asked.

Jojo chewed his inner cheek. "I felt some kind of way. It's like when you're doing a project and stop before it's done because you're frustrated with it. Unfinished business. You don't feel satisfied at all."

"I understand."

Jojo wiped his forehead, which had broken out in a sweat.

Sowah smiled. "You were afraid I would disapprove of you?"

Jojo was both anxious and sheepish. "Yes."

"I'm only concerned about the private lives of you and your colleagues if it adversely affects your work," Sowah said, unconsciously twirling the pen on his desk. "I'm grateful and proud you stopped seeing Marcelo to safeguard your job as a private investigator, and now you recognize a conflict of interest in this case."

"Yes, sir."

"I will team Emma up with Manu instead without divulging these details."

"Thank you. I appreciate that."

"Of course. Anything else?"

"No, no, that's it, sir. Thank you so much."

As Jojo rose to leave, Sowah said, "Oh, wait. I wanted to say one more thing."

As he sat down again, Jojo's stomach plunged. He felt there had to be a catch to the boss's positivity, a reprimand, a *but*.

"You know," Sowah began, "when I was a kid—long before you were even just a cluster of cells in your mother's womb"—Sowah chuckled—"it was normal for male friends to hold hands in the street, even if they were *hetero*sexual.

Sometimes, I would do that with my best high school *paddy*, but nowadays, we might be beaten up by civilians or the police. What has happened to Ghanaians? We've become vindictive and cruel."

Sowah momentarily closed his eyes, despondently resting his forehead on two fingertips. But he looked up again with a smile. "Don't mind me, Jojo. Just venting. Off you go."

Once Jojo had left the room, he leaned against the wall trembling as the tension in his body slowly dissipated.

CHAPTER FIVE

AFTER SPEAKING TO JOJO, Sowah called Emma and Manu in to let them know there was a change of plan.

"I've decided to switch the team," he announced. "The two of you haven't worked together on a major case before, and I think it's time."

"Sure," Emma said more sanguinely than she really felt about working with Manu.

"Okay, sir," Manu said, apparently abandoning his previous excuse for not taking on a new project.

"I think you can learn a lot from each other," Sowah observed. "Let's review our first steps. Top of the agenda is to contact Mr. Quao, who was allegedly Marcelo's boyfriend and worked or works at Ego's Club."

EGO'S IN OSU, the area of Accra with the most restaurants, bars, and clubs per capita, was on the corner of Sixth Lane and Justice Annie Jiagge Street, after Ghana's first female court of appeals judge. They had named the street but hadn't paved it, so it was dusty in the dry season and often muddy in the wet, which was fast approaching. A few patrons sat on the front terrace, sipping drinks and eating underneath a canopy with a serrated edge resembling a shark's teeth. Music was playing from somewhere, but it was generally quiet. Emma imagined that nighttime was when Ego's made most of its money.

She allowed Manu to take a slight lead as they walked up
to the bar, where a short, compact bartender was rinsing out
glasses.

"Good afternoon," Manu said. "We're looking for Abraham Quao. I understand he works here?"

"I don't know much about that," the man replied. "You
can go upstairs and talk to the manager."

Emma trailed Manu up a split-level flight of steps to a cav-
ernous, open space that smelled of bleach and had another,
smaller bar. A lanky man with salt-and-pepper dreads and a
green tracksuit was instructing two men on ladders as they
hitched up a large banner that read: *Smooch Night @ Ego's.*

"Raise it a little on your side, Ebenezer," he said to one of
them before turning to Emma and Manu. "Can I help you?"

"Good afternoon," Manu said. "My name is Mender, and
this is Ruby."

Mender? That's an interesting new alias, Emma thought. She
rather liked it. Manu chose a different one for each undercover assignment, while she stuck to "Ruby."

"Okay," the man said. "I'm Festus."

"We are looking for one Abraham Quao," Manu said as
they shook hands.

"And you are who?" Festus asked evenly.

"I'm his uncle," Manu said, then gestured at Emma.
"She's his cousin."

"I see." Festus nodded and gestured toward an office to
the side. Emma and Manu followed him and sat down on
a couple of chairs while Festus perched sideways on a desk
with a laptop. "What brings you here looking for him?"

"One of his aunts—my dear sister—has just died in the
Eastern Region," Manu said. "To be honest, Abraham
knows little or nothing about the aunt, but the family wants
me to inform him about the funeral in a couple of months."

"Ah, okay," Festus said, before scrutinizing Emma. "And you, young lady? Did you know Abraham? Is that why you're also here?"

"I've never met him, no," Emma said. "Uncle Mender doesn't know Accra well, so I've been taking him to the places he needs to go. The last we heard, Abraham was working at Ego's."

Festus nodded. "That's true, but he left."

"Do you know where he went, please?" Emma asked. When she saw Festus hesitate, she added, "If it was something else besides a funeral, we wouldn't be bothered. But this is important."

Festus took a breath. "You have to keep it as confidential as possible."

"You have our word," Manu said.

"He went to his hometown, Weija," Festus said, "and that's all I know right now."

"Why is it confidential, if I may ask?" Manu asked.

Festus cleared his throat in visible discomfort. "Because he thought—this is what he told me—he thought someone was after his life."

This is starting to get interesting. "Did he explain what he meant by that?" Emma asked.

"No," Festus responded.

She didn't believe him. "You don't need to worry that you'll give something away," she said quickly. "We know about him and his boyfriend Marcelo, who is now dead."

"Oh?" Festus was surprised. "How did you know all this?"

"Long story," Manu said. That always worked; no one ever genuinely wanted to hear a long story. "So, did something happen between the two of them—Marcelo and Quao?"

"If it did," Festus said, "then I never saw it. All I know is that he told me he was scared someone was going to kill him the way they did to Marcelo. I was the one who advised him to go to Weija for a while."

"Ah, okay," Manu said, nodding. "And what day was that?"

"Saturday, same day they found Marcelo's body. He was crying and shaking—very scared."

"I think it was good advice to seek safety," Emma said with approval.

Festus's shoulders lifted a centimeter as he turned a palm upward. "What else could I do? I was afraid for him."

"Have you heard from him at all?" Emma asked.

Festus shook his head. "Nothing. I've texted him but I think he's changed his SIM card."

"Do you have a recent pic of Abraham?" Manu said. "I haven't seen him since he was a kid."

"Yeah," Festus said, pulling his phone from his back pocket to scroll through his photos. "Here's one with Abraham, who is on the right."

Abraham was of medium height, shorter than Marcelo, with closely cropped hair and a luxuriant beard, while Marcelo's facial hair wasn't as lush.

"Wow," Manu said, smiling. "Abraham is a big man now. Thank you for showing that and for the info you gave. We'll try to find him in Weija."

Emma and Manu descended to the ground floor and into the street.

"I suppose we'll be going to Weija, then," Emma said. They walked toward Oxford Street, where it was easier to get a taxi or Uber.

"We'll ask the boss if we can take the office car," Manu said, nodding. He seemed lost in thought for a moment. "Wow," he muttered.

"What's up?" Emma asked.

"Seeing that pic of Quao and Marcelo," Manu said. "I was expecting something else."

"How so?"

"Well, both of them are so manly—you know, thick beard and all. I thought they would be looking like a woman, you know, *Kojo Besia*. I just wonder how they . . . I mean, who is the woman and who is the man?"

Emma shot him a look. "Is that a serious question?"

"But have they tried a woman before?" Manu continued, obliviously. "I mean, maybe they'll find out it's nicer."

"Have you tried a man?" Emma asked dryly.

Manu looked stricken at the thought, but before he could respond, someone behind them called out to get their attention. It took Emma a few moments to recognize that the man running up to them was one of the two people hanging the banner at Ego's.

"Good afternoon," he said. "Please, I heard you asking Festus about Marcelo Tetteh and Abraham Quao."

"Yes?" Manu said.

"I didn't want to say anything there, but I would like to help you."

"Good!" Emma said eagerly. "Thanks so much. How can you help?"

"You need to talk to Henrietta Blay," he said. "She knows a lot and she knew Marcelo and Quao too. She's my friend."

"Do you mean the singer?" Emma asked in some surprise.

"Yes."

Manu looked lost, so Emma explained. "It's Henrietta Blay who performs that song everyone is playing now, 'Mi Fie.'"

"Okay." He was blank. "And?"

"I'll explain later," Emma said, not wanting to waste the man's time. "What's your name, please?"

"I'm Ebenezer," he said.

"Ebenezer, isn't it tough to get an appointment with Henrietta? She's now a big star in Ghana, so . . ."

"I have her number. If you text her and say you're a friend of Ebenezer's, she will answer."

"Oh, nice!" Emma said. "We're grateful to you."

Ebenezer shared Henrietta's contact information with Emma and Manu, and then with a single "bye," he turned and hurried back to work.

"This is good, Manu," Emma said.

"Who is this Henrietta Blay?"

"She's one of Ghana's only openly trans women, if not the only," Emma said as they resumed their walk. "Just google her and you'll find her, but anyway, she's also a singer. In her hit song, she tells everyone that gay people are all around us—at work, home, in the family, your plumber, tailor, barber, doctor, teacher, whoever."

"Okay, that may be true," Manu said, "but just one thing—any *Kojo Besia* better stay away from me and not try to convert me."

"Don't flatter yourself," Emma said. "Let's start out to Weija, Manu. We still have time."

EMMA DIDN'T DRIVE, so it was Manu at the wheel. As they left the densest parts of Accra behind, she called Dr. Rosa Jauregui, the brilliant, Cuban forensic pathologist she had collaborated with on previous cases. She answered on Emma's second attempt.

"My dear Emma," she said, sounding delighted, "it's been too long!"

After pleasantries, Emma got down to business. "Doctor, I'm here with my colleague, Mr. Manu. Do you mind if we talk on speaker?"

"Not at all."

"Thank you. Do you know anything about a case of a gay man murdered on Friday night? His body was found on Saturday morning."

"Marcelo Tetteh?"

Emma's heart soared. "Yes!"

"I did his case yesterday. What's going on?"

"His father has asked us to investigate."

"Well, I can tell you it was a brutal attack with multiple deep tissue wounds inflicted by a machete or ax—more likely a machete," Jauregui said. "He would have died from massive blood loss. No evidence for strangulation or anything like that."

"I see," Emma said. "Mr. Tetteh said as much, but I wanted to confirm it with you."

"But there's one interesting aspect," Jauregui said. "From the injuries, I suspect there were two assailants, not one."

"Really?"

"Yes, the two distinct patterns suggest that they struck from opposite sides of Marcelo's body and one culprit was stronger than the other."

"Wow," Emma said, looking at Manu.

"Hi, Doctor," he called out. "Thank you very much for letting us know."

"Where are you at the moment?" Jauregui asked.

"En route to Weija," Emma said. "We're looking for Marcelo's boyfriend as a person of interest."

"I see. Strong possibility?"

"It's too early to say, but I'll keep you updated."

They said goodbye to Jauregui and Emma hung up.

"So," she said, "if the doctor is right, we have *two* suspects instead of one. Does that make it harder or easier?"

"Harder," Manu said. "We have to work double."

"On the other hand," Emma said, "if we catch one, he could tell us who the other one is, which cuts the work in half."

Manu scowled at her. "*What?* That makes no sense."

AS THEY APPROACHED the town of Weija, Emma frowned. "What's going on up there?"

"Where?" Manu asked, squinting.

"Up ahead. There's a crowd at the roadside, and traffic is backed up."

Like the vehicles ahead of them, Emma and Manu's car had come to a stop.

"Probably an accident," Manu suggested.

"I'll find out," Emma said, opening her door.

As she got closer to the crowd, she heard their animated discussions and saw a portion of the road was flooded. Some vehicles were cautiously negotiating the depths and at least one had gotten stuck.

"What's happening?" Emma asked a young woman soaked to her waist.

"Weija is flooded—see?" She pointed.

The roadway was at a higher elevation than the town, and Emma didn't appreciate the scope of the flood until she had pushed her way to the front of the gathering. She gasped at the sight of water engulfing one-story houses and small vehicles like a swollen river. People were half wading, half swimming to reach higher ground or taller buildings.

"*Awurade!*" Emma exclaimed. "What's happened?"

A man next to her began to explain in rapid Twi. "They opened the Weija Dam to release some of the water. Every year they do this stupid thing."

"But this is the worst it has ever been," a woman next to him said bitterly. "This is too much. Some people have even died."

"When did the flood start?" Emma asked.

"This morning," the man said. "We thought maybe it wouldn't be as bad as the previous years, so some of us stayed in our houses, only to find we were trapped."

"How did you get here?" Emma asked. "Did you swim?"

"*Ei,* I can't swim, o!" he said, laughing. "No, the army came with rescue boats. See? Over there."

"Yes, I see them now."

There were three man-powered rescue boats various distances away. Ten or so rescued civilians huddled in the closest one while soldiers on each side paddled. For extra power, a chest-deep young man tugged the boat with a long rope tied to the bow.

The water was an opaque grayish-green color. At intervals, piles of trash went floating by, and Emma shuddered to think what else could be in the water. At each house, the soldiers shouted in Twi, "Is anyone there?"

Spotting a frail, bent elderly woman in the rising water, a soldier yelled out to the paddlers, "Go left, left, *left!* There's an old lady there!"

They changed the boat's direction, but the woman lost her balance, fell, and was instantly submerged.

"Oh, *no!*" Emma said.

One of the soldiers dropped his paddle and leaped out of the boat to swim the distance to the drowning woman. In seconds, she was in his arms at chest level, which was just enough to keep her out of the water. Against the current, the soldier buoyed her up as the rescue boat arrived.

"Take her," he said, lifting the woman up to another soldier, who grabbed her and laid her down gingerly on the floor of the boat.

Emma could see the woman was stirring, albeit feebly. *Thank God.*

A long column of people lined the stairs zigzagging up the side of a three-story building. They were safely above the water level, but they were also stranded, and for how long?

The soldiers called out to them, asking if they wanted to be rescued. A man waved frantically at them and pointed to a small boy he was carrying in the crook of his elbow.

A nimble soldier jumped in and made his way to the staircase as the man brought the boy down as close as possible to the water's surface and handed him over to the soldier.

"Were you also rescued from your home?" Emma asked a sharp-featured woman beside her.

The woman nodded. "By God's grace, I'm alive."

Lowering his voice, Manu said to Emma, "We should start returning to Accra. I think the flood will soon reach the road, and cars will be swept away."

"You're right," Emma agreed. "Let's go back."

She was turning away when she caught sight of something bulky bobbing and swirling in the current of the rising waters. It could have been a mound of *bola*, but was it?

"What's that floating in the water?" Emma said.

"Where?"

Emma pointed.

"Trash," Manu said.

"Are you sure? Don't you think it looks like a body?"

"What? No."

Emma moved closer to the water level and Manu yelled at her not to approach the swell.

It's not trash. Emma was certain it was a dead body, and in an intuitive flash, she knew it might well be Abraham Quao.

As she slid into the murky water, a soldier in a rescue boat saw her and went berserk, screaming, "What are you doing? Stupid woman! *Stop!*"

But Emma was already up to her neck, and the strange,

floating object was quickly riding away from her with the current. Just at the submerging point, Emma became buoyant as she began the swim strokes she knew well. With the direction of the water's flow in her favor, she gained on the object and grasped it, pulling it up and out. She gasped and choked. What she had clutched was the body of a man dressed in a T-shirt and dark pants. The head was bloated and gray. The eyes protruded grotesquely. Deep slashes were cut into its neck, throat, and torso.

For a moment, she wanted to release the body, but she clung on and dragged it through an open gate to a house with shallow steps and up to the porch yet untouched by the flood. With her footing on a step, she pulled the spongy, water-bloated body up to the porch and let it go in revulsion. She backed up, soaked with foul water, her chest heaving as she eyed the body.

A rescue boat approached half full of people. A soldier shouted, "What's happening?"

"Dead body," Emma said. "Floating. So I went to get it."

"Why?" the soldier barked.

"You want to just let it continue down the river?" Emma responded incredulously. *What's wrong with these people?*

The soldier had no answer.

"Can we get an empty boat for the body, please?" Emma called.

"Yeah, okay. I'll try to get one as soon as possible.

That took far longer than Emma would have preferred, but at last, two soldiers arrived in a small, motor-powered boat to remove the dead man from the canoe and carry it to the roadside. Gasps broke out from the crowd as people shifted their gaze away from the flood to the sodden corpse, so distended that it seemed to be bursting out of itself.

Two policeman materialized, one yelling at the looky-loos

to back up. The other, whose badge read "Amoah," turned to Emma, who was close by resting her hands on her knees as she tried to catch her breath. "Do you know how foolish you've been?" he snapped. "You could have drowned."

Emma didn't have the energy to reply. Amoah circled the reeking body, took a few photographs, and then used a stick to reposition the body so that its balloon face turned to the crowd. Several people spun away in revulsion and left. Someone retched.

Officer Amoah stopped and peered at an indentation over the dead man's pocket. Gingerly, he brought his fingers and thumb together like forceps and eased out a wallet. He flipped it open, examined one of the cards inside, and then held it up to the crowd.

"Anybody here know this man? His identification card says Abraham Quao."

CHAPTER SIX

EMMA LET OUT A scream and lunged toward the dead man, but Amoah stopped her. "What's wrong with you?" he bellowed

"He's my cousin!" Emma wailed. "Oh, Abraham, *Abraham!*"

The policeman narrowed his eyes at her. "How did you know it was him?"

"I didn't, I didn't!" Emma said, weeping. "I just had a bad feeling."

Manu appeared, resting a hand on her shoulder and playing it just right. "Ruby, Ruby, calm down, okay?"

"You know this woman?" Amoah asked. "Who are you?"

"She's my daughter," Manu said. "My name is Mender, Abraham's uncle. We've been looking for him since he went missing on Saturday. We heard he had come to Weija, so that's why we came."

The officer's features softened. "Oh, very sorry, sir."

"Thank you, sir. I'll take her. Come along, Ruby."

Amoah released her to Manu, who put his arm around her shoulders in a comforting manner. Manu shot a horrified look at the dead man, shook his head in feigned anguish and said, "*Awurade*, how could this have happened?"

Emma wondered if this much putrefaction could have occurred in the relatively short time Quao's dead body had been submersed. That was for an expert to assess, but Emma's impression was that Quao must have been dead for a while before the onset of the flood this morning. By then, the gases of putrefaction would have been sufficient to cause the body to float in water. Otherwise, it would have remained submerged for some period.

"How will you remove the body, Officer Amoah?" Manu asked.

"I'm calling the nearby police stations to see if they have a vehicle," he replied, his phone to his ear. After having spoken to someone, he shook his head. "Lapaz doesn't have one to spare; let me try Kasoa."

Kasoa police said they could send a pickup truck, but it would take time. That meant the dead body would have to wait and people would continue to stare, take pictures, and record videos. Emma eschewed posting gruesome images on the internet, but it was going to happen, especially on the notorious Nairaland.com.

Emma turned to Amoah. "Please, for dignity's sake, can we get something to cover my cousin's body?"

"You are right." Amoah looked around and spotted a man in a reflective yellow jacket, probably a construction or utility worker, and called out to him. The man pointed to himself with a "do-you-mean-me?" gesture.

"Yes, you," Amoah said gruffly.

The worker trotted over. "Yes, sir?"

"Find a tarp or something to cover him up. Can you do that?"

"Yes please."

"Okay, then go. Hurry up."

The man disappeared to return about five minutes later with a wet, medium-sized piece of canvas full of holes. It would have to do. Emma was relieved as the officer closer to the body draped the canvas over it. Quao's legs were still exposed, but the head and torso, the most important, were now shielded.

"Where will you take the body when you're able to transport it?" Manu asked Amoah.

He hesitated. "Well, I'm not sure yet."

"Please, Officer Amoah," Emma said immediately, "send him to the Accra Police Mortuary. I trust them."

"I can try." He cleared his throat. "That will take some additional effort, you understand."

Manu fished in his wallet and gave Amoah a ten-cedi bill. "Thank you, Officer."

"God bless you," he responded, smiling. In Ghana, one tipped the police for any favor, large or small.

"I DON'T THINK you should have jumped in to go after the body," Manu said sullenly to Emma as they got back into the car. "We could have waited for it to wash up somewhere and then retrieved it."

Emma looked at him with one eyebrow cocked. "Somewhere like where? We might have lost Abraham forever had we not intervened. This way we can be sure the body gets to the right place."

Manu grunted in reluctant agreement. "I must say you are a powerful swimmer," he commented. "Who taught you?"

"My dad. We went swimming in Lake Bosumtwe."

"What!" Manu exclaimed. "Weren't you scared?"

"At first, yes, but I got used to it."

"I've never heard of a father teaching his daughter to swim."

"My dad was special in every way. I've always wanted to be like him." Emma's voice caught slightly.

Manu nodded in approval. "From the way you've described him, I'm not surprised. Come on, let's get going. I'll drop you home."

JUST AS MANU was about to drop Emma off, she slapped her forehead and said, "We've committed an embarrassing blunder."

"What?" said Manu.

"We haven't visited Marcelo's crime scene at the Trade Fair site. There may have been clues left behind."

"Clues?" Manu frowned. "I'm sure the police have already collected everything."

Emma looked at him askance. "Are you talking about the same Ghana Police Service I know? Seriously, Papa Manu? And what are we going to tell the boss when he asks us if we found anything at the crime scene?"

Manu groaned. "Emma, you're killing me. We can go tomorrow."

"We have other stuff on the agenda tomorrow. Let's finish this up today. I'll clean up and change clothes quick."

"Traffic is really bad right now," Manu said desperately.

"Traffic is always bad. Come on, you always do the right thing, that's why I admire you so much."

Manu's mouth dropped open at the audacity of this flattery while Emma tried to keep a straight face. She failed and her expression crumpled into mirth. Manu, in spite of himself, began to laugh as well. "Okay," he said, shaking his head in resignation. He had lost the debate. "But you owe me one *fufu* meal."

"Of course!" Emma said, grinning. "Any time. I'll even pound the *fufu* myself."

"Oh, yah. I'm sure you will."

MANU'S PREDICTIONS WERE confirmed: the traffic was excruciating, and the trip from Emma's home in Madina to the Trade Fair site was no short distance. In one way, that was good because it gave Emma a chance to call Dr. Jauregui.

"It's bad news, Doctor," Emma said. "The person of interest I described, Abraham Quao, is dead."

"*Dios mío,*" Jauregui muttered. "I'm sorry to hear that."

"Please, I wanted to ask you if you could do the autopsy," Emma said, "in case there are similarities to Marcelo's findings. The two murders might be connected."

"Yes, of course. Do you know the ETA of the body?"

"By this evening, if luck is on our side."

"Very well. I'll put Mr. Quao on the schedule for tomorrow."

Emma's next call was to Detective Chief Inspector Boateng, their most important contact and ally in the police force. The agency and the sometimes-grumpy Boateng had a fair-trade agreement between them: if both parties were on the same case, each gave to the other as much information as possible. There was no doubt that Boateng was worth more than his weight in Ghana gold, because he was privy to police matters and unafraid of sharing them with Sowah. Boateng, smarter than many, had long understood that it wasn't a zero-sum game of "police versus private investigators." Each could thrive with the other's help.

"How are you, DCI?" Emma asked. "It's been a while."

"I'm good, and you? What can I do for you?"

"Do you know about this case—a man called Marcelo Tetteh murdered in the Trade Fair area this past Friday night?"

"I heard something about it," Boateng said, "but I don't know the details. My colleague has the case. Why—you have a client asking about it?"

"Yes, his dad came to the boss."

"Ah, okay. What do you need to know?"

"We want to visit the crime scene but we don't know the exact location—all we've heard is 'behind the Trade Fair site,' but that's a large area. Do you know it?"

"Not really, but I can ask my guy if he can enlighten us. Do you need photos too?"

"Oh, *yes!*" Emma said excitedly. "That would be so great if you could get that for us."

"I'll work on it and get back to you. Give me at least an hour."

"No problem. Thanks so much. You're the best."

Boateng grunted and muttered a half-hearted "thanks." Compliments slid off him like rain on an oilskin. Emma grinned. *Classic DCI Boateng.* She wouldn't have it any other way.

Courtesy of the long drive, Emma and Manu were still en route when they heard back from Boateng.

"I talked to my man on the case," he told Emma. "I'll send you the GPS coordinates and also the crime scene photos."

"You are a godsend! I owe you a *fufu* meal."

Which makes two, Emma thought.

Within a few minutes, Boateng had sent the coordinates via the GhanaPostGPS app, which would guide them to the precise location. In gruesome detail, the police photos of the crime scene showed Marcelo's blood-drenched body lying prone in an abandoned minivan with his head and limbs angled in the bizarre, almost impossible anatomical positions only death could create. Marcelo's blood had drenched the floor of the vehicle. *Why was he dumped in a minivan, and by whom?*

Perhaps Boateng had had access to only some of the

available photos, but if this was all the detectives had taken, they were incomplete in that they didn't include the minivan's surroundings, which were almost certainly part of an extended crime scene.

"Bad?" Manu said, taking his eyes off the road for a moment to glance at her.

"Yes," she said. "Very. It's a slaughter."

FOR THE FINAL half mile, Emma used the app to direct Manu. They had exited the main highway and the sound of traffic had diminished noticeably. For the few minutes they were on a paved road, trees and tangled foliage obscured the view of the Trade Fair.

"Soon as you get to Zenith College, take a left," Emma said.

The turnoff was a dirt road with overgrown brush on either side.

"Is this the rear exit to the Trade Fair?" Manu asked in some surprise.

"I believe so," Emma said uncertainly, but the only sign of security was a leaning, flimsy sign that had faded so badly the words KEEP OUT were all but invisible.

The road was rutted and potholed, forcing Manu to slow down. The entire sprawling area known as Trade Fair was an odd mix of built-up commercial areas; residential buildings, many incomplete; and untended bushes in large patches so dense they resembled mini-forests.

"If they had any sense," Emma muttered, "they'd make this a park."

Instead, people were using it as a dumping ground for their discarded junk.

"Slow down," she said, consulting the map. "We're here. Oh—there. See the minivan on the left?"

"Yes," Manu said, as he pulled the car over, "but there's also one on the other side of the road."

"You're right," Emma said, as she spotted the battered skeletal remains of another old minivan engulfed in the bushes.

"I'll check that one," Manu said. "You take the other."

Picking her way through the bosky terrain, Emma approached the closer minivan, which was submerged in weeds like a sinking ship. She peered into the interior through one of the windows. No seats meant that they had probably been pilfered. The steering wheel and most of the dash were also gone. Emma couldn't open the door on the driver's side, so she went around to the other, where the absence of any door at all enabled a better view of the van's interior.

Now she could better see the dried blood on the vehicle's floor intermingled with rust. Poignantly, the iron content of both substances rendered them similar in color, although the blood had a deeper tint.

Training her flashlight on the walls of the vehicle, Emma now made out blood splatter, which the casual eye might have missed. She discerned a partial handprint on the farther side, and just to her left, another curving trail around the doorjamb. It could have belonged to the assailant or Marcelo himself. The vehicle was in no shape to have transported Marcelo from some other location, but that didn't mean he hadn't been killed elsewhere, moved to this location, and dumped. Why the minivan? Emma had no answer to that.

"Manu!" she called out.

He hurried over and she shared what she had seen. Manu nodded and then shuddered. He had always been strongly hemophobic.

Emma spotted something else and craned her neck forward. "What's that?"

"What? Where?" Manu asked, attempting to follow her gaze.

"In the corner."

Before Manu could respond, Emma climbed into the van and stooped her way to the mystery object in the far rear corner: five or six gray, heavily bloodstained pebbles stacked like a pyramid.

Manu leaned forward to get a better view without clambering in.

"Stones?"

"Yes," Emma said, "but smooth, like what you would find on the beach or a riverbank."

"To be honest," Manu said, "it looks like a juju object."

"Ahh," Emma said. "You could be right." She took photos from several angles. "Is there something in the car I can use to collect them?"

"Awurade, just leave the thing alone."

"But what if it has something to do with the murder?" Emma objected.

"I'm sure whatever that is has been there long before that. I'm just saying, don't mess around with juju stuff."

"Papa Manu," Emma said with some irritation. "We're not leaving here without these pebbles."

"Okay," Manu said heavily. "I'll be back." He scuttled away and returned with his police notebook.

"Brilliant idea," Emma said.

Manu ripped out several blank pages from the notebook and Emma used a sheet to pick up each pebble without letting them make contact with her bare hands. "I'll take this to Dr. J. Maybe she can have them checked for DNA."

"Good luck," Manu said sourly. Their general past

experience with the police forensics lab had been unsatisfactory. "Still, it's worth a try."

"Yes," Emma said, backing out. She took more pictures of the van and its surroundings in case she would need to refer to them at some point. In vain, she walked around looking for bloodstains on the ground.

"Are you done?" Manu said, looking at his watch. The sun was beginning its descent to the horizon.

Emma smiled at him. "Yes, I think so. I know you want to get home. Let's go."

In the car, Emma said, "Assuming Marcelo's body wasn't transported here, why do you think he was here in the first place? Someone must have lured him here on a pretext."

"Saying what?" Manu asked. "Let's go to have sex in the Trade Fair forest?"

"Actually . . ." Emma said reflectively, "that's not as unlikely as we might think. You know, sometimes people have nowhere private to go."

Manu grunted. "I suppose you are right. I've forgotten how tricky it was sometimes to find a place when I was at the university. Wait till your dorm roommate is away and then sneak a girl in."

Emma snapped her fingers. "University."

"You say?"

They had reached the junction with the main road. "There it is, right in front of us." Emma pointed to Zenith University's blue-and-white entrance. "What if the killer is a student and he invited Marcelo to his dorm room?"

"So you mean," Manu said, "when Marcelo arrived, the killer said, 'Let's go to the bush?'"

"Right," Emma said, nodding slowly as she tried to piece a scenario together. "Oh, wait, wait! What about this? The killer meets Marcelo somewhere in town and tells him, 'I'm a student at Zenith, why not come chill in my dorm room for a while?' So they take a taxi to the front of the Trade Fair and the killer says it's easier to take a shortcut through the forest to Zenith. Marcelo says okay, and follows the guy, and they end up on the dirt road. There is where the killer attacks. Maybe he has an accomplice because Dr. J thinks there might have been a second attacker. When they get to the spot with the old minivans, the accomplice emerges from the shadows with not one, but *two* machetes, and together they murder Marcelo."

Manu nodded. "Could be. Only thing, if someone told me to accompany them alone through a forest, I would be very suspicious."

"True," Emma conceded. "Okay, drop me off here and you can go on to your family."

"Why?" Manu asked, slowing down. "What is it now?"

"Someone at the college might have seen or heard something that night. Maybe even the guards who patrol the premises—well, I presume they have guards. Anyway, I want to ask people around the campus."

Manu looked skeptical and torn. "Emma, that's a chance in a million."

"Yeah, but it *is* a chance. Go home, Manu! I'll handle it and report back tomorrow."

"Okay," Manu said falteringly, "but be careful. I mean, do you want me to wait for you?"

"No, thank you," Emma said, getting out of the car. "I'll be fine. Call your wife and kids and tell them you'll be home soon."

She grinned at him and waved before turning to the college campus.

UNFORTUNATELY, MANU'S PREDICTION had been accurate. After asking a laconic and unforthcoming security officer who had been at the university entrance the night in question, Emma went onto the campus to approach random students with the same inquiry. She showed them her phone picture of Marcelo when he was alive, but few people were helpful or the least bit interested, many of them puzzled by Emma's quest. It was early evening now, when students headed to the library for "prep"—essentially homework—or to study for exams. Some bizarre concern over a murder was irrelevant to them.

As Emma left Zenith feeling like she'd been on a fool's errand, she came away with one insight that even if anyone had seen or heard anything suspicious from the Trade Fair grounds, including the screams of a person being murdered, only an idiot would go out at night to investigate. As for strange noises, well, a lot of those floated over to the campus on the night air. Whether it was a bunch of drunk students on the street causing a ruckus or some unknown call or growl of a nocturnal animal, no one cared.

Before Emma finally left, she stood with arms folded gazing for a while at Zenith's campus. She was worried that there could be a connection between Marcelo, his murderer, and the college. A student killer on campus was entirely possible.

She turned with a sigh to request an Uber, which arrived before long. Heading home, Emma was weary and unable to get the image of Marcelo's bloody, twisted body out of her mind.

CHAPTER SEVEN

CHRISTOPHER CORTLAND AND HIS sister, Gertrude, were firmly at the helm of the International Congress of Families.

Although Christopher's wife, Diana, was less involved with the inner workings of the enterprise, her passing resemblance to Marilyn Monroe (including her blond hairstyle) certainly helped cement her a role as ICF's glamorous unofficial mascot. Both in their late thirties, Christopher and Diana were a beautiful and telegenic couple. They had two equally pretty strawberry-blond teenage daughters.

Diana was upstanding, moral, and entirely devoted to her husband and his work. She wasn't flirtatious and feigned not knowing when a man was lusting after her. She was invaluable at her husband's side at meetings or dinner parties with would-be sponsors, who saw Diana as the consummate representation of white middle America, as clean and pure as new, powdery snow. She was warm and attentive and easily left the people she encountered with a good feeling. On the other side of the coin, Christopher was a good-looking, gregarious, and affable redhead who easily lured powerful people to his side.

The Cortlands made good money through sponsorships, fundraising soirées, and charity events. They had tax shelters in the Caymans and the state of Delaware. Right-wing US entities like the American Center for Law and Justice and the Family Research Council, also active in Africa, strongly allied themselves with the ICF and helped sustain its international anti-gay agenda.

The Cortlands had already achieved successes in Nigeria, Kenya, and Uganda, where homosexuality could result in the death penalty. Now the ICF had turned to Ghana.

While Christopher worked with members of parliament, Diana concentrated on influential female figures like entertainers and politicians. On a scorching Wednesday, Diana hosted brunch for Ghana's First Lady, Madam Abigail Nartey, and six other women of note at the five-star Kempinski Hotel. Diana had been debriefed earlier by Christopher, who told her what he had learned from his conversation with Peter Ansah, and was up to speed on their three-pronged approach.

On the menu was kale or caprese salad; goat or wild mushroom soup; jollof rice with spicy chicken, sirloin steak, chicken escalope, salmon filet, or veal zurichoise; and finally, for dessert, Belgian chocolate lava cake or New York cheesecake.

Diana looked fetching in a businesslike lemon-chiffon blouse and an olive-green skirt. Madam Nartey, the most important guest, sat to Diana's left. Tall and bespectacled, she wore her hair in a low bun with a front puff. With tasteful pearl earrings, she looked rich and distinguished.

"Thank you all so much for attending," Diana began, as waiters in crisp white uniforms served the appetizers. "Please enjoy the lunch as we talk. I don't stand on ceremony, so feel free to interrupt me or ask a question at any time.

"I don't think it would be too much to say that the work my husband, Chris, and I do in promoting family values is the Lord's work. We've been to Uganda and other wonderful African countries, where we've successfully collaborated with their leaders to draft laws that preserve the sanctity of marriage in their societies."

The women murmured approval, including, Diana noted, Madam Abigail, who said, "I have a question, Mrs. Cortland." Her voice was as smooth as warm honey.

"Oh, absolutely!" Diana said enthusiastically, flashing her smile. "But do please call me Diana."

"Thank you," Abigail said. "How can we get rid of these sick, gay people? Like you said, they hide, so how do we identify them?"

Diana nodded with enthusiasm. "That is *such* a good question, and Madam Abigail, I'm so glad you asked it, because that segues perfectly into what I was going to talk about next, but let's get started on the entrées and then we can talk some more."

Diana had ordered the sirloin cooked to medium-rare perfection. She waited a little until her guests had dug into their meals and unanimously expressed delight. "So," she continued, "I like Madam Abigail's question because it ties into what my husband, along with his devoted sister, Gertrude, has drawn up as the legislative blueprint that the Ghana government can use to fashion the Proper Sexual Rights and Ghanaian Family Values Bill. It's similar to what we used in other African countries, but we've modified it a bit for Ghana because you're more advanced than the others and your police force is superior."

The women tittered with pride.

"First and foremost," Diana continued, "the bill, once passed, will authorize people to report these LGBT people to the police, who can then arrest them. For example, if you see two men holding hands in the neighborhood, you could report them, or if there are enough people to help, they can detain the men by citizen's arrest until the police arrive. Or you might report a man with obviously effeminate mannerisms—you know, the limp wrist and swishy hips and so on.

But above all, if you come across men engaged in sexual intercourse, including family members, you must go straight to the police. The bottom line is, *be vigilant!*

"Second, the bill will provide funding for conversion therapy. I'm not sure if everyone around the table knows what that is?"

Flora Ansah, wife of the Tourism, Arts, and Culture Minister, and most of the others shook their heads.

"Conversion therapy is a very effective method to turn homosexuals into heterosexuals," Diana continued authoritatively. "It's been used *very* successfully in the States to convert thousands of gay people. The way it works is that the homosexual is given an electric shock every time he responds to gay pornographic material. After about a month or two of treatment, most of them are cured."

"Wow!" Flora exclaimed. "I didn't know this. So, the situation is not completely hopeless for these people?"

"That's right. The thing is, though," Diana cautioned, "they have to *want* to change, kind of like with alcoholism."

"But we don't imprison alcoholics just for being alcoholics, do we?" Madam Abigail pointed out.

"Well, I think that's because alcoholics don't really want to be that way," Diana replied. "But gay people have actually *chosen* to be gay even though they know it goes against the world order. They're very sick people. The American Psychiatric Association categorized homosexuality as an illness in the 1950s."

"Then if it's an illness," Madam Abigail pushed, "why should they go to jail for it? I mean, I'm not casting doubt on your work, Mrs. Cortland. I just want to be sure we think this through."

"Absolutely!" Diana said, sweetly. "Because they've

willfully turned their illness outward in a way that endangers the normal family unit," Diana explained. "That's how it becomes a crime."

Madam Abigail didn't appear wholly convinced.

Diana moved on. "Third, the law will prohibit anyone from advocating for the LGBTQ lifestyle, and by that I mean, showing or expressing a positive sentiment toward being gay—on social media, for example—or promoting it by wearing rainbow colors, displaying a rainbow flag, putting up pro-LGBTQ billboards, hosting homosexual gatherings, or contributing to a gay organization."

"I think the billboards are the worst of all," Flora said with fierce energy, "because they are out there in the public and our children can see the filth; and you know, some of them might even become gay from that."

"You're exactly right," Diana said. "These billboards should never have been erected in the first place, but since they have, there should be grave consequences. So, as you can see, there is a three-pronged strategy to eliminate homosexuality: imprisonment, which will get these people off the street and deter other people from choosing the gay lifestyle; conversion therapy to return these people to heterosexuality; and the criminalization of any kind of promotion of the LGBTQ way of life."

"These LGBXYZ and whatever all those letters are claim to have been born that way," Flora said.

"That's the excuse they use," Diana said, "but scientific studies have demonstrated that *no one* is born that way. This bill becomes even *more* important for the Ghanaian extended family, because imagine how one gay male family member can destroy the continuation of the family line, especially if he's an only child."

"Well," Abigail said with a slight smile, "maybe it's not

the same in America, but we Ghanaians like to have more than one child."

"Absolutely!" Diana said. "I hear you, Madam First Lady, and I think that's the right approach. Children are among the Lord's many blessings. I think of my own dear daughters who have brought Chris and I so much joy."

"But how did this thing—this homosexuality thing, I mean—start?" Flora piped up. "Where is it from? I really don't understand it. Is it that some of the men want to be women? I heard they dress up in girls' clothing."

"Well, the painful truth, Flora," Diana explained, "is that homosexuality originates with the European explorers who brought the filthy practice with them and introduced it to Africans, and that's a fact. In my humble opinion, the Europeans' worst legacy is homosexuality, because once it takes root, it is very hard to remove. Before colonization, Africa did not suffer from any homosexuality whatsoever."

"I would like to respectfully raise one point," Madam Abigail said evenly, just before she took a bite of her steak. She took her time chewing and swallowing, while they all politely waited. "Homosexuality may be a legacy of the European colonizers, but in the present day, Americans are part of the reason it continues. These gay American men and women are flowing into Ghana and turning our people into homosexuals, trans people, and so on.

"I liken it to the drug trade. The supply side introduces deadly substances into a country where the market exists, but if the supply were to be completely shut off, drug abuse would cease. So, extending the analogy, what is being done to stop the flow of homosexuals into Ghana, and what institutions are active in that regard?"

"That's an excellent question, Madam First Lady," Diana

responded, "and your analogy is perfect. There are a number of things we are doing to stem the supply of homosexuality from our side. The ICF has formed partnerships with organizations with the same values. For example, there's the Traditional Values Coalition, the Americans for Truth About Homosexuality, and so on. I mention AFTAH because it's doing excellent work fighting against the indoctrination of children. My heart has always been with children, who are so very vulnerable. They need our protection. So, yes, Madam First Lady, we have many allies in this global, existential battle."

Madam Abigail was slowly nodding with apparent understanding and approval. Diana felt that her answers to the First Lady's concerns were having a positive effect and was grateful. Abigail was essential to the ICF cause, because behind every successful man—in this case, Ghana's president—was a woman advising him. The president had the bully pulpit and would be instrumental in passing the Family Values Bill.

"Besides the government," Diana continued, "there are two other institutions we must keep in step with: the clergy and the medical profession. We've gained the support of the Christian Council of Ghana, and we'll be donating money to all the major churches to enable them to carry on their anti-LGBTQ campaigns."

"Yes, you're right," Madam Abigail said, "religion is a powerful force in this country, some say more than the political establishment. If our pastor or minister preaches that homosexuality is a sin, people listen and accept it as divine truth."

"Praise God!" Diana beamed. "Isn't it wonderful to have the Lord in your heart?"

The wives agreed verbally or by gesture.

"You said something about the medical profession," Flora said. "What do you mean?"

"We thought of this only recently when we spoke with Ghanaian doctors and nurses," Diana said. "They told us about the young gay men who come in with horrible injuries."

"From the beatings they get?" Flora said. "A group of vigilantes beat one gay man almost to death in Nima recently."

"And worse," Diana said, wincing. "I'm talking about—and I don't want to be too graphic—I'm referring to their, um, sexual injuries."

"Ohh," Flora said, "you mean from the sodomy?"

Diana felt the blood leave her face and return red hot. Madam Abigail sent Flora a withering look. That was uncalled-for and inappropriate in any setting, let alone this one.

"So, continuing," Diana resumed hastily, "we are going to suggest that the Ghana Medical Association give doctors and nurses the option to refuse medical care to the gay people who have obviously been sexually harmed."

"I think that's a good idea," another of the ministers' wives said. "If the gays know that they might be denied medical treatment, that will make them reconsider being gay."

"I agree," Flora said vigorously. "It's a good deterrent."

"On that point," Madam Abigail said, "it's vital you meet the man who will fiercely oppose you from the medical standpoint."

"Excuse me?" Diana said, momentarily derailed.

"A Ghanaian doctor who probably knows half the population of Accra because he's taken care of so many people. He's in his early seventies and says he'll retire from his practice the day he dies because then he will have no choice."

Diana and the group laughed. "So, what is it about this man?" she asked. "What's his name?"

"Dr. Newlove Mamattah," the wives chorused at once.

"Wow, quite a name," Diana said, laughing nervously. "Are there any special concerns regarding this gentleman?"

"Don't worry, Mrs. Cortland," Flora said, brushing the notion aside. "He's just an old doctor who can't shut up."

"Ah," Diana said. "I know exactly what you mean. I'm sure we can easily handle him."

CHAPTER EIGHT

EMMA ARRIVED AT THE police mortuary before the scheduled time of noon on the day after the Weija flood. Dr. Jauregui was running late by about an hour, par for the course at an overwhelmed morgue. While she waited outside, Emma went over what she knew so far about the case. It wasn't much: a gay rights activist was butchered mercilessly to death; an odd juju-like object made of half a dozen pebbles had been left at the unlikely crime site of an abandoned minivan on the Trade Fair premises; the gay activist's boyfriend surfaced in the Weija flood, time or manner of death unknown. Were the two deaths related?

Masked, gowned, and gloved, Dr. Jauregui popped her head through the entrance. "We're ready, Emma. Sorry to keep you waiting."

"No problem," she replied, joining the doctor and steeling herself to the sights and smells of the morgue. Since it had been over a year since she had last visited, she was out of practice.

Despite its renovation, the police mortuary was in a perpetually backlogged state, and Emma supposed the Covid pandemic had only exacerbated the issue. Added to that was the perennial challenge of unclaimed bodies. At least once a year, the Ghana Police Service conducted a mass burial of up to two hundred unaccounted-for corpses. Often, family members never showed up to claim a body.

Following Dr. Jauregui to the changing room, Emma smiled at her in admiration. Even shrouded in scrubs and PPE, the doctor was tall and elegant, her glossy, burnt-sienna hair gathered underneath a surgical cap. Because she ran a tight ship, none of the morgue attendants, almost all of them men, dared slack off for fear of a good tongue-lashing from the boss. At the same time, Jauregui was fair, kind, and respectful of the dead.

"*Lista?*" the doctor asked with a smile.

Emma didn't know a lot of Spanish, but that much she had picked up from the doctor. "*Sí,*" she replied. *As ready as I'll ever be.*

Jauregui left her to change into the protective clothing provided, and minutes later, Emma emerged for her first blast of the odor of putrefying bodies, blood, and the bleach used to clean the floor. Her saliva curdled.

At Emma's last visit to the morgue, only three autopsy tables had been present, but Dr. Jauregui had lobbied for two more with additional space to place them. Three tables were occupied now, and Emma picked out Abraham's cadaver on the first. With the march of putrefaction not entirely halted by refrigeration, the body appeared in worse shape than she remembered.

"So," Jauregui said, "tell me all about it."

Recounting the tale of the Weija flood and how Abraham's body had surfaced in the surging waters, Emma described her rescue of the body. Jauregui listened intently and in silence, but at the end of the story, she exclaimed, "*Dios mío*, Emma! Weren't you afraid to dive into that water? I would have been."

"I didn't have time to be afraid. I couldn't see many details from where we were standing, so I thought, 'What if the person is actually alive?' And I'm a strong swimmer."

"You've done very well," Jauregui said, smiling. "I'm proud of you."

Emma's face went hot with self-consciousness, but she was pleased; a compliment from the doctor was golden.

"What about the gentleman's next of kin?" Jauregui asked. "Do we know of any?"

Emma shook her head. "Me and Manu, one of my colleagues, pretended we were relatives to be sure the body didn't get out of our hands and disappear."

Jauregui grinned. "Very clever of you," she said before turning serious. "Well, let's proceed."

They turned to Abraham's supine body while one of the attendants stood ready for the initial autopsy steps. He was a balding little man whose tranquil mien suggested he had been doing this work for decades.

The doctor stood on the right-hand side of the body and touched it on the shoulder. "Sorry, Mr. Quao," she said quietly. "Allow us to find out what happened to you."

Emma thought this gesture of feeling from a living person to a dead one extraordinary. Her own sentiments were mixed. She felt terribly sorry for Abraham, while also being repelled by his decomposing flesh, swollen and bursting with large grayish blisters and sloughing sheets of tissue.

"Now," Jauregui said, holding up a finger, "it's time to turn off our emotions, Emma. This is the lesson you must learn. It doesn't mean we are callous or anything like that. It is so that we can assess what we have before us and do justice by him. Okay?"

Emma nodded and immediately felt as if she had donned a suit of armor. Her surgical mask helped to dispel some portion of the stench and the rest she banished from her consciousness.

"What you said was correct," Jauregui continued. "This

decomposition could not have occurred within the period of submersion yesterday morning during the flood. I would estimate that Mr. Quao had been dead up to three days before you found him. The question is, what exactly caused his death?" She circled the cadaver, peering closely at it and probing the slick, rubbery tissue. "What do you see here on the right side of the face and throat?"

Emma followed the doctor's lead. "I . . . I'm not sure."

"Watch as I trace along here. It dips into a fissure, which isn't easy to spot because of the distension of the flesh." Jauregui's inserted finger made a squishy sound. "Now . . ." Jauregui moved her hand to another location. "There's the same thing here. On the torso, we see another one of these gaps in the tissue on both sides. The arms as well."

The doctor looked to the assistant and made a circular motion with her finger. He stepped to the table and deftly turned the body over.

"Here is the clue," Jauregui said. "On the back of the skull is a gash, and if I probe it . . . if I probe it, there's a depression, probably a skull fracture as a result of a strike."

"So, something like a machete," Emma suggested.

"Exactly. Maybe two machetes, two assailants."

"Really? Why do you say that, Doctor?"

"The angles of the lacerations are different on the front of the corpse than on the back. We go to his upper extremities and we see what are probably defensive wounds on the palms and forearms. If there were two attackers, perhaps the first one hits Quao on the side of the neck; Quao tries to defend himself by raising his forearms in front of his face; as he's trying to back away, the second assailant comes up behind him and strikes him in the body and head. I suspect it's the skull hit that was the fatal blow. We'll see the extent of the skull damage when we open the cranium."

"Do Mr. Quao's injuries resemble Marcelo's?"

"Yes and no. As they appear now, they do not. But if we had discovered Quao's body early on, as we did Marcelo's, we would probably find similarities between the respective wounds. Unfortunately, that doesn't mean the assailants in both cases are necessarily the same, because machete wounds by themselves are nonspecific."

"It seems too coincidental to me that two boyfriends should be murdered in a similar way only a day apart," Emma said. "Maybe it was a vendetta against them."

"Like either Marcelo or Abraham rejected another guy who then killed them both out of spite and jealousy?"

"Yes, that's what I was thinking."

"*Puede ser*," Jauregui agreed. "Then you should try to find someone who was involved with either Marcelo or Abraham who could perhaps give you more information."

I already have, Emma thought. *Jojo.*

When the autopsy was over, Emma showed the doctor the pebbles she had found in the minivan. She picked each one up gingerly with her gloved hand and examined the blood pattern.

"No bloody fingerprints," she murmured. "What a pity. Still, I'll have a courier take it to the forensics lab, though I'm not sure if they have anyone who can process it for DNA right away."

"What are the chances we could get an analysis very soon from the lab, Doctor?"

With an ironic smile, Jauregui sent Emma a sidelong glance. "Is that a serious question?"

Emma tried in vain to suppress a snort, which made the doctor giggle, and before long the two women were sharing a round of contagious laughter.

"If I get any news, my dear Emma," Jauregui said, sobering up, "I will inform you immediately."

BACK AT THE office, Emma was pensive. She saw the need to probe Jojo some more about his relationship with Marcelo, while simultaneously feeling skittish about getting into Jojo's business. Later in the afternoon, Jojo sidled up to tell her that he wanted to meet afterhours and Emma's heart leaped. She hoped he was going to unwittingly save her from making the awkward overture.

"Sure," she said. "No problem."

By six that evening, the coast was clear, everyone having left for the day. Jojo and Emma met in the break-room.

"What's up?" Emma asked.

"I feel bad," Jojo said, phone in hand. "After finding out the date of Marcelo's death, I went through my WhatsApp messages and realized he had texted me that same night."

"Oh," Emma said. "Why was he texting you?"

"Take a look." Jojo handed Emma his beat-up phone and she read the exchange.

I want to see you again.
8:16 PM

Why for what?
8:17 PM

I've missed you a lot
8:18 PM

First you go and cheat on me
and now you want me back?
Ur not serious at all
8:20 PM

I made a mistake and now
I'm telling you I'm sorry.
U too did some bad stuff
8:21 PM

> What bad stuff? I never
> went behind your back!
> Don't try to lie.
> 8:22 PM

Ok but let's talk, can
I come over to your
place?
8:23 PM

> That won't be good
> for either of us bro
> 8:24 PM

Emma looked up at Jojo, who said, "You see? If I'd allowed him to come over to see me, he might still be alive."

"You feel guilty?"

"Yes, I do."

"I get it. Those 'if only' things can really worry your mind. Although, the bottom line is that if someone had been determined to kill Marcelo, they would have gotten to him eventually. Maybe not at that time, but later."

Jojo heaved a sigh. "Yes."

"Who do you think might have wanted him dead?"

"Have you been to Ego's yet?"

"Yes, I went with Manu."

"Who did you meet there?"

"Festus."

Jojo grunted and brooded.

"Why—is that bad?" Emma said.

"It's complicated," Jojo said wryly. "You see, Festus had secretly liked Abraham, but Abraham wasn't attracted to married men. Festus has a wife and three kids. Marcelo went to work at Ego's last July, about two months after breaking up with me. When Abraham joined Ego's, six months later, he and Marcelo fell in love."

"How do you know about that?" Emma asked. "Were you in touch with Marcelo at that time?"

"No, but I heard it through the grapevine, and my friend Henrietta Blay confirmed it, and you know if she says something is true, it is."

"*The* Henrietta Blay? I didn't realize you knew her."

"Yes, I met her at an event for her organization, Trans Life. If you think Marcelo was out there, you should check out Henrietta. The only thing people hate more than a gay person is a *trans* gay person."

"I can see that," Emma said. "Manu and I met Ebenezer at Ego's. What can you tell me about him?"

Jojo sighed and gave a rueful smile. "I told you it was complicated. From what I understand, Ebenezer was after Marcelo, but the sentiment wasn't mutual."

"Which means Ebenezer could have resented both Marcelo and Abraham. Enough to kill them?"

"That I can't say, but I heard Ebenezer has a hot temper."

"Okay," Emma said quietly. "Is there anything else, Jojo?"

"That's all," he said. "I hope it helps." He heaved a sigh. "I wish none of this had happened."

Emma was concerned. "Do you miss Marcelo?"

"It's not even about me," Jojo said. "He was an important figure for a lot of gay people—the leader who made us become braver—and now he's gone. It's sad."

CHAPTER NINE

AFTER REPEATED ATTEMPTS, EMMA finally reached Henrietta Blay by phone on Thursday. Her voice was in the alto range with a slight huskiness, like the rustle of dry leaves.

"Hello, my name is Emma Djan. I got your number from your friend Ebenezer at Ego's."

"Okay," Henrietta said, sounding cautious. "How can I help?"

"I work at a private investigation agency, and we've been asked to look into the death of Marcelo Tetteh, whom you knew, I understand."

"Yes, I did know him."

"Can we meet to talk? This isn't suitable for a phone conversation."

She hesitated a moment. "All right. But just one thing: you cannot let anyone know where I live, and please come alone."

"You have my word on that. When is a good time for you?"

"Make it this evening at five. First, go to Suncity Hotel on La Road. When you get there, call me, and I will direct you."

SUNCITY WAS A six-story hotel of luxury apartments with a pool deck at the top. The sun was still burning brightly only an hour before sundown, and Emma moved to where the building gave her some shade as she called Henrietta, who answered after two rings. "Okay, cross the street," she instructed Emma, "and take the path to where it connects with the next road. Go straight. You'll meet First Kaadzaano Street, keep going to Second Kaadzaano and make a right. If you see a white horse eating grass on the corner, that's the correct one. Keep going to a snack bar restaurant on your right called Fika, and come through the gate into the courtyard, turn left past the clothesline, and you'll see my apartment straight ahead, number eleven. I'll be waiting. Are you alone?"

"Yes."

"Okay." She hung up.

Emma walked quickly, following the directions. There was, indeed, a tethered white horse munching contently on grass along the verge. Emma's best guess was that it offered beachgoer rides on popular Sundays. La Bamba Beach wasn't far away. *Was the horse a good omen?* She liked to think so.

The metal gate squeaked and rattled as Emma shut it behind her. A woman in the courtyard was washing clothes by hand, and she exchanged good evenings with Emma. Then came the clothesline as specified exactly by Henrietta, whose directions were better than most people's.

Emma tapped on the door and waited a few seconds. It opened.

"Henrietta? Hi. I'm Emma."

"Come in, please."

The small sitting room had a three-seater couch, TV, and a small dining table.

"Have a seat," Henrietta said. "Would you like a Bel-Aqua?"

"Thank you. That would be nice." Bel-Aqua was Emma's favorite water bottling company, and she swore that, even if blindfolded, she could distinguish it from other brands.

Henrietta went to the kitchen on the side. It was small but fully equipped with a stove and refrigerator. On the whole, the apartment was compact but comfortable enough for one or two occupants.

Emma, sitting on the farther end of the couch, took a few gulps of the chilled water, realizing how thirsty she had been. Come to think of it, she hadn't had lunch. Mama had always said that one day Emma's stomach would eat itself alive, whatever that meant exactly.

Henrietta sat at the other end of the sofa. Free of makeup, she was androgynously pretty with beautiful skin and a petite frame. Her naturally styled hair was perched high on her head with resplendent, cascading curls. She was wearing short shorts and a bright-yellow T-shirt that read, *I'm the T in LGBTQ,* with a rainbow flag arcing over the words like an umbrella.

"So," Henrietta began, "how did you meet my friend Ebenezer again?"

Emma let her know what had transpired on the visit to Ego's.

"It's been a long time since I've been to the place," Henrietta said, sounding wistful.

"You used to spend more time there, then?" Emma asked.

"Years back, when the political climate wasn't so hot as now. These days, I hardly go out, and if I do, I try to go with a girlfriend for only a short time. My mother buys all my clothes."

"That's tough," Emma said. "Being so confined, I mean."

"But necessary," Henrietta said. "At least, if I want to live. Sometimes I wonder if it's worth the trouble."

"The shaming and heckling?"

"Yes." Henrietta sent her the slightest of smiles. "Seems like you understand."

"I try."

"So, what is this agency you work for? I didn't quite understand the details."

Emma gave her a brief account of how she moved from CID to Sowah's agency going on four years ago. Then, she asked Henrietta how she'd gotten to know Marcelo.

"We had a common friend," Henrietta said, folding her legs beneath her. "Frank was an older man, an LGBTQ activist himself, who mentored me and then Marcelo. When Marcelo's dad kicked him out of the house, Frank took him in with barely the means to do it.

"Then, Frank died suddenly two years ago—they said heart attack, but I'm certain he was poisoned. I don't have proof, but"—Henrietta shrugged—"I don't believe their heart attack story. His death inspired Marcelo to establish his own organization, Rectify Ghana. I gave Marcelo moral support—and a little financial, after I had my first hit song. It didn't make me rich, but it did get me some money."

"I love your 'Mi Fie' video," Emma said enthusiastically. "Congrats."

Henrietta smiled sweetly. "Thank you. Marcelo did, too."

"When was the last time you saw him, if I may ask?"

Henrietta looked down at her manicured fingernails. "Two or three days before they killed him, he came to pay me a visit."

"By 'they,' you mean . . . ?"

"It's both hard and easy to say. So many people of importance hated or feared Marcelo. Take Minister Peter Ansah, for example. I can easily see him contracting professional killers to get rid of Marcelo. People like to say that a gay person should just shut up and go away. But Marcelo always said that visibility was the most important thing in changing people's minds. There was a time you would never see a woman wearing trousers, but now, it's commonplace because brave women started to do it. Marcelo was more on the political side, while I'm on the artistic. So my song 'Mi Fie' is a way to put our LGBTQ issues in people's faces. That's the only thing that will make people change."

Emma nodded in appreciation. "You are so right."

"The problem is," Henrietta continued, "that we put ourselves in danger. So, for Marcelo, a lot of his fellow Ga people in the La district also hated him, and you don't mess with the Gas. Hm, they are no joke. In the La district, it would be simple to get one or more people to gang up on another. Accra is an easy place to kill and be killed. I'm glad you're doing this investigation because the police won't do anything about Marcelo's death. They side with the killers, can you imagine that? I was at a drag show once when a gang of hooligans came in and robbed us at gunpoint. When the police arrived, they arrested *us* instead of the bad guys."

Emma grunted. Had she remained with the Ghana Police Service, would she have become that corrupt and wrong-headed? She would like to think not.

"What's the story with Abraham Quao?" she asked Henrietta, and then faltered. "Oh, wait. I'm sorry—you've heard about his death, right?"

Henrietta heaved a sigh, staring at the ground. "It's terrible. Poor guy."

"Do you think his death is connected to Marcelo's?"

"Yes, of course," Henrietta said fiercely.

Her phone buzzed from the coffee table and she picked it up. "It's my mom. She's asking if I'm home because she's in the area." She called back. "Yeah, Mama, I'm home. You can come around."

Emma hesitated. "Well, maybe I should take my leave now . . ."

"No, no," Henrietta protested. "I'd like you to meet her. Unless you have an appointment somewhere?"

"Not really, no."

"Then sit. You're going to get a free dinner, too. Mama always cooks for me when she comes over. I don't cook well."

"My mother's the same way," Emma said. "Loves to cook for me and always trying to make me eat more."

"We're in the same boat, then."

HENRIETTA HAD BEEN accurate. Her mother, Georgina, arrived with a bag of goodies and whipped up a luscious meal of boiled yam and fish *kontomire*. The three women sat at the small table and ate with their fingers. That food always tasted better that way was an undisputed fact.

Every so often, Emma caught Georgina glancing fondly at Henrietta.

"You resemble each other so much," Emma said.

"She's my rock," Henrietta said. "Always stood by me, never abandoned me to struggle alone as a trans woman."

"When did you first feel like you were more a girl than a boy?" Emma asked.

"Maybe around five or six, would you say, Mama?"

"Oh, before that, my dear. You won't remember it the way I do, but I believe you felt like a girl almost from the start. After you were born, people kept bringing pink outfits as gifts."

"Interesting," Emma said.

"There was no problem with how I looked when I was small, up to about age six," Henrietta said, "but things turned ugly when I started primary school. The boys, and even some of the girls, teased me mercilessly. I liked playing with the girls while the boys played football, but sometimes the girls couldn't be bothered with me either. So, I was stuck in the middle with nowhere to turn."

"That's a bad feeling."

"Very bad, very bad, and once I started wearing feminine clothing, like a blouse instead of a boy's shirt, everyone started to talk."

"Sometimes, Henrietta would come back from school crying because of the bullying. On the advice of one of my uncles, I sent her to a boarding school. That was a mistake. Tell Emma what it was like, dear."

"I was scared the boys would see my body when we were taking our showers in the morning before classes," Henrietta began, "so I used to get up at three in the morning to have my bath, get dressed for classes, and then go back to bed until six when everybody got up. But then they were curious why I didn't want them to see me naked. One afternoon, three or four of them ganged up on me to pull off all my clothes. They laughed because my body was girlish."

Georgina squeezed her daughter's hand.

"So, you've been dealing with this practically all your life," Emma said.

"Sometimes I just think about ending it all, you know?" Henrietta said despondently.

"Stop," Georgina said, her voice wavering slightly. "Take strength from the Lord. And from me," she added.

"You care, I know, but I'm not sure the Lord does. Why does he put me through all this?"

"God has a plan for everyone," Georgina assured her.

"You sure?" Henrietta asked.

"Of course." Like Georgina's, Henrietta's eyes had moistened.

"When did you discover you were good at singing?" Emma asked.

"In high school," Henrietta said, smiling. "I entered a song and dance competition and won. People couldn't stop talking about it. Then I started to do national contests and one of the music label owners noticed me."

"Well done," Emma said. "Did that lift your spirits?"

"A little bit for a while," Henrietta responded. "But people are strange. They praise you from one side of their mouth and insult you on the other. Some of the same people who publicly shame me also direct message me on Facebook asking for sex."

Emma grunted. "Hypocrisy is alive and well."

"There's more food," Georgina told Emma. "Don't be shy."

"Oh, thank you, Mrs. Blay. I'm good."

Georgina shook her head. "What's wrong with young people that you all want to be a bag of bones? Eat! Henrietta, have some more."

"Mama, did you see how big my first helping was?"

"Ho! That small amount you call a helping?"

Henrietta looked at Emma. "See what I mean?"

Georgina began clearing the dishes away, and Emma jumped up to help.

"Oh, no!" Georgina said. "Sit and relax."

Emma sat down with Henrietta, but only for a bit longer. "Please, I must take my leave, Mrs. Blay. Thank you for the delicious dinner."

"Please come back. We would love to see you again."

"I'll walk you to the gate," Henrietta said. Outside, she grasped Emma's forearm and said, "Please stay safe in your investigations."

"I appreciate that," Emma said. "And you do the same. It's dangerous in the city, so be vigilant."

"You're right; thank you. I should be fine."

But as Emma said goodbye, she could see the anxiety in Henrietta's eyes.

CHAPTER TEN

BACK HOME, EMMA TURNED on the TV in her bedroom
and watched the news as she folded her clothes from off the
clothesline. She was done before nine o'clock, when one of
her favorite shows, *Tough Talk with Gus*, came on. She
propped a pillow against the wall and sat on the bed cross-
legged, eager to watch them cover the timely topic: the
"Anti-Gay Bill."

Gus Seeza, the anchor who had reinvented himself after
a scandal two years before, welcomed his guests: Minister
of Tourism, Arts, and Culture Peter Ansah and Dr. Newlove Mamattah. Emma was familiar with the MP but not
with the doctor, whom Seeza described as "Ghana's most
renowned physician caring for LGBTQ people."

Bald on the top with sparse gray hair at the sides, Mamattah
had a round face and a keen but kind expression, and glasses.

"As an introduction to those of our viewers who may
not be familiar with this topic," Seeza began, "the proposed
law, the complete name of which is quite a mouthful—The
Promotion of Proper Human Sexual Rights and Ghanaian
Family Values Bill—would criminalize anyone identifying as
an LGBTQ+ person or having a gay relationship or intercourse with up to five years in prison, and ten years for a
person seen as promoting prohibited identities or campaign-
ing for the rights of LGBTQ+ people, or using media to even
discuss homosexuality."

Seeza, seated in between the two men, swiveled to the MP. "Most Honorable Ansah, let me start with you."

Ansah smiled tolerantly and nodded his ginger head. "Yes, of course."

"Why does Ghana need this law?"

"There are three main reasons, Gus," Ansah began. "First, we need to tackle the crisis of LGBTQ+ people pushing their dangerous agenda of recruiting innocent boys and girls. Second, as you know, Gus, homosexuality isn't indigenous to Ghana. It's an import from the West contrary to our values and cultural norms. The practice of homosexuality or gayism has no place here, nor does transsexualism. Third, homosexuality is already against the law—and has been since colonial times. It has just never been enforced as it should be. This bill will ensure that the law is followed."

"Okay," Seeza said, "let's examine those points individually. Dr. Mamattah, Minister Ansah states that the first rationale for the law is that the existence of LGBTQ people is now a crisis and needs to be curbed. Comments?"

Mamattah appeared serene. "Well, I'd be curious whether the minister can back up his claim of boys and girls being recruited. I'd be surprised if he produces any figures."

Seeza turned to Ansah. "What about that, Honorable? Do you have those figures?"

Ansah, apparently unconcerned, replied, "I don't need any figures. We know this is happening."

"Only scientific study can confirm or refute your opinion," Mamattah said. "What you think or believe is irrelevant. There have been vigilante attacks on gay and trans people. If the LGBTQ community has an agenda, so do the government, press, and the clergy, all of whom are pushing hatred-based propaganda against our lesbian, gay, bisexual, and trans citizens."

"'Hatred-based' is a strong term, Doctor," Seeza said.

"What would you call it?" Mamattah asked. "Assaulting gay people for being who they are is a hate crime, and it's increasing exponentially."

Seeza nodded. "Anything to add, Honorable Ansah?"

"All I can say is my belief is firm. There is a gay crisis in this country."

"Let's look at your second rationale for the bill, Minister Ansah," Seeza continued. "Doctor Mamattah, what do you say to those who insist that homosexuality was brought to Africa and Ghana by Westerners?"

"Was *hetero*sexuality brought to Ghana by the West?" Mamattah asked.

Ansah laughed. "This is not a valid question. Heterosexuality is the norm in Africa. It has been the custom and tradition for centuries."

"But so has homosexuality," Mamattah returned. "It was documented by the early explorers in the seventeenth century. There are ancient rock paintings by the San people depicting same-sex relations, and right here in Ghana, the Nzema people had a long tradition of adult males marrying younger men."

"I don't believe a word of it." The minister scoffed. "Ghana is in charge of our own destiny, Doctor. We are a sovereign nation, and we must protect ourselves from Western values."

"Are you a Christian, Mr. Ansah?"

"But of course!"

"And where do you think Christianity came from? Christianity is a Western value. Who are the International Congress of Families and the Family Research Council?"

"What about them?"

"They're American far-right organizations who have

influenced Uganda and Kenya in passing their anti-LGBTQ laws."

"Honorable Mr. Ansah," Seeza said, "outside influence of African governmental policy is troubling, don't you think?"

"Like I said, Ghana remains a proud sovereign nation. We don't take instruction from anyone or any country outside our own."

"Really?" Mamattah said. "Honorable Ansah, can you assure me and the viewing audience, right here, right now, that you aren't receiving any campaign funding from the ICF?"

Ansah looked for a moment as if he'd been slapped. He jabbed a finger in the doctor's direction. "If you don't drop that accusation, I will sue you, Doctor."

"It will be my great pleasure."

There was an awkward pause, which Seeza rushed to fill. "The third issue you mentioned, Honorable—and Doctor Mamattah referenced it as well—is that Ghanaian law already prohibits same-sex intercourse, but you, Minister Ansah, say that the law isn't adequately enforced."

"The law as it is written now is not specific enough," Ansah said. "The proposed new law delineates that it is not only LGBTQ people who will be penalized, but supporters as well."

"This isn't a law; this is a witch hunt," Mammatah said. "It's barbaric, unnecessary, and I must say, very un-Ghanaian."

For the remaining part of the program, the opposing sides went back and forth like a tennis ball across the net, and, unsurprisingly, they were at a stalemate at the conclusion.

"Thank you, Honorable Peter Ansah and Dr. Newlove Mamattah," Seeza said. "You've given us all a lot to think about. Until next week's edition, I'm Gus Seeza."

Curious about the doctor, Emma was already on her phone searching Newlove Mamattah. He had an impressive set of credentials apart from his MD, including an MSc in Tropical Medicine, multiple awards, and dozens of published papers.

Emma wanted to meet him.

CHAPTER ELEVEN

"HOW FAR?" SOWAH ASKED Emma and Manu the next morning.

Manu related their visit to Ego's and the encounter with Ebenezer. Then, it was Emma's turn to discuss her visit with Henrietta.

"Henrietta told me many people in La felt Marcelo had dishonored their community. She believes anyone from there who hated him enough could have killed him or had him killed. Contract executions aren't difficult to arrange," Emma said, keeping her account brief.

"Interesting," Sowah said. "It's good that you've both been establishing good rapport with people who may be able to help us."

"Boss, last night," Emma said, "I watched MP Peter Ansah debate a doctor called Newlove Mamattah—I love that name—about the anti-gay bill. The doctor mentioned Marcelo in a kind of more personal way, and I got the impression he might have known Marcelo. Perhaps he had been to Dr. Mamattah's practice once or twice."

"Aha, interesting," Sowah said. "As a matter of fact, I know the doctor."

"Oh, nice!" Manu exclaimed. "You know him well?"

"Not to that degree, but I met him before at some function I don't recall, and we had a brief chat."

"I was thinking of contacting him to see if he'll agree to meet, or at least talk on the phone," Emma said.

"Start working on that. He may remember me, so feel free to mention my name. We also need to work more on the Ebenezer and Festus angle."

EMMA CALLED DR. Mamattah's office and spoke to his assistant, Maude, who thought Emma was either a prospective patient or the press.

"No, madam," Emma said. "It concerns someone the doctor and I know. I can't give much more detail than that."

"He's out of town right now," Maude said, "but he'll return this evening, and I'll let him know you called. That's all I can do."

THE FOLLOWING DAY was Saturday, and Emma had strong doubts that Doctor Mamattah would call on a weekend, but in the morning, after she had gotten dressed, her phone rang. She dove across the bed to snatch it off the nightstand. But it wasn't Dr. Mamattah. It was Courage, Emma's boyfriend of four years. A member of the Ghana police SWAT team, he was on an extended assignment in the Eastern Region. So far, he had been gone three weeks with no word on when he would return except that it "might be very soon."

"How is it going in general?" Emma asked him.

"I'm bored, honestly," Courage said, "and I miss you a lot."

"I miss you too."

Emma detected a hesitation in Courage's voice. "Babe," he said, "are we okay?"

"How do you mean?"

"Well, these assignments keep me away, and when I'm in town, both of us are so busy. I mean, we're not drifting apart, are we?"

In the time Emma had known Courage, this question had never come up.

"Oh," she said blankly. "No, em, no, I don't think so." She was stammering, which was not a good sign. "I mean, do *you* think we're drifting apart?"

"No, I don't, but . . . just wanted to check."

"Oh," Emma said, again at a loss.

Courage cleared his throat. "Like . . . you know, the sex has definitely gone down, right? I mean, sometimes I'm tired, or you're tired, have a headache, or whatever."

"Yeah," Emma said. She gulped audibly. "You're not saying it's me, are you?"

"No, no, no, babe—of course not. I'm not blaming it on any one particular person. I love you, you know that."

"And I love you, Courage, but now you've got me worried. Why did it come to your mind?"

"I think I jumped the gun. Sorry, babe—it was just a stupid thing to say."

Emma's face had grown hot with distress. "You must have had some kind of feeling; otherwise, you wouldn't have said it. Maybe . . . well, have I been mistreating you?"

"Emma, *no.* Of course not. Listen, I need to get off now, but we can talk more about it when I return."

"Okay," Emma said haltingly.

She hung up with her mind in confusion. *Had* she been taking Courage for granted? On the force, he was a tough guy with dead-accurate sniper aim, but away from work he was a teddy bear who liked TLC.

Rattled, Emma sat on the bed awhile. This was a bolt from the blue. Had she missed something? Or . . . wait, did Courage have an ulterior motive?

She started as her phone rang again with an unknown number.

It was a man on the line. "This is Dr. Newlove Mamattah. I received a message that an Emma Djan wished to speak to me?"

From being down in the dumps a few seconds ago, Emma's spirits now soared. "Yes, this is Emma speaking. Thank you so very much for returning my call, Dr. Mamattah."

"You're quite welcome. How can I be of help?"

"I saw you on TV a couple of nights ago discussing the anti-gay bill with Minister Ansah."

"Oh, right."

"You massacred the other side, Doctor."

"Thank you. I don't think the bar was high."

"I called because I work at the Sowah Private Investigators Agency. We've been contracted to find out who killed Marcelo Tetteh, and I noticed you referenced him briefly toward the end of the interview with Gus Seeza. During our daily briefing, we were wondering if he was in touch with you before he was murdered."

Mamattah paused awhile before speaking again. "Listen, I have a little time this afternoon after one if you'd like to talk about this in person. I don't feel comfortable discussing it over the phone."

Emma sent up a silent prayer of gratitude. "I'll be there. Just tell me where to go."

MAMATTAH COULD HAVE built a clinic in the upscale Airport Residential neighborhood or East Legon, but where it started in the raggedy Lartebiokorshie locality of metropolitan Accra is where it stayed, more or less unchanged until a recent extensive expansion and renovation. Around the corner was his residence, where he lived with his physician wife.

His home was modest by contemporary standards. The

maid who greeted Emma at the door led her to the back porch, which faced a green yard with an avocado and jacaranda tree.

Mamattah, who was shorter than he had appeared on TV, invited Emma to sit in the comfortable cane-backed chair identical to his and separated from it by a round coffee table.

"I was about to have some coffee," he said to Emma. "Would you like some?"

"I'm fine, thank you, Doctor. Such a lovely, peaceful spot."

"Thanks. Yes, I come here to de-stress, meditate, and contemplate."

When Mamattah smiled, small wrinkles appeared around his kind eyes.

The maid brought the coffee tray and set it down on the table.

"What about some water, Miss Djan? I beg your pardon, is it Miss?"

"Yes, but Emma will suffice. Thank you, sir. Water would be fine."

"Still or sparkling?"

"Oh, em, still is okay," Emma stammered. It hadn't occurred to her that there would be a choice. She realized she was bashful in the doctor's presence. He had a grace and wisdom about him. She could imagine how much solace his patients in crisis drew from him.

The maid poured Mamattah's coffee, which he took black.

"And bring water for Emma, would you?" he said to the maid.

"Yes, please."

"So," Mamattah said, "Mr. Marcelo Tetteh is the topic at hand."

The maid returned with a glass and bottled water, and Mamattah paused as she poured for Emma.

"I first met Marcelo in July of last year," the doctor continued. "I need to let you know from the outset that I won't be discussing his medical issues. He may be dead, but he still deserves the dignity of his privacy. In addition, whatever else we discuss here should be kept as confidential as possible."

"I understand, Doctor."

"You know, I liked that young man. He wasn't just an activist. He also had artistic talent and dreams. He was soft-spoken and highly principled. We had a good rapport. It's no secret that I treat gay patients without discrimination or judgment, and that might be the reason he confided in me. I had high hopes for Marcelo, whom I saw for the second time in January. He appeared happy then, maybe a little giddy, confessing he was in love with someone at his workplace." The smile on Mamattah's face vanished as he continued. "The third and last occasion Marcelo came to see me was in March of this year. By then, his mood had changed radically. He didn't have anything physically wrong with him. I perceived he was there for psychological support. He seemed despondent and afraid.

"I asked him if anything was amiss. His answer surprised me. He told me the visit may be the last, so I asked him why. He said people were out to kill him, that he had always known that, but now the word was stronger that one or more members of a group called the International Congress of Families were plotting to kill him. I asked him how he knew that, but he declined to say. And indeed, two months later almost to the day, he was murdered."

"I wonder how he knew," Emma said.

"Or sensed it. Is there perhaps a more radical wing of the ICF that carries out killings? I mean, you know there's been a string of murders of gay men in Accra. It's not unreasonable to ask if there's a vigilante squad—associated or unassociated with the ICF."

"Yes, that's been on my mind as well. Doctor, did Marcelo name the man he said he had met in January?"

"He didn't, no. Do you know who it was?"

"It must have been Abraham Quao, whom we found dead on Tuesday during the Weija flood."

Mamattah sat up straight and shifted his body to face Emma directly. "Is that so? Do you believe there's a connection?"

"Well, there could be. The pathologist who did both Abraham's and Marcelo's autopsies said that the inflicted wounds in the two cases bore a strong resemblance."

"I hope it was Dr. Jauregui who did the postmortem?"

Emma smiled. "Yes."

Mamattah let out a contented sigh. "Ahh! Excellent pathologist. Wonderful woman. If Jauregui says so, then it's so. What was the nature of the wounds?"

"Deep—inflicted with machetes, most likely."

"Yes, I see," Mamattah said soberly. "This is a messy business. Tragic." He leaned back in his chair and gazed at nothing in particular. "What has happened to us as Ghanaians? You're too young to know this, but when I was growing up, money and greed weren't the primary determinants of our behavior like they are now."

Emma kept silent as she watched anguish bloom in Mamattah's expression.

"And what about you?" he said, unexpectedly shifting subjects. "How did you get into the investigation business?"

Emma gave him the short version: starting with her brief time at the Criminal Investigation Department Headquarters and then switching to Sowah's agency.

"You're happy?" Mamattah asked.

Emma nodded. "Very much. Mr. Sowah is like a dad to us all. We love him. My colleagues are all great as well."

"Yes, that's good." After a moment, the doctor continued. "Did you know that practicing medicine is similar to solving a murder mystery?"

"I . . . well, no, I hadn't given that any thought, Dr. Mamattah. How so?"

"When I get a medical case with an unknown diagnosis, that's like your dead body. At the beginning, you may not know who or what killed the victim, just like I don't know what disease is present. Both the doctor and the detective have to ask questions. I take a detailed history of the present illness or anything that came before that may be relevant. You question witnesses and suspects. We both look for clues, you on the body itself and at the crime scene, the doctor during the physical examination, with the help of subsequent laboratory tests and imaging studies. Some leads may be red herrings, and medicine has those too. Finally, after all the pieces come together, you have your killer, and I have my diagnosis."

Emma nodded slowly with a smile. "I never thought of it that way."

Mamattah looked at his watch. "I must pick up my wife from the hospital, and then we're going to a function. Please, keep my number, and let's stay in touch."

"I appreciate your having met with me, Doctor."

"And I appreciate your coming. Keep me posted, and the best of luck."

CHAPTER TWELVE

Youngstown, Ohio

THREE WEEKS BEFORE THE Cortlands' second visit to Ghana in May, they hosted a few friends for Easter Sunday dinner. After the last of them had left, Christopher lounged on the sofa while Diana tinkered around in the kitchen putting pots and dishes away. The arrangement was that Christopher, who had graduated from culinary school before establishing ICF, did the cooking, and Diana cleaned up. She didn't know how to boil an egg. She looked around to ensure the kitchen was scrupulously tidy, switched off the light, and joined Christopher on the sofa with a long sigh.

"It was nice having them over, don't you think, honey?" she said.

Christopher grunted. "I guess. I'm waiting for the day *they* have us over."

She took his hand. "Oh, Chris. It's not a zero-sum game, you know. Remember what Jesus tells us. We need to love without condition."

"Yeah," he muttered.

"Want to watch the news?" she asked, locating the remote.

"Not really." He stood up. "I'm turning in."

"Okay, honey."

Upstairs, he washed up and got into a true crime show on the bedroom TV, which he was still watching when Diana came up. She went to the bathroom to wash up and apply face cream before changing for bed.

"What you watching?" she asked Christopher as she folded the covers back on her side of the bed. "Oh, why did I bother to ask? True crime on HLN, what else?"

She slipped in under the sheets.

"Hey, I like it, okay?" he said. "Let me enjoy what I like."

"I didn't say anything," she said defensively.

When he didn't respond, Diana stealthily sneaked her hand to his crotch.

"Diana," he said warningly.

"What?" she said with a giggle as she stroked him in a futile attempt to jump-start the engine. "It's been a while, honey bunch."

"Stop," he said, removing her hand.

"All *right* then," she said, annoyed. "Be that way."

She amused herself with TikTok videos until Christopher's show ended.

He switched off the TV. "Remember, we go to Ghana again on May second for the big conference and to tie up any loose ends from last year's visit."

"Oh," she said heavily.

He frowned at her. "What's that tone?"

"Nothing. Just that . . ."

"That what? *Spit it out.*"

"I was just hoping we could get a little reprieve from all the traveling. It does wear on me a bit. That African heat and humidity and all the Ghanese names I can never pronounce."

He let out a breath and eye-rolled. "It's *Ghanaian*, not Guyanese."

"I didn't say *Gu*yanese."

"Well, either way, it came out wrong."

"I'm sorry, okay?" she snapped. "I suppose Gertrude is coming with us?"

"Of course. She's essential for these kinds of trips."

"What am I, chopped liver?" Diana said, with a resentful laugh.

"You're my wife, not my assistant or business partner. You're there to support me and look gorgeous. That's plenty enough. What more do you want?"

"I want a little more say in what we do on these journeys and where we go. I have no say in the policy-making at the executive level. You just stick me with the politicians' wives."

"Don't sell yourself short. The wives are important too. You don't have any organizational or implementation skills. That's Gerty's forte, and she likes being in charge. She's always been that way, so we might as well embrace it and use it."

She sighed. "'No organizational skills,' huh? Wow, that hurt."

"As the truth often does." He grinned. "Come on—nothing wrong with being pretty, blond, and brainless."

"Honey, don't. Please."

"Don't what?"

"Don't start with the name-calling."

He laughed. "Dumb, blond."

"That isn't fair," Diana said, her voice shaking.

"I'll say one thing, though, you sure look good hanging around like decoration, not doing shit." He chuckled.

"That's it," Diana said, getting out of bed. "I'm not gonna lie here and take this abuse." She stopped at the door and turned. "You've got issues, Chris, and I can't solve them for you. Just because your dad bullied you and Gerty doesn't mean you get to do the same to me."

She left the room. Christopher rose and followed her as she marched down the hallway to the guest bedroom.

"Aw, come on, Lady Di," he taunted, "you're not really all that bad. You're only a tad dumber than the average rock. Or would you prefer being a 'pudden-head?' How about 'lame-brain'?"

She let out a sob as she tried to slam the bedroom door behind her, but he caught it and came up to her side.

"Don't you walk away from me. Come 'ere." He pulled her by the hair to the bed.

"You're hurting me. *Stop!*"

He pushed her onto the bed face down.

"Why do you get like this?" she shouted. "Chris, *please*."

He straddled her thighs and pushed her nightgown up to her waist. "Remember homecoming week way back when we did it under the bleachers? We were both drunk as fuck." He slapped her buttocks with relish, and she jumped. "Jiggle, jiggle," he said. "That ass is inviting me in."

"No, Chris!" Diana wailed. "I don't want it that way."

"Don't lie," he grunted, entering her aggressively without warning. "Come on—you know you do."

She shrieked with pain, which excited him. He reached a guttural orgasm and lay like dead weight on top of her for a moment. Then, abruptly, he got up and dackered to the bathroom, leaving Diana whimpering as she rearranged herself.

Trembling, she rose from the bed. As she heard Christopher turn on the shower, she retrieved her phone from the nightstand and went downstairs. She curled up on the sofa in the fetal position. At times like this, Diana needed someone to talk to, and although she sometimes envied or even resented her sister-in-law's esteem with Christopher, Gertrude knew how to render comfort.

"Gerty?" Diana whispered into the phone.

"You okay, love?" Her voice was warm and soothing. "Did you get hurt?"

"I don't know what to do when he gets like this. He's out of control." Diana wept bitterly.

"I know, love," Gertrude said softly. "I know. You want me to come pick you up?"

"You think you should?"

"Yes, you need to be in a safe space right now. I'll make us some hot chocolate with marshmallows the way you like it."

"Yes," Diana said, smiling through tears. "I'd love that. Thank you for always being there for me."

"Get to somewhere secure in the house till I arrive."

"Yes . . . yes, I'll stay in the guest room downstairs."

"Okay, love. I'll be there soon."

Diana went to the guest bedroom and locked herself in, lying on the bed and listening for Gertrude to open the front door with the spare key Diana had given her for emergencies like this.

DIANA WAS SNUG in a borrowed fleece dressing gown as she sat at Gertrude's kitchen table drinking hot cocoa. Somehow, Gertrude knew just when to listen quietly to Diana and when to speak. After a while she could even crack a couple of benign jokes that made Diana smile, albeit wanly.

Gertrude's phone rang. It was Christopher crying on the line.

"I messed up, Gerty," he blurted. "I feel so bad."

"Chris," Gertrude said gently but firmly. "It needs to stop. You need help."

"I've prayed, Gerty, I really have. I've begged for the Lord's forgiveness."

"God works through counseling too. There's nothing wrong with getting professional help."

"Yes, yes. I'll do that. I promise."

"You always say that, Chris. I go to counseling, and so should you. We both have unresolved family issues. It's a continuous process of healing, right?"

"I'm going to change, I swear. I've asked God for forgiveness and guidance."

Gertrude didn't respond. Diana was watching intently.

"Can I talk to her, please?" Christopher asked.

Gertrude covered the bottom edge of her phone. "Talk to him? Only if you want to."

Diana took the phone. "Hello."

Gertrude could hear him clearly from where she sat. "Baby, I'm so, so, so sorry for what I did. Can you forgive me? Will you?"

"I don't know, Chris."

"I would just die if I didn't have you. I would literally shrivel up and die. I really, really need you. *Please*, forgive me. *Please?*"

"I can't go on like this."

Christopher began to cry again. "Baby, right now, you don't even know how much I'm hurting inside for what I've done to you—the terrible, *terrible* things I've done. I need you. Will you come home?"

Gertrude shook her head vigorously at Diana and mouthed the word *no*.

"Not tonight, Chris," she said. "We need time to calm down in separate spaces."

"You're absolutely right, baby. Even though I won't be able to sleep tonight, I'll let you have a little time away from me. But I need you back tomorrow morning, okay? I'll even make breakfast for you, all right?"

A weak smile broke out on Diana's face. "Okay."

"See you tomorrow, then. I love you so, so much. You're my right hand. I'm nothing without you."

"You mean that?"

"Every single word of it. Tell me you love me, I need to hear you say that."

"I do love you, Chris."

CHRISTOPHER WAS WAITING outside the house when Gertrude's car pulled up at eight o'clock in the morning. He opened Diana's side and eagerly embraced her. They cried on each other's shoulders.

"I couldn't wait till you got back," he said. "I'm so glad you're here." He bent down to the open door. "Thanks for taking care of her and bringing her home, Gerty."

"Remember what we talked about, Chris."

"I will. I promise."

He walked back into the house with his arm around Diana's shoulders. Inside, the house smelled deliciously of pancakes and sausage.

"Oh, my goodness," she exclaimed.

"Breakfast just for you, sweetie," Christopher said. "Sit down and let me treat you like the queen you are. My queen."

CHAPTER THIRTEEN

ALL DAY, JOJO HAD felt the urge to get in touch with Henrietta, who picked up his call right away.

"Hey, stranger!" she cried. "We haven't talked in so long!"

"I know," Jojo said. "I've been bad not calling you all this time. Sorry, baby girl."

"It's okay—you my honey anyways. But how have you been?"

"Well, it's been tough of late with Marcelo's and Abraham's deaths."

"I know, I know," Henrietta said softly. "How are you holding up?"

"It's strange. The agency is working Marcelo's case, and I've never been involved in an investigation that strikes so close to home. I'm very uncomfortable because, you know, I was dating Marcelo for a while. I feel as if I got some of his blood on my hands."

"Oh, *no!* Why do you say that?"

"Well . . ." Jojo started, "the thing is he and I had been texting each other the night he was killed."

"And so?"

"Marcelo said he wanted to get back with me. He threatened to come over to my place, but I rebuffed him, and now I feel if only I'd let him, he might be alive today."

"Don't blame yourself, dear," Henrietta said. "You were setting the right kind of boundaries."

"Thanks. You always make me feel better."

"Do people at your job know about you and Marcelo?

"Only Mr. Sowah and Emma."

"You're going to be okay, Jojo. Why don't you come around one of these evenings to see me?"

"I would love to," Jojo said. "I'm free tomorrow and Tuesday evening. How about you?"

"I'll be at a TV interview with Gus Seeza tomorrow night, but Tuesday will be fine—let's say six."

"Perfect. I can't wait to see you."

CHAPTER FOURTEEN

With the radio on in the background, Henrietta began preparing for her TV interview. What used to take her hours she could now do in half that time or less. After building up her cleavage with duct tape, a push-up bra, inserts, and dark bronzer, Henrietta pulled in her waist with a firm compression garment. She finished up her facial makeup and then donned her outfit—a sequined black blouse and skintight fuchsia pants flared at the bottom over contrasting black heels. Her last items were her dangling diamond earrings and flowing black wig.

A little past six, Henrietta posed in the full-length mirror and turned around slowly to check that she hadn't missed a single detail. It all looked good, and she felt sexy and secure. From her jumbled closet, she chose the knockoff Gucci purse that went best with the outfit.

She turned in surprise at a knock on her door.

Henrietta was to arrive at the Metro TV station at seven to start taping the show at eight. Unlike most of Gus Seeza's programs, Henrietta's interview would be pre-recorded and shown later.

The Metro TV vehicle arrived outside her home at six-thirty to take her to the studio, a safety measure Henrietta had demanded.

The driver, Mahama, called Henrietta's number, but she didn't pick up. He texted her, then gave her about five minutes before making another call with no luck. He got out of the car and went through the squeaky gate, then asked a little girl skipping by and humming a tune where Henrietta Blay lived. The girl pointed vaguely ahead. Mahama went in that direction, tried knocking on one door, and then another. As he stood wondering what to do, a neighbor came out of the opposite apartment.

"Please," Mahama asked, "is this where Henrietta Blay lives?"

"I don't know anyone like that," the man replied sullenly.

The time was almost six-fifty. Mahama called back to the station. "I don't know where she is," he told the producer.

"What do you mean?"

"I can't find her and she's not taking any of my calls."

"Hold on. Let me try. I'll call you back."

Mahama waited. The little girl came back carrying a large pizza. "Please, have you seen her?" she asked Mahama.

He shook his head. "Is this her place?"

"Yes please. That's her door." Balancing the pizza box in one hand, the girl knocked a few times with the other and called out for Henrietta. Nothing.

"Sorry," she said. "Please, I'm going now."

"Sure, sure, no problem," Mahama said absently. "Thank you."

The producer called back, sounding resigned and annoyed. "I can't reach her either."

"Should I go back to the studio?" Mahama asked.

"Nothing else we can do. We'll call it a day and try her again in the morning. Thank God this wasn't live."

Forty-five minutes earlier

HENRIETTA HADN'T BEEN expecting anyone so soon. She put her ear to the door and called out, "Who is it?"

"Uncle Richie. Can you open, please?"

Henrietta hesitated. What did he want? They hadn't had been estranged for years, nor did they like each other. She opened the door cautiously. Preceded by his potbelly, Richie pushed through with two large men Henrietta didn't know behind him. Both wore caps and Covid masks.

"What's going on?" Henrietta said, scowling at them. "What are you doing here?"

"Henry," Richie said calmly, "let's talk, okay? Sit down."

"What do you want? And don't call me Henry."

Richie's eyes were bloodshot and he smelled of *akpeteshie*. "You just sit down and relax, okay?"

"Uncle—"

"I want Pastor Timothy to try casting out your demons again."

"What demons?" Henrietta snapped. "What are you talking about? I've told you, I don't have any demons!"

She backed away as Richie approached her with his hand outstretched.

"Come," he said, "we can go right now."

She stood her ground then. Richie nodded at the other two men, who exploded into action and grabbed Henrietta by the arms and trunk.

"No!" she shouted. "Stop! What are you doing?"

Henrietta writhed, kicked, and twisted as the men took her to the floor. She screamed once, and Richie pressed his hand over her mouth. "Don't make noise, or I'll hurt you."

One of the other men fumbled for a roll of duct tape in his hoodie and handed it to Richie, who taped her mouth shut with several layers.

"We have to tape her feet too!" Richie bellowed, sweat dripping from his forehead.

They grappled with her, trying to bring her ankles

together and secure them with duct tape, and then they got her wrists.

"We'll take her outside through the back door," Richie said, gasping for breath. "Get the car . . . *be quick!*"

Pastor JB Timothy, a Nigerian evangelist about as famous in Ghana as in his home country, was known for his ability to cast out the demons possessing their hapless human hosts. He was a slight man whose boyish looks belied his actual age of forty-seven.

The vast space seated a congregation of several hundred in its crescent-shaped, stadium seating. No one ever knew how many deliverances would take place in an evening because dormant demon possession could spontaneously erupt from any number of congregants. JB Timothy's deliverances could last into the early morning hours.

Watching the parade of the demon possessed being dragged, carried, or assisted to the stage by ushers, Kwabena Mamfe and George Mason sat next to each other in the last column of the uppermost row.

"I heard a rumor Henrietta Blay is coming for deliverance," Kwabena said, leaning closer to his friend.

"You think so?" George said. "I thought she doesn't want that."

"They're bringing her by force," Kwabena said.

As time passed, it seemed doubtful that Henrietta would make an appearance and Kwabena and George debated whether to leave.

"Wait, wait," Kwabena said, as a ripple went through the crowd. "Something is happening."

The audience appeared to become especially alert, craning their necks and leaning to the side for a good view of the back of the stage, where two ushers were dragging a woman with long black hair, a black sequined blouse, and fuchsia pants that showed off her curvaceous figure.

"That's Henrietta!" George whispered excitedly.

She was fighting the ushers, episodically shrieking as they brought her closer to JB. He regarded her with studied wariness and then spoke into his mic.

"What is your name?" he asked her.

"Let me *go*!" Henrietta shouted. "This is illegal! You've kidnapped me!"

"Tell us your name!" JB commanded.

Sweating heavily, panting for breath, and leaning against the ushers for support, Henrietta appeared exhausted. Her wig was askew and her blouse had a rip in the right shoulder.

"You already know me, Pastor," she said into the microphone. "I'm Henrietta Blay."

"Henrietta, why have you possessed Henry's body?"

"Henry? What Henry? Is this a joke?"

The crowd murmured. As Henrietta briefly wriggled away from the ushers, she stumbled, but they prevented her from falling.

JB held his Bible over Henrietta's head. "In Jesus's name, *leave Henry!*"

He pushed on her forehead. In return, she took a wild swipe at him.

"You cannot overcome the power of *Jesus!*" JB growled. "Leave Henry! I command you in Jesus's name, *come out!*"

For several minutes, Henrietta struggled in vain with the ushers until she slumped and went limp, wholly spent. They lowered her to the ground, where she lay gasping for breath.

JB knelt beside her. "What is your name?"

He put the mic to her mouth and she whispered something unintelligible.

"*Yes!*" JB shouted. "Yes, you are Henry. Praise God, praise *Jesus!* You have had deliverance by the power of the Lord!"

He roughly pulled off her wig and threw it aside.

The congregation sprang to its feet, clapping and cheering wildly.

JB handed his mic to an assistant and quietly told two ushers to take Henrietta to his quarters behind the church. "Lock the door," he added.

"He did it," Kwabena said, his eyes shining. "She's been delivered from the demon."

"We'll see," George replied, looking skeptical. "I'm not so sure."

THE TWO MEN who had dragged Henrietta to Pastor JB's vestry chamber left as a female usher sat on the couch with a traumatized Henrietta.

"Are you okay?" the usher asked softly.

"Why did they do this to me?" Henrietta whispered, her voice shaking with fury.

"Don't mind them," the usher said. "Have a little water."

She opened a plastic water bottle and brought the top to Henrietta's mouth.

Henrietta drank frantically to slake her thirst and moisten her dry mouth and throat. Within five minutes, she felt light-headed and nauseous, her forehead was wet with sweat, and her surroundings appeared blurry.

"Oh, God," she moaned, falling back, "what was in the drink?"

"You don't worry, okay?" the usher said. "Just rest."

Henrietta stretched out on the couch and slowly slipped into a daze. When she returned to full consciousness and her eyes fluttered open, she saw JB sitting at the edge of the couch with one hand in her underpants and the other pleasuring himself. Henrietta gasped and pulled away from him.

"What are you doing?" she cried. "Get away from me!"

JB jumped off the couch, zipping himself up at the same time. "Sorry, sorry," he stammered. "I wasn't trying to hurt you . . . are you okay?"

"You've abused and assaulted me, and now you ask if I'm okay?" She stared at him in disgust. "How dare you. Why did you try to deliver me? This is the second time and you know very well I have no fuckin' demons, so *why* do you keep trying?"

"Henrietta, I'm sorry. Uncle Richie has been pressuring me constantly."

She sat up. "You can't withstand pressure? Are you so weak?"

He sighed. "Richie and I are like—"

"Yes, yes, I know," Henrietta said impatiently, swinging her feet to the floor. "You've known each other since primary school and you're like brothers. I've heard that bullshit so many times."

"Right."

"What did he pay you for this?"

JB dropped his head. "Come on, Henrietta."

"You'd better hand over some of that cash if you want me to keep quiet."

JB looked startled. "You don't mean that, do you?"

"I'm a hot item," she said, "and you know that. Radio, TV, magazines, newspapers all want me because I'm a sensation. If I start spilling names—you and your cronies who pay to fuck me—well, I'll be an even bigger sensation and you'll be seen as the sick individual you are."

"No, no, please," JB said hastily. "No need for that. I'll . . . I'll send you some cash tomorrow."

"You made me miss the show I was to tape at Metro TV this evening."

"I'm very sorry about that," JB said, chastened.

"That 'sorry' had better add a whole lot more to the money you send. I'm not joking, o!"

"I get it, okay?" JB said, becoming irritated.

They were quiet for a moment.

"Will you do the final surgery?" JB asked.

"I haven't made up my mind," Henrietta said sullenly.

"Okay, but when you do, let me know. I'll help with the surgery and travel. Will it be Spain?"

Henrietta nodded. "Or Thailand."

"Whatever. I promise. But, please, just . . . I mean, don't tell anyone I've been seeing you. It will destroy me."

She cheupsed, stood up, and went to the mirror on the wall. She winced at the sight of her unadorned head and smeared makeup.

"Your wig is in the top drawer there," JB said.

She put it back on and adjusted it. "I want to go home."

"I'll send the car for you," he said.

Past midnight, Jojo was on the phone listening to a furious Henrietta telling him about the kidnapping and botched "deliverance."

"This is sick," Jojo said, disgusted. "Do you know the two men who helped your uncle?"

"I couldn't see their faces because they wore masks and caps, but they were huge. I mean bodybuilder physiques." Henrietta paused. "I feel like exposing JB to the public tomorrow night when I tape with Mr. Seeza, the TV show I missed."

"Too dangerous to be worth it," Jojo cautioned her. "Someone will come after you in revenge. Pastor Timothy's followers are crazy."

"I already threatened to talk."

"Oh," Jojo said, worried. "How did he react?"

"He was scared. Started offering me more financial support."

"Besides you and Timothy—and me—does anyone know what's been going on between you?"

"No, I don't think so."

"All right. Let's keep it that way."

"Can you still visit Tuesday evening?" Henrietta asked. "I'll cook for you and we can talk."

"That will be great. I'll be there around eight."

"You can't make six anymore? Earlier is better for me."

"I have a family function, but I'll try to slip away."

CHAPTER FIFTEEN

EMMA MISSED THE MONDAY morning briefing because of an early medical appointment, but she went straight to the boss's office on arrival at the agency around ten o'clock.

"Everything okay?" Sowah asked lightly.

"Yes, thank you. Just a routine visit." She could not reveal that she had discovered a worrying lump in her left breast.

"Good."

Sowah updated her briefly with details of the morning meeting. Manu had spoken to Ebenezer over a Sunday afternoon beer to learn more about the complex relationships at Ego's, but Manu had come away frustrated, with very little new information. Ebenezer had been guarded and evasive.

"How did your meeting with Dr. Mamattah go?" Sowah asked Emma.

"It was fruitful. I met the doctor at his home and found him to be a caring person. Marcelo visited him in July of last year and January and March of this year. In January, Marcelo seemed joyous about starting to date someone at work. But at the final visit to Dr. Mamattah, Marcelo's mood had changed. Despite putting on a brave front, he was afraid that people were out to kill him, especially Minister Peter Ansah or the ICF."

"I see," Sowah said, rubbing his chin. "What's your next step?"

"Sir, I need to go undercover at the ICF to find out if

anyone in the organization had a vendetta against Marcelo or thought he needed to be silenced. There's no time to waste because the next ICF event is at the Labadi Beach Hotel this evening. I need to be there."

IN HIS LABADI Beach Hotel room, Christopher sat with Gerty, making last-minute changes to his speech for that evening. Diana, standing in her bra, underwear, and stockinged feet in front of the closet, was deciding on an outfit. She picked an olive-green frock with a sash at the waist and dark-green suede pumps for contrast. She had a newly styled hairdo, shorter, blonder, and straighter than before, with the left side tucked behind her ear.

"What do I have after the speech?" Christopher asked Gerty.

"Elder Simon Thomas from the LDS will be here to meet with us," she said.

"What's that about?" Diana asked, shimmying into her dress.

"We're devising a plan to provide a community center for the La township," Gerty said. "LDS will bear most of the cost, but we'll put something into it as well with proceeds from AFTAH—"

"What's AFTAH?" Diana asked.

"Americans for Truth About Homosexuality," Christopher said. "They're based in Columbus. You forgot the abbreviation already?"

"I don't keep all that stuff in my head," Diana said airily. "I'm not Miss Walking-Encyclopedia Gerty."

"Whatever," Chris muttered. It was true, though: his sister retained impressive amounts of information.

"And we've got the Alliance Defending Freedom and the Family Research Council on our side as well," Gerty said. "We can never have too much support."

Christopher, wearing a cream-colored linen suit, slipped into his butter-soft Italian leather loafers. "The Ghanaian politicians are mostly a done deal, right?"

"They're well covered, I'd say," Gerty said, "but there are a couple outliers we need to bring into the fold. Peter is working on it, but they want perks so we'll see what we can manage—a weekend at one of the five-star out-of-town resorts, maybe."

"And what's the latest with the religious organizations?"

"The Catholic Council and Anglican Church are on board, but we should pay courtesy calls to them before we return to the States. There's this one pastor named JB Timothy who does deliverances, and I'd like to ask him if he could focus on casting out the gay demons from people."

"Do you think that really works?" Diana asked.

"If you believe it works, yes," Gerty said. "Anyway, I'm working on setting up an appointment with Timothy after we meet with the LDS and the chief of the La town."

"Could you explain the whole La town thing?" Christopher asked. "I'm confused about it."

"The Greater Accra Region has several districts, including the La-Dade-Kotopon. Its capital is La, which is pretty much on the beach. There's some protocols when we meet a chief, so I'll be sure to be up on those."

"You're a genius," Christopher said.

Gerty smiled, pleased. She turned back to her laptop to put the finishing touches on her brother's speech.

"What did I say?" Diana muttered under her breath. "Walking encyclopedia."

THE LABADI BEACH Hotel conference hall offered a breathtaking view of sunset over the Atlantic Ocean. A crowd milled around, looking at ICF merchandise spread across long rows of tables: pamphlets and leaflets depicting a white, blue-eyed Jesus with flowing auburn hair, ICF pens, T-shirts, notebooks with the ICF logo, crucifixes, Bibles, and a book by Christopher Cortland called *Let Your Light Shine for the Glory*. The conference attendees were buying copies so quickly that new boxes had to be opened to replenish the supply.

Bible in hand, Emma went quietly from table to table. Behind one of them, a young, enthusiastic man asked her what her interest was.

"I want to volunteer to work for the organization," Emma said. "Do you know if that's possible?"

"Oh, wow! That's really great! I'm Nathan, and you?"

"Ruby," Emma said. "Nice to meet you."

"Yeah, you too. I know they have one volunteer program they call Angel Ambassador."

"What is that?"

"The ambassadors pay visits to different neighborhoods to bring the word of God to the people and promote Ghanaian family values."

"Oh, okay," Emma said, sounding interested. "What are the Ghanaian family values?"

"Well, you know, the man is the head of the house," Nathan said, "and the wife is there to support him and bring up the children in the sight of the Lord."

"What if you're not married yet?" Emma asked.

"That's okay," Nathan said with a broad, gap-toothed smile. "Remember what the apostle Paul said to the Corinthians, that those unmarried or widowed can remain single as Paul himself was, but if they burn with the passion of lust, they should marry."

"Yes, you're right," Emma said, beaming. "Wow, you really know your Bible!"

He laughed bashfully. "Thank you. Yeah, marriage is a holy union in the sight of God. That's why in Genesis, God said, 'It is not good that the man should be alone, so I will make him a helper fit for him.'"

"It's our duty as women to help men out," Emma said neutrally.

"Now you're getting it, Ruby," Nathan said, looking happy.

"Back to the volunteer thing," she said. "Who should I talk to about it?"

"I think either George Mason or Kwabena Mamfe. They are the senior Ghanaian officers of the organization. They're around somewhere."

"Could you help me find them?"

"Wait here," Nathan said. "Let me check in the conference hall."

He trotted to one of the double-door accesses to the hall and knocked. Someone on the other side opened the door a crack. Emma overheard Nathan saying a "certain young lady" was looking for George or Kwabena. Nathan glanced over his shoulder at Emma, and the person behind the door also took a peek.

The doors shut again, and Nathan returned.

"Kwabena's in the conference hall," he told Emma. "They'll tell him, and if he has some time he'll come and talk to you." Nathan's attention turned elsewhere. "Look, there's George Mason right over there. I'll introduce you to him."

Emma followed his eyes to a short young man as round and soft as a pillow. His face was open and pleasant, with a dimpled smile. Nathan called out to him and George walked up.

"This is Ruby," Nathan said. "Ruby, meet George."

They shook hands. George's skin was baby-soft, reminding Emma of Jojo, except that Jojo was better looking.

"Ruby wants to volunteer with the ICF," Nathan said.

"Really!" George exclaimed, enthusiasm lighting up his face. "That's great! In our Angel Ambassadorship, you'll represent the ICF to communities around the city. Would that interest you?"

"Absolutely!" Emma said. "That sounds exciting."

"Only thing to remember," George cautioned, "is that you'll need to be ICF-trained and adhere to certain guidelines."

Nathan excused himself to return to his table.

"How did you learn about us, Ruby?" George asked.

"To be honest, I've been following you on social media for some time," Emma said, smiling sweetly. "I missed your event earlier this month, so I caught this one."

"Nice!" George said. "We are happy to welcome you, and I see you're ready with your Bible."

"Yes, it's my strength," Emma said, holding the Bible to her heart. "So, what shall we do next about my volunteering?"

George beckoned. "Come with me into the auditorium. Hopefully, Kwabena will be free to talk to you, and if you're lucky, Gertrude Cortland will also be there."

"Who is she?" Emma asked, shortening her stride for George's benefit.

"That's Chris Cortland's sister. We collaborate with her to organize the events."

George had a key to the auditorium door, which he pulled open for Emma to pass. "Please, sit here and let me talk to him to let him know what's going on."

Emma sat in a random seat near the door to observe. A technician was doing a sound check as a man and a woman who looked like hotel employees conferred with each other at the side of the stage. Another couple of people were rearranging outlying chairs to fit the seating pattern.

The group George had joined was interesting. A tall man, George's corporeal opposite, was talking to a white woman in black-and-white *kente*. Emma guessed they were Kwabena Mamfe and Gertrude Cortland, respectively. A Ghanaian woman at the group's periphery was writing on a clipboard.

But most noticeable and spectacular was one of the most beautiful women Emma had ever seen. Almost Kwabena's height, she had luminous light-brown skin. Her lush, curly black hair perfectly framed a heart-shaped, blemish-free face. About thirty, she was lean with a pale-violet sleeveless blouse showing off well-defined shoulders. Emma would kill for shoulders like that.

George turned and beckoned to Emma to join the group for introductions. Emma had been correct about Gertrude and Kwabena. The gorgeous woman's name was Paloma. From her adoring glances at Kwabena, Emma guessed that they were a couple; whether married or not remained to be seen. She had a British accent, and was likely the product of a Black-and-white union in England.

"Please, madam," George said to Gertrude, "Ruby is interested in the Angel Ambassador program the ICF."

"Oh, that's wonderful, Ruby!" Gertrude exclaimed, smiling at Emma. "We're just getting started with that, so it's nice you've come in at the beginning."

"Yes please," Emma said with suitable respect. "I look forward to it."

"My brother, Chris, will talk more about it during his speech, so, Ruby, I hope you can stay for the entire program."

"Yes, madam," Emma said. "I wouldn't miss it for the world."

"We don't have time to talk right now," Gertrude continued, "but after Chris's speech, you and Kwabena should get
together to discuss next steps."

"Okay, yes," Emma said. "That will be fine."

"You can sit with us, if you like," George said, smiling at
Emma and then allowing his eyes to drop salaciously to her
breasts without much effort to conceal his interest. Emma
wasn't particularly endowed in that department, but apparently George felt she was adequate.

Just then, the conference doors opened and attendees
began to stream in. Emma joined George and the rest of
the group in the first row before the stage. Like a good host,
Gertrude sat at the very last seat to make it easy to get up at
will for any reason. Then came Paloma, Kwabena, George,
and Emma.

To begin, the Bethel Revival Choir performed a rousing,
welcoming hymn. Christopher Cortland strode onto the
stage to deafening applause. Although Emma had expected
enthusiasm, this degree of exaltation surprised her. Curious,
she glanced down the row at Gertrude, whose face practically glowed with pride and joy.

Christopher spoke in sweeping, grandiose language. At
one point, he passably quoted a Twi proverb, prompting
delighted laughter and another round of applause. Moving
on to the heart of his address, he began with intense gravity.
"In Second Corinthians, chapter five, verse twenty, we read,
'Therefore, we are God's ambassadors. We invite you, on
behalf of our Lord Jesus Christ, to be reconciled to God.'
Who are God's ambassadors? What does that mean? They
are his authorized messengers or representatives. Therefore,
Christ speaks through his ambassadors. They receive his
word and then message it to others through prayer, joyful
singing, or quiet discussion."

In the periphery of Emma's vision, she could see Kwabena and George nodding at intervals as Christopher spoke, at times even murmuring approval under their breath. Using this Bible verse, Christopher spoke about the new ICF Angel Ambassadorship, inviting audience members to sign up at the tables outside. George leaned closer to Emma and whispered in her ear, "You don't need to sign up. We'll get you started today."

She nodded and whispered back, "Thanks."

Uninvited, George squeezed her hand, and she flinched inwardly. She was uneasy with George, but she had to remain neutral somehow, so she didn't push him away. For a moment her mind strayed to Courage, and she again experienced her disquiet over their recent phone conversation. When would he be back home?

Christopher finished to a standing and prolonged ovation.

"Wasn't he good?" George said excitedly to Emma. "Wow!"

She nodded enthusiastically and exclaimed, "One of a kind!" which wasn't inaccurate.

As Christopher left the stage, both Kwabena and Gertrude got up to join him at the bottom of the short flight of steps.

"Let me introduce you to him," George said to Emma.

"That would be great."

The number of people crowded around Christopher at the side of the stage had grown. Some had a copy of his book, which he autographed with a flourish. Others wanted to thank him or tell him how much they had enjoyed his speech. After eight to ten minutes, the band of admirers began to disperse as Kwabena politely thanked them for coming. Only Christopher, his sister, and Kwabena remained now. Emma noticed Paloma standing off to the side with her arms crossed and thought her body language projected less enthusiasm than she saw in the core ICF team. At least for now, Paloma's role was difficult to figure out.

"Come along," George said to Emma, gently touching the small of her back to usher her closer to the rock star. "Mr. Cortland, may I introduce Ruby—" He looked at Emma to supply the rest.

"Mensah," she prompted.

"Ruby Mensah. She's a newcomer to our family, but she wants to be an ICF Angel Ambassador."

"Nice!" Christopher said, with a friendly smile. *Not bad-looking*, Emma thought, now that she was up close.

"Your speech was inspiring to me, sir," she said. "I can hardly wait to get started as one of your ambassadors."

"Well, we would love to have you," he said. "Kwabena and my sister, Gertrude, will make the necessary arrangements."

"I can also help," George said, a little pointedly.

Christopher put a kind hand on his shoulder. "Yes, of course, absolutely! We work as a team, right?"

"That's right, sir," Kwabena agreed.

"So," Christopher said, turning to Gertrude. "Where next? We meet with the LDS elder?"

"Right," Gertrude said, looking at her watch.

Emma said quietly to George, "Excuse me one moment."

She slipped away and joined Paloma, who gave Emma an immediate, exquisite smile. "Enjoying yourself?"

"Very interesting," Emma said, without a total commitment. "Paloma, do you know where the ladies' washroom is?"

"Come with me, Ruby. I'll show you."

Perfect. Emma needed to pull her away from the flock. Almost equal in height, the two women had matching strides.

"Is this your first time at an ICF event?" Paloma asked.

"Yes. And you?"

"My third, actually. I came for the one earlier this month and the first last year after I'd met Kwabena."

With a standard, middle-class English accent, she emphasized "Kwabena" incorrectly on the first syllable.

"Oh, interesting," Emma said. "Where did you meet?"

"Jazz concert."

"Aha, nice."

"So, I heard you were interested in the ambassador thing," Paloma said as they crossed the lobby past a crew of airline attendants checking in.

Because Paloma was a different kind of audience, Emma deliberately tamped down her enthusiasm. "I'm only considering. I'm unsure of the whole thing, but that's between you and me."

"Got it. Here's the ladies' room. I'll wait for you here."

"Thanks so much."

Emma went into a stall briefly, emerged, and washed her hands out of habit. Outside, Paloma was checking her phone.

"Thanks for waiting," Emma said. "Very nice of you."

"Not at all," Paloma said cheerfully. She hesitated a moment. "Ruby, could I have a word, please? Would you mind?"

"Of course not. Shall we sit down?"

They took one of the crescent-shaped sofas in the lobby and sat facing each other.

"Actually," Paloma said, looking rueful, "I'm not even sure why I'm telling you this, but you seem cool and level-headed, especially since you said you were a little on the fence about joining the ICF."

Emma laughed. "Well, thanks. I hope I don't disappoint."

"Um . . . I'm in a bit of a dilemma. When I met Kwabena, I saw only one side of him—you know, hip-hop and jazz lover, and he's pretty sophisticated with a really nice personality, and all. The thing is, I discovered this religious part of him later on. It kind of popped out like a jack-in-the-box, and I have to say, all this Bible stuff is a little bit much for me. I mean, it's not a one hundred percent condemnation, and I still like Kwabena a lot, but, to be honest, right now, I'd rather be somewhere else with him. Like on the beach." Paloma laughed in a flowing, musical tone, then lowered her voice and looked around to make sure no one was watching or listening. "If you do begin working with Gertrude, Chris's sister, just don't say anything that's even remotely ungodly, or she'll turn as cold as a block of ice. That woman is super-religious and plays by the book. She writes Chris's speeches for him, you know. As a matter of fact, she runs the whole show—gets all the meetings set up and so on."

"I see," Emma said. "Powerful woman."

"Yeah, and I admire that, but she's rigid. She's kind of like your stern secondary school teacher. I know you've had your share of those, Ruby!"

"Absolutely," Emma said, casting her mind back. "How about Chris's wife, Diana?"

"She doesn't get into the weeds of the day-to-day running of ICF, but if you ever need something, you can go through her and she'll send it up the chain."

"Thanks for the tip. May I ask if you've come to stay in Ghana, or if this is only a visit?"

"Both, sort of. I expect to go back and forth between here and England," Paloma responded. "I'm setting up a home care business with my mother, who is Ghanaian and a nurse by training. As you've probably already figured out, I was born in the UK. My father was from London, where he met my mum."

"How long have you been in Ghana on this occasion?"

"Four months, so far. Things are moving a lot slower than I'd anticipated."

Emma nodded. "It can be hell getting a business going in Ghana."

"Kwabena has helped sort out a few things for me," Paloma said, "and I really appreciate him for doing that. What bothers me is his subscribing to all this anti-LGBTQ stuff. I disagree with him on that. That might influence whether to stay together or part ways."

"Let me ask you a question," Emma said. "Do you know anything about Marcelo Tetteh, the gay activist who was murdered recently?"

"The same lad who confronted Chris Cortland at the Mövenpick?"

"That's the one."

"I thought his death was horrendous. Very upsetting."

"What was the reaction from Chris, Kwabena, and the others?"

"They were quiet about it," Paloma said. "As if they didn't want to talk about it. It bothered me that they were so stone-faced. I know they oppose LGBTQ people, but there's no need to be heartless."

"I see what you mean. Did you ever hear anyone in the group make threats against Marcelo?"

Paloma shook head slowly. "No, I didn't. It never struck me that the ICF could be connected to Marcelo's death. I mean, they're pretty extreme, but I don't think any of them are killers. If I did, I wouldn't have anything to do with them."

"Yes, of course."

"Why, did you hear something?"

"Nothing more concrete than rumors in the air, and there'll always be those."

"Right. But I can keep my eyes and ears open for you," Paloma added.

"Thanks, I appreciate that. Let me get your number and flash you back."

CHAPTER SIXTEEN

PETER ANSAH WAS WAITING in the morning at the entrance to the hotel as Elder Simon Thomas arrived from the Church of Jesus Christ of Latter-Day Saints' spired temple, a ten-minute ride away on Liberation Road. He was a striking man who stood at least six-foot-two, with a slight stoop; a lean, craggy face with gouged-out brows; and a full head of shocking silver-white hair.

Ansah greeted him heartily, switching on his charm and allowing his ginger eyes to perfectly capture the bright sunlight. He led Elder Thomas to the small meeting room they had reserved. Christopher stood up from the table and came forward enthusiastically. "A pleasure, Elder Thomas."

"Do have a seat, Elder," Ansah said, as he and Christopher circled around to the other side of the table to take their seats opposite Thomas.

"Welcome, Elder," Ansah said. "We are very happy to see you."

"Well, I thank you for that," Thomas responded in a strong baritone. "We like to interact with the public and to go out into the community. People often mistakenly think our church members are secluded or excluded from the outside world. This is what our missions are all about."

"Well said." Christopher nodded vigorously. "Well said."

"So I'm especially interested in what you said on the

phone was a proposal you had for me," Thomas said, leaning forward slightly.

"As you might know," Christopher said, "I'm the CEO and Director of the International Congress of Families, ICF."

"Yes, of course!" Thomas exclaimed with almost a smile.

"My sister, Gertrude, is the one who makes our appointments and schedules—you know, the important stuff." Christopher grinned, but his weak half joke didn't appear to register on Thomas's expression. "Anyway," Christopher continued, "our God-given mission of the ICF is to guide African governments back onto the righteous path and away from the abomination of homosexuality."

"It *is* an abomination," Thomas said, gravely.

"To wield influence," Christopher continued, "we in the ICF have been working with the highest levels of government, the chiefs, the clergy, and members of parliament like the Most Honorable Mr. Peter Ansah here. Of course the chief or king is in charge of the subjects within his jurisdiction, so there are different areas and towns with their own chief, or *mantse*. For instance, there's the La *Mantse*."

"Understood," Thomas said, with a slow, tolerant blink.

"And it's that town, La, that interests me," Christopher continued, looking at Ansah. "Peter, I think you have some relevant information."

"Yes, I met with Chief Nii Lante II and Elder Brown several weeks ago," Ansah said. "The La region badly needs a recreation and community center where the youth can go for activities like soccer, boxing, even after-school classes, and to hold events. The idea here is to channel youthful energy constructively to keep them away from drugs, sex, and crime. Of course, what I—and now potentially you—get in return is the assurance that chiefs and kings will continue to emphasize that sin and crime, homosexuality in particular, have no place in the community."

"That is an excellent idea," Thomas said.

"And then it occurred to me that among the leading religious influences, the Church of Jesus Christ of Latter-Day Saints is one of the greatest of them all."

Thomas nodded as if that were elementary.

"I feel that if LDS were to share the cost of the community center with us, it would be a win-win all around. Both our organizations would be contributing a significant resource to one of the most important and traditional segments of Accra. And then, of course, best of all, we have the buy-in of a mighty chief. We go where the power is."

"This potential project could really be worthwhile," Thomas said, suddenly alive. "I'm certainly going to pass it on to the administration and we'll see if we can get their approval."

Thomas looked at Ansah. "Thoughts?"

"I've approved the idea immediately, and once we've put some plans together, I suggest we visit Chief Nii Lante II to let him know all about it."

ONLY THE LA Highway separated the La Royal Palace from Labadi Beach. Two black gates etched with rooster silhouettes formed the entrance to the property. A crimson-red sculpture of a rooster stood between the gates. Far to the right, by some two hundred meters, stretched a long wall decorated with *adinkra* symbols. Looking above the wall, Manu could see the tops of the second stories of the palace and the adjoining building marked *La Traditional Council*. In a sentry box, a security guard lounged casually on a chair with his legs stretched out.

"Good morning, sir," Manu said.

The guard came out of repose and sat up. "Yes, sir?"

"My name is Manu. I wish to meet with Chief Nii Lante."

"Hold on one minute," the guard said, putting a phone to his ear. "Yes, madam," he said after a pause. "Yes, he is here and says he needs to see Chief Nii Lante II. His name is Mr. Manu."

Whoever was at the other end of the line issued an order, and the guard performed a cursory pat down on Manu. "I will show you the secretary's office," he said, leading the way. "Her name is Madam Dolly. She can make you an appointment."

Following the guard across the compound, Manu realized how vast the space was. There were only three structures: the sandstone-colored royal palace directly ahead, the La Traditional Council on the left, and another building too low in profile for him to have seen from behind the wall.

"What is that?" he asked the guard.

"The building? District court, but it's not in operation right now."

The palace housed the office of the chief. The guard knocked politely on the open door. "Please, madam, Mr. Manu is here."

Madam Dolly was no doll. Large in dimension, she seemed to engulf her desk. She looked over her half-glasses and dispassionately said, "Yes?"

The guard left.

"Good afternoon, Madam Dolly," Manu said.

"Good afternoon." She raised her eyebrows. "How can I help you?"

Manu flashed her a friendly smile. "I heard you are the boss around here."

She grunted, but she was more flattered than not. "What can I do for you, Mr. Manu?"

"Please, I wish to have an audience with Chief Nii Lante II."

Dolly gestured at the chair facing her desk. "The meeting concerns what?"

"I work for the Sowah Private Investigators Agency," Manu said, taking a seat. "We are looking into the death of Marcelo Tetteh, who was killed not far away from here."

Dolly leaned back, making her chair squeak. "Hmm, this Marcelo *wahala*."

"Please, you say?"

She dismissed it. "This is what you must do, Mr. Manu. You must write a letter to this office detailing the purpose and mission for your meeting with the chief. Then, we will consider it and let you know. Can I have your phone number, please?"

Manu recited it mechanically as he wondered how long this protocol would take. He thought of something. "Madam Dolly, may I write the letter here?"

She looked surprised. "Write it how?"

"On my phone, and I'll send it to you right now, either via email or WhatsApp."

"But you have to print it and sign it," Dolly pointed out.

Manu glanced meaningfully at the tabletop printer in the corner.

"The public is not allowed to use our equipment," Dolly said frostily. "You can get the letter printed, sign it, and return tomorrow."

"Ohh, Madam Dolly," Manu said, allowing his expression to collapse with disappointment. "Why should I waste money outside when I can just give it to you?" He had already armed himself with a twenty-cedi bill, which he dropped on her desk. "This is for your trouble. Thank you very much."

Dolly feigned not seeing the inducement. "Okay," she said. "No problem."

"Madam Dolly, you are great."

She grunted again.

Manu began drafting the letter, first asking Dolly how to address the chief and how to sign off. That took about ten minutes to complete. Manu emailed it to Dolly and within a short while, the printer woke up and whirred. Dolly heaved herself out of her chair, looked over the copy, and handed it to Manu.

"Is it okay?" he asked.

"It's fine."

Manu signed it and handed it back. "Please, may I know when to expect a reply?"

Dolly turned the corners of her mouth down and shrugged. "Depends on Chief Nii Lante."

"Oh, madam, I beg you. Time is of the essence, so if you could, you know . . ."

She eyed him for a moment. The fact was, the twenty cedis Manu had forked over was a decent but not quite sufficient incentive. "It will mean more work for me to set it up on emergency basis."

"Of course, I understand," Manu said, dropping another twenty. "You should be rewarded for your efforts."

"All right," she said. "I will try for you."

"I really appreciate it," Manu said.

Having flattered and bribed his way hopefully to the top of Dolly's pile, Manu left.

EMMA KNOCKED AT Suite 612, and a few moments later, Madam Gertrude unlocked the door.

"Oh, hi, Ruby!" she said to Emma. "Good to see you."

"Madam, I'm sorry I'm a little late. I was held up."

"That's all right," Gertrude said airily. "You're still within the twenty minutes allowed by APT."

"APT?" Emma said, following her into the luxurious suite.

"African Punctuality Time."

At first, Emma didn't know how to take the comment, but then she had a good laugh. "True," she admitted ruefully.

"I'm teasing, of course," Gertrude said, gesturing to a plush forest-green chair. "Please, take a load off. Kwabena should be up in a minute." She sat down opposite Emma. "Tell me a little bit about yourself, Ruby. What do you do for a living?"

"I work part-time as a nurse's assistant," Emma said, "but they've cut my hours, so I'll have more free time to volunteer with your team."

Gertrude's face lit up. "Great! I see a lot of dedication in you."

"Thank you, madam."

"Call me Gertrude. Formality isn't necessary."

"All right, then," Emma said, smiling and feeling guilty that she had prejudicially formed an impression that Gertrude was rigid and perhaps cold. Paloma's admonishment too, at least so far, seemed off the mark.

"So, a little bit about my background," Gertrude said. "I'm more familiar with your lovely country than you might imagine. My first visit to Ghana was almost twenty years ago when I got a two-year appointment to teach at Winneba High School, or 'secondary' school as they called it back then. My major had been biology at Ohio State, and when I graduated, I joined a Catholic NGO as a volunteer to work in West and Central African countries. I did lots of different things—teaching in schools, helping to build houses, providing running water for villages, setting up refuges for street children, and so on. On my first trip, I simply fell in love with Ghana. Since then, I've been returning every three or four years."

"No wonder you know about African Punctuality Time," Emma quipped.

They laughed in unison.

"At the time I started volunteering," Gertrude continued, "my brother, Chris, was studying at divinity school at Emory University. Our father had also been to divinity school, and he always told me to listen to the voice of God. I remember clearly the day God spoke to me. I was standing alone by Pine Creek in southern Ohio, and dusk was falling. I heard God instructing me to be Chris's right hand as he sought to build his own church. I joined him in his endeavors, raising money, reaching out to religious community members, and all that."

"I understand," Emma said. "In that way, you became your brother's keeper."

Gertrude's expression registered delight at the biblical reference. "How clever of you! You're absolutely right—my brother's keeper. I've been with him ever since the early days of his church. We were very close as kids, but he's always been a bit all over the place, if you get my meaning. He needs to focus more, and that's something I help him with. Besides, I'm older than him, so . . ."

"I understand you write most of your brother's speeches?"

Gertrude nodded. "That frees him up to concentrate on other things."

"What about Mrs. Cortland? Do you also help her?"

Emma thought she detected a fleeting disquiet in Gertrude's expression. "We certainly coordinate when we can," she said. "What did you think of Mr. Cortland's last speech?"

"It was uplifting and inspiring."

Gertrude was obviously pleased. "I'm so glad. And thank you. So, Ruby, what inspired you to come to us here at the International Congress of Families?"

"I've always been a loyal member of the church," Emma said, "and I'm also a great believer in the Christian family, so when I read about your organization, I was interested. I saw online that you would be coming to Ghana, so I made sure I didn't miss Mr. Cortland's speech. I guess I was just lucky that I bumped into George and he introduced me to you."

"Which church do you attend?"

"Accra Ridge Interdenominational Church."

"And are you a true believer?"

"God guides me every day," Emma responded soberly. "Without Him, I am nothing."

"Amen! What do you know about the Angel Ambassadorship?"

"Well, I'm sure you'll tell me more, but the way I imagine it is that as ambassadors, we go out to the people with a message from God so pure that we can be called angels."

Gertrude nodded. "Yes, that's about right. And underlying our ministry is the importance of family and traditional family values. That can't be overemphasized. It's at the core of our beliefs, and because of that, we must fight the outside satanic forces that want to bring us down with their agenda. Do you understand what I mean?"

"If you can explain the last part, please."

"There are people who want to taint marriage between a man and a woman by forcing same-sex marriage down our throats. What do you think about that?"

"The book of Genesis says, 'Therefore a man shall leave his father and his mother and hold fast to his wife, and they shall become one flesh,'" Emma quoted. "And the book of Hebrews tells us that marriage should be held in honor among all. 'Let the marriage bed be undefiled, for God will judge the sexually immoral and adulterous.'"

Gertrude's eyes filled with light as Emma recited these verses. "Very good, Ruby," she said. "*Very* good. I can see you're well-versed in the Bible. There is no place in God's eyes for same-sex marriage or activities. Homosexuality is an abomination, and Leviticus tells us that. The role of the ICF is to strengthen the traditional family and push back against this abomination. You've probably heard about the bill before parliament for proper sexual rights and Ghanaian family values?"

"Yes, I did hear about it," Emma said. "I only wish they would hurry up and pass it."

Gertrude smiled. "So do Chris and I. Then, abhorrent acts such as sodomy can be stopped."

"I've read the bill," Emma said, "and I approve of it, but I think the sentences are too lenient. For example, I believe giving support to gay organizations or advocating on their behalf should have a penalty of fifteen to twenty years rather than up to ten. To send the strongest of messages, the punishment must be severe."

Intrigued, Gertrude stared at Emma. "Wow!" she said softly. "That's a statement of incredible clarity."

Emma smiled bashfully and then grew serious again. "Madam Gertrude, I need to tell you something about myself that will help you understand why I cannot condone homosexuality, and sodomy in particular."

"Please do," Gertrude said earnestly.

"Forgive me for some of the descriptions I will give. I worked briefly at the clinic of Dr. Newlove Mamattah. Have you heard of him?"

"Oh, of course we have," Gertrude said, pressing her lips together. "As far as we're concerned, he's an offender."

"Yes, he accepts and treats these, you know, homosexual guys at his practice," Emma continued, "and while I was there, I saw things that were—I don't even know how to describe them—beyond abomination. One teenager came to the clinic with a"—Emma sighed and squirmed—"a terrible infection in the rectum from having unprotected sex. What personalized it for me was that young man was my brother. You can imagine how horrified I was, Madam Gertrude."

"I'm so sorry." She paused. "Would you have recommended your brother go to prison for what he did?"

"If he refused to repent and completely change his ways, then yes."

"Yes, I see. As tough as I know that must be for you, that's the right course of action. How painful to see those things, but I believe it was for a reason. God wanted you. He chose you."

"Do you—do you really think so?" Emma said, widening her eyes and allowing a quiver in her voice.

"I do," Gertrude said, nodding vigorously. "God really does move in mysterious ways."

They were silent and reflective for a moment.

"How else can we fight against this plague, Madam Gertrude?"

"We must have a comprehensive approach," she said, steepling her fingers. "We are speaking to the clergy, the chiefs, and even the doctors to help scoop out the rot that will spread if it isn't curtailed."

"Do you believe that homosexual tendencies can be cast out of a person?" Emma asked.

"In some cases, yes," Gertrude said decisively. "Have you heard of Henrietta Blay, the singer?"

"Yes, I have."

"I hear she continues to show progress after her many deliverances by different priests."

"We praise God for that," Emma said, clasping her hands together.

"And how do you feel about the violence against the gays by vigilantes?" Gertrude asked.

"Well, I can't condone violence, of course," Emma said cautiously, "but . . . but these people brought this on themselves, don't you think, Madam Gertrude?"

"You mean—"

"I mean they kind of deserve it." Emma shuddered inwardly at the cruel remark, but she needed to make a strong impression.

Gertrude stared again, apparently startled. "Is that right?"

Emma nodded. "Apart from the bill—if it's passed, that is—there must be deterrents built into the society."

"Deterrents?"

"Sometimes, in Africa," Emma explained, "we take care of things ourselves rather than waiting for the police."

"Like . . . beatings? You approve?"

"Well, Madam Gertrude," Emma said slowly, "do you believe in capital punishment?"

"I do."

"It's a kind of physical punishment, right? A deterrent, don't you think, Madam Gertrude? Certain behaviors warrant that."

Gertrude sat very still, as if thunderstruck. "Ruby, please do not let what I'm about to tell you leave this room. Can you promise me that?"

"I can, Madam Gertrude."

"I agree with you," she whispered. "I think these people should be flogged or stoned to death."

CHAPTER SEVENTEEN

AFTER EMMA HAD LEFT, Gertrude made a call. "Hello, Pastor Timothy?"

"Yes, my dear Madam Gertrude! How are you?"

"I'm very well," she replied, "and how are you too?" Over the years, she had learned this unique Ghanaianism, a direct translation from local idiom. "George and Kwabena told me they enjoyed themselves Sunday night at your church. You put on quite a show, I understand."

"I'm glad they had a good time."

"What would you say is your deliverance success rate?"

"It depends. On the first try, it may be sixty percent, but if the failed forty percent return, I achieve almost ninety percent."

"That's outstanding. Kudos to you."

"Thank you so much."

"Of course, the highlight was Henrietta Blay's deliverance."

"Of course," he echoed.

"Have you had any feedback on that? How successful it was?"

There was a pause, and for a moment, Gertrude thought she had lost the connection. "Are you there, Pastor?"

"Yes, I'm here. Sorry about that. Well, Henrietta is a tough case. She's headstrong and wayward and she is more intertwined with her demons than most other people."

"Okay. Go on."

"I did hear back from Henrietta this morning, and rather than being at peace with herself, she was angry with me about the event. She's no less demonic than before my attempt at delivering her."

"And so, what does that mean?"

"I'm not sure how we can arrange to do it again if she isn't willing."

"Do drugs work?" Gertrude asked. "Make her more placid, perhaps?"

"The problem is that when you do that, the demons may overpower whatever small amount of will is left in her."

"I see," Gertrude said heavily. "That's a shame because I'd rather not have her getting all that air time advocating for LGBTQ rights."

"I understand," Timothy said. "She's not an asset."

"Yes," Gertrude said slowly. "There's no way you could . . ."

"Could what, Madam Gertrude?"

She cleared her throat. "Well, some of your guys up on the stage with you at the church are goliaths, so to speak. Perhaps they might be useful where Henrietta is concerned? You know what I mean?"

"I understand."

"We need these voices silenced, Pastor Timothy. That's all I'm saying. While we wait for that bill to pass through parliament, we need to crush the diatribe that comes from people like Henrietta. She sabotages not only the work of the ICF but yours as well. You are a clear voice for what's right, and we don't need you to be drowned out."

"Agreed. Thank you, Madam Gertrude, and let me think it over. God bless you."

"You as well."

As Gertrude hung up, there was a knock on the door.

She opened it to find Diana looking gorgeous in a sleeveless cobalt-blue blouse and formfitting white slacks.

"You wanna go for coffee with me, Gerty?"

"Sure! In the hotel?"

"No, let's get out of here. How about Cuppa Cappuccino?"

"I'm in," Gertrude said. "I'll grab my purse. Where's Chris?"

"He was exhausted, so I let him sleep in and left him a note in case he wakes up while we're out."

OFF VOLTA STREET in a quiet, tree-lined spot, Cuppa Cappuccino was a full-service café, restaurant, and refuge from the stress and din of Accra's punishing traffic. It was a cool enough day to sit outside on the porch. Gertrude was a latte person while Diana ordered an impossibly sweet mocha, and both had a fruit pastry each.

"I was speaking to Pastor Timothy this morning," Gertrude said.

"Oh," Diana said blankly. "Which one is he again?"

"You remember—he has a megachurch and performs deliverances."

"Uh-huh. Wait, have I met him?"

"No, but I told you about him."

"If you say so," Diana said. "Well, anyway, what was it all about?"

"You remember Henrietta Blay?"

"The transvestite?"

"Diana, dear," Gertrude said witheringly, "she's not a transvestite. She's a trans woman."

"Yes, yes, I knew that. I just get them mixed up sometimes."

"He attempted to cast out Henrietta's demons last night. Didn't work."

"Does it ever *really* work?" Diana asked skeptically.

"Well . . ." Gertrude began, interrupting herself with a sip. "It's complicated. It all has to do with belief systems. In Ghana, the spirit world is responsible for a lot of stuff—physical and mental illness, bad luck, death, and stuff like that. So, for instance, a spiritual death has no obvious cause except a curse or something like that. If you've invested in this kind of belief system, then you may not only become ill through it; you can be cured by it as well."

"I don't get it," Diana said, frowning. "What if you're a schizophrenic? You don't have demons; you just need to be on some good medication."

"What about those schizos who are resistant to medications? How do you explain that?"

Diana shrugged. "I dunno. Isn't it that way with all medications? None of them work one hundred percent of the time, and with the schizophrenics, they often don't take their medication consistently."

"Sure," Gertrude said, "but I feel some people hold on to illness for whatever reason. Or maybe they can't let go, and maybe the casting out of demons is what gives them that spiritual release."

Diana laughed. "Okay, now you've lost me. And you're telling me that a trans woman can be 'untransed' by casting out her demons? I don't see how."

Gertrude inclined her head. "I admit there's a lot of theater mixed in. This thing with Henrietta Blay was a big show."

"I don't get the trans thing," Diana said. "Just be the sex you were born with and stop whining."

"And she sure does whine," Gertrude agreed. "Ever see her on TV?"

Diana snorted. "Have you ever known me to watch Ghana TV?"

"True." Gertrude grinned. "I can't stand that woman, Blay. In other news, this morning I interviewed the girl— well, young woman, I should say—who's interested in becoming an Angel Ambassador."

"And? Who is she?"

"Her name's Ruby. She's something else! Has a way about her and seems to be all in with our cause even before Kwabena has worked with her. She could be a real asset. She's obviously astute."

"Good, then," Diana said, draining her cup. "Seconds? I'm going for more."

"I'm good, thanks."

Gertrude waited for Diana to return with another sweet drink topped with whipped cream. How she kept her figure was a mystery to Gertrude, who was built like a rectangular block.

"Ruby also made an interesting point," Gertrude said as Diana sat back down. She leaned forward a little and lowered her voice. "She didn't exactly condone assault on gay people, but she suggested that in a way, they've made their bed, and now they have to lie in it. They reap what they sow, as it were."

"Including getting killed?" Diana said, studying her sister-in-law's face. "Do you really believe that?"

Gertrude hesitated. "I'm on the fence about it."

"Really? Interesting."

"Why do you say that?" Gertrude asked.

But Diana's attention had strayed.

"What are you staring at?" Gertrude asked, turning in the direction of Diana's gaze.

"Nothing."

But Gertrude had spotted the object of desire: near the restaurant on the sidewalk, a fit, well-dressed Ghanaian man with broad shoulders and a V-shaped torso was on his phone.

Gertrude rolled her eyes. "Diana, you're not a teenager anymore."

Diana's face and neck turned a bright red. "I know, I know. But my *God*, Gerty, these hunky Ghanaian men . . ." She trailed off with a moan laced with lust. "I mean . . . his ass alone!"

"Whatever," Gertrude said dismissively as she finished her coffee. "How are you and Chris getting along?"

Diana's eyes clouded over immediately.

"Hey, hey, hey," Gertrude said, reaching across the table to squeeze Diana's hand. "What's going on? Talk to me."

Diana looked up, her eyes pleading, "All I ask from him is some respect. The only person he really respects is you, Gerty. He approves of every single thing you say, but me? I'm dumb, worthless."

"Come on, Diana," Gertrude chastised gently. "You know that's not true."

"Yes, *I* know I'm not dumb, but does he?"

"Of course he does."

"Well, then he has no right to disrespect me like that."

"Honey, why do you need his respect so much?" Gertrude said in a harsh whisper, looking around for eavesdroppers. "Don't keep crawling back to him for approval."

"Oh, no," Diana said, her eyes suddenly glacial, "there's not going to be any crawling; oh no, sweetheart. This is all about getting even."

"That's the spirit!"

The women laughed.

AFTER RETURNING TO the hotel, the two split up to go to their respective rooms. When Diana entered hers,

Christopher was in the shower. She quietly slipped out and hurriedly tapped out a text: Coming now but not much time.

She had to do this fast. The elevator was taking too long to arrive. Come on! Ding. It was empty. Perfect. Diana got off on the fourth floor and half ran, half walked to the right while texting to say, Omw. As she grew closer, her eagerness rose. As if by magic, the door to the room Diana had reserved opened the instant she arrived in front of it, and she hurried in.

Kwabena was wearing torn jeans but was shirtless. He lifted her up and carried her to the bed.

"My love, may I give you my sweet milk?" he said in her ear.

Diana giggled throatily and rolled her eyes up in mock derision. In fact, she loved the way Kwabena talked—so ridiculously over-the-top as if he didn't know or care how goofy it sounded. He made her feel young and beautiful and special.

"Where is he?" he asked, kissing her neck.

"Taking a shower," she gasped, pushing down her pants.

He pulled her lacy panties aside.

"Do you give sweet milk to Paloma, too?" she whispered jealously.

"My beautiful, beautiful Diana," Kwabena said, "Paloma is only my show trophy. You are my treasure."

She went limp with submissive ecstasy. "Do whatever you want to me."

CHAPTER EIGHTEEN

EMMA WAS OVERJOYED TO receive a call from Courage early that evening. "Are you back?" she asked him eagerly.

"Yes, I am," he said, sounding weary. "Can I come over?"

"But of course! I've missed you! Can you stay the night?"

"Yes, yes, I could," he said with the slightest of hesitations.

"Good. Are you hungry?"

"I'm fine. I ate a little earlier on."

"Okay, then. I'll take a shower and wait for you."

As they hung up, Emma felt odd. By nature, Courage was bubbly even when exhausted, but he hadn't sounded like himself. Trying to dismiss the nagging discomfort, Emma took a shower and came out refreshed.

While waiting for him, Emma took a look at the biographies of the three people in command at the International Congress of Families: CEO Christopher Cortland, second-in-command sister Gertrude, and wife Diana. First, Emma examined the Wikipedia entry for ICF.

International Congress of Families (ICF)

The International Congress of Families (ICF) is a global nonprofit organization established in 2009 to promote and advocate for heterosexually based families worldwide. Based on its Christian belief system, the organization is known for rejecting alternatives such as same-sex marriage and general LGBTQIA+ rights, asserting that these contradict their values.

History

ICF was founded by CEO Christopher Cortland, an ambitious business leader born and raised in Columbus, Ohio. With a master's in business administration, and having attended divinity school, Cortland recognized the potential for an organization dedicated to preserving traditional family structures. He drew inspiration from his personal life, which was rooted in a long-standing relationship with his childhood sweetheart, Diana.

Leadership

Christopher Cortland is the head of the organization. His leadership is complemented by the support of his wife, Diana, known for her charm and as the homecoming queen at Bishop Patterson High School in Columbus, Ohio. Cortland's leadership approach is profoundly influenced by his Christian values and dedication to maintaining what he considers to be the natural family structure.

Notably, Christopher's sister, Gertrude Cortland, plays a significant role in the organization's operation and public image. After a scandal in Youngstown involving her former husband, business tycoon Charles Kinney, and the mayor of Youngstown, she relocated to Columbus and embraced Christianity. Her new path led her to missionary work in Ghana, West Africa, further affirming her commitment to her faith. Now, Gertrude is integral to the running of ICF, with her zealous dedication to the cause contributing significantly to the organization's influence.

Beliefs and Controversy

The ICF's promotion of heteronormative families has sparked controversy due to its outright rejection of alternative family structures and LGBTQIA+ rights. The organization's beliefs, founded on strict Christian principles, have been critiqued by LGBTQIA+ advocates and various human rights organizations for their exclusionary practices.

While the ICF maintains its stance, citing religious and cultural reasons, its critics argue that the organization's beliefs are discriminatory and incompatible with human rights and equality principles. However, ICF continues its work, leveraging its networks and resources to promote its conception of family worldwide.

Interesting, Emma thought, but she didn't understand what homecoming queen meant. She looked it up.

The tradition of a "homecoming queen" is predominantly associated with high schools and universities in the United States as part of the homecoming celebrations, a series of traditions centered around welcoming alumni back to a school.

The homecoming queen is a female student selected and well-regarded by her peers.

The homecoming queen is often crowned during the homecoming football game.

Emma thought that was interesting as well, if not odd. To see more, she searched for Diana Cortland on Facebook. It didn't take long to find her.

Welcome to the official page of Diana Cortland, radiant spouse of Christopher Cortland, CEO of the International Congress of Families. Join us in celebrating Diana's inspirational journey from

homecoming queen at Bishop Patterson High School to the dynamic woman she is today!

The cover photo caption read:

Diana Cortland: A vibrant journey from a queen in Columbus, Ohio, to a queen of hearts worldwide.

Emma scrolled through the page, looking at the photos. Without a doubt, Diana was beautiful at her present age, and back then as homecoming queen, beyond stunning.

The photos and their captions covered the present and past.

Homecoming Queen: Once a queen, always a queen. Diana's sparkling moment as Homecoming Queen at Bishop Patterson High School. #TBT #HomecomingQueen

Diana Cortland, lighting up Bishop Patterson High School with charm and elegance. #HighSchool-Memories

Behind every successful organization, there's a dedicated woman. Diana at the International Congress of Families event. #EmpoweredWoman

From the queen of the school to the queen of our hearts, Diana Cortland with the most precious jewels of her crown. #FamilyFirst

Beauty with a cause. Diana Cortland extending her royal touch to those in need. #CharityWork

Emma felt she had a much better idea of who these people were, which was essential for undercover work.

She opened the door to Courage's taps. "There you are!" she exclaimed.

"Yes, love," he said, smiling. "I'm back."

They embraced for quite a while before sitting beside each other on the sofa.

"So," Emma said, "how did everything go?" She didn't expect a detailed account; Courage liked to avoid his work as a conversation piece.

"Same old stuff," Courage said in resigned tones. "Never changes that much. How about you—still on the case you mentioned to me?"

Emma told him how far they'd come in the investigation, which wasn't far enough.

Courage squeezed her hand. "Little by little, babe."

Emma squinted at him. "I don't remember ever seeing you look so tired," she said. "Everything okay? You seem a little down—is it the guy at work you said is lazy?"

"Oh, no," Courage said, dismissing it. "Not at all."

Emma stared at him, but he wasn't returning her gaze. They *always* made eye contact. "Courage, what's wrong?"

He put his forehead in his palm and to Emma's shock, began to cry. "Emma, I'm sorry, I'm very sorry."

"*What?* Courage, what's going on?"

He continued weeping, staring at the ground, apparently unable to look up at her.

"Courage, slow down, slow down. Take a breath. What's happening? You're scaring me."

"We had a light day last week," Courage began in mechanical tones, "and me and a couple of guys got together for some drinks at one of the bars. I think I had a little too much. There were a couple of girls hanging around, of course, because what is a bar without a few *ashawo*. I was chatting with one of them, and I don't know what I was thinking . . ."

To Emma's dismay, he began to cry again. It was the most crying she'd ever seen from a man, funerals included. "Courage, please continue."

"I went to one of our vehicles with her, and we were just talking when she started to . . . rub me, and I got excited and she pulled out my . . . to start to perform oral sex—"

Emma drew back as if she had received an electric shock. "*What?* Courage!"

"But, but wait," Courage stammered, holding his palms out defensively to stem the coming fury. "I swear, Emma, I stopped her; she never even touched me. I told her to leave, and the whole thing was over in less than a minute, seriously, Emma."

"Jesus," Emma whispered. Then her voice rose. "You know what *really* makes me angry? It wasn't even some gorgeous runway model; that you would go so low as to be defiled by a cheap *ashawo*. What, I'm not good enough for you?"

Still crying, he apologized over and over again. "I feel so ashamed. I had to tell you because I would feel even worse if I didn't. I beg you to forgive me, but if you would rather not see me again, I'll understand."

A thought dawned on Emma. "Is this why you were asking if we were drifting apart?"

"No, no," he said, "it didn't really have anything to do with that. I mean, I did feel that maybe we were drifting, but we can easily work on that."

Courage leaned back against the sofa with his eyes closed. Emma stared blankly at the floor and both were silent until she said abruptly, "You can leave now."

Head down as if he had been guillotined, Courage stood up. "So . . . I mean, will we see each other again?"

"Courage, I don't know," Emma snapped. "I don't know how to handle this. I thought you were different from other men, but it turns out you're just the same. Can't keep your dick in your pants. And meanwhile, you *knew* how anxious I was for your return. Why did you have to go and spoil everything? This is disgusting."

"I know," he whispered. "Oh. God."

"Wait," she said. "Is this the first and only time you've cheated on me? Because I need to know."

"I swear to God, Emma. The only time."

"I need to be absolutely certain," Emma insisted. "I need you to get yourself tested for HIV and all the other sexual infections, and I want to see the results."

"Okay," he whispered. "I'll make an appointment tomorrow at the clinic, and I'll send you the results when they come in."

"I'm going to bed," Emma said, "so make yourself scarce. And I want my spare key back."

He nodded and removed the copied key from its ring. "Bye," he said glumly.

Emma didn't reply. Once Courage had left, she locked the front door and went to her bedroom, where she sat bereft at the edge of her bed.

She lay down and drifted to sleep with the bedroom light on, waking up not more than an hour later to darkness. Pulling aside the window curtain and looking out, she saw the whole block was dark, courtesy of the Ghana Electricity Corporation's rolling blackout program to conserve power. *And tomorrow they'll raise the cost tenfold*, Emma thought bitterly. For a moment, she couldn't remember why her heart was heavy, and then it all came rushing back. She tried to drive from her mind the image of Courage in the vehicle with that *ashawo*, but it wouldn't leave her alone.

Emma sat up again and put her head in her hands. She was passing the numb stage, and the fury was just beginning.

CHAPTER NINETEEN

JOJO ARRIVED AT HENRIETTA'S place at 8:20 Tuesday night, later than he had wanted to. He had texted her to let her know his family had kept him and so he was running late. Both Henrietta's mosquito-blocking screen and the front door behind it were ajar. He caught a whiff of something cooking, but more like burning.

"Henrietta?" he called out, pushing the door back.

There was no answer. The lights were on, but the house was eerily quiet. Jojo felt a quiver travel from the nape of his neck down his spine. Something wasn't right.

"Henrietta? *Henrietta?*"

He went to the kitchen. An open, smoking pot sat on the stovetop. What was once a stew was now a charred mass at the bottom of the pot. Jojo switched off the gas and spun around to the door at the kitchen's rear. It opened onto a small back patio, which was dark. Jojo fumbled for his phone and switched on the flashlight. Henrietta wasn't there.

"Henrietta, where are you?" His voice shook as he hurried to her bedroom. A pile of washed clothes waited on the bed to be folded. The bathroom door was ajar, and the light was on. Jojo pushed it open and staggered back with a gasp. Engulfed in a congealing red pool, Henrietta was lying naked and twisted on the floor of the shower stall.

"No, no, no, no," Jojo cried out. "Henrietta, *no.*"

Kneeling in blood, he turned her body toward him, but

her head, partially detached by a deep wound to the throat, lolled the other way. Jojo tried to cradle her body and lift it in one piece, but Henrietta was so bloodied that she slipped from his grasp. He stood up, hyperventilating and whimpering. He blacked out for a moment, but then his wits returned and he ran out the door into the yard, where a couple of guys were playing chess in an alcove. They looked up as Jojo approached, covered in blood.

"*Ei!*" one of them exclaimed at Jojo's appearance. "What happened?"

Jojo began to feel strangely disconnected from the scene, as if he were watching a performance from a distance. He heard himself stammer in Ga, his mother tongue, "It's Henrietta. I don't know. She's dead. I don't know. Oh, God."

"*What?*" one of the men said, staring at him in disbelief.

Jojo swayed, bent forward with hands on his knees, and threw up.

One of the chess players jumped up and sprinted to Henrietta's apartment.

Jojo collapsed, then sat up weeping with his face buried in his bloody hands.

The other chessman crouched beside Jojo. "Are you okay? What's your name, bruh?"

"Jojo."

"I'm Edinam. Don't cry, eh, Jojo? It will be all right."

Within less than a minute, the other chessman reappeared with a stunned look. "Jesus."

"What happened?" Edinam asked.

"It's terrible," the other responded. "The woman is dead. Butchered. I'm going to the station to bring a policeman. Stay with the guy, okay? Don't go anywhere or let him disappear."

"All right." Edinam returned to Jojo. "Are you her friend? I haven't seen you around here before."

"Yes, I am, but I don't come often."

"She knew you were to visit her this evening?"

Jojo nodded.

"Oh, sorry, bruh."

Jojo felt numb. In an instant, his world had become warped and unfamiliar.

"But," Edinam started hesitantly, "but you didn't do anything to her, right?"

Jojo shook his head.

"All right. You don't worry, eh? When the police comes then you can tell them everything. I'll stay with you, okay? You don't worry."

JOJO COULDN'T SAY how much time passed before the police officers—an inspector and two constables—arrived. A small crowd of curious neighbors had gathered in front of Henrietta's apartment, and the inspector and one of the constables entered to inspect the crime scene. Standing a few meters away, the second constable kept an eye on Jojo. Ten minutes later, the inspector emerged. He was a thin man whose uniform was a size too large.

"Is this is the gentleman who found the body?" he asked Edinam.

"Yes please."

The inspector bent forward. "What's your name, sir?"

"Jojo Ayitey."

"Okay, Mr. Ayitey." He drew up the two chess players' chairs. "Please take a seat."

Jojo got to his feet as if he were an old man and slumped in the proffered chair while the inspector sat down opposite. His name was Jeremiah Boseman.

"Tell me what happened," he said.

Jojo cleared his throat. "I came to see Henrietta for dinner at eight-twenty. I knocked on the door, but no one answered. The door was open, so I entered, and after looking in the kitchen and the back of the house, I went to the bathroom and found Henrietta there. Dead."

"Was she your girlfriend?"

"No, just a friend."

"Were you having any kind of disagreements or arguments?"

"Not at all. We got along well with each other."

"I see." Boseman paused before looking up at Edinam. "Do you live here? Your name?"

"Yes please. Edinam."

"Where were you when Mr. Jojo says he arrived here?"

"Me and Kofi—my friend over there—we started playing chess around seven-forty-five."

"All right. Then if you started chess at seven-forty-five, you must have seen Jojo arrive at eight-twenty?"

"No please."

"How is that possible?"

"You can't see the front gate from where we were, sir."

"But don't you have to pass by this way to get to the victim's apartment?"

"There's a path on the other side of this compound, please." Edinam pointed behind them, and Boseman briefly followed his gesture before resuming.

"Which way did you pass?" Boseman asked Jojo.

"The back way."

To Edinam, Boseman said, "When I came here, I noticed the gate squeaks when you open or close it. Can you not hear it from this distance?"

"Yes, sometimes, please."

"What do you mean, 'sometimes'?"

"People don't always close the gate, and if it's a little bit open, you can enter without pushing it."

"Is that so?" Boseman said, standing up. "Come with me, Jojo and Edinam. Kofi, you stay here."

The inspector took the lead and Jojo and Edinam followed him to the front gate, which was fully shut.

"You go outside, Edinam," Boseman instructed, "and come back in the way you normally would."

The gate groaned on Edinam's way out and did the same when he came back into the compound.

"Okay, don't close it," Boseman said quickly. "Just let it be."

The gate whined once more as it swung back, but it stopped ajar with about a foot to spare.

"So that's what you're saying? That it doesn't close?" Boseman asked Edinam.

"Yes please."

"But an adult can't easily fit through that space," Inspector Boseman pointed out. "Unless he *wants* to be sure the gate doesn't make a noise." He looked sharply at Jojo. "How was the gate when you came in? Was it wide open, a little bit open, or closed all the way?"

"It was a little bit open," Jojo said. "I think."

"So you had to push it wider to pass, then."

"Yeah . . . yes, I think so, sir."

"You don't seem sure."

"I might have pushed it a little," Jojo stammered. "I don't remember exactly, sir."

Boseman smiled one-sidedly and stared at Jojo for a moment.

He suspects me, Jojo realized, beginning to panic.

"Okay. Mr. Edinam, please return to your friend. I need to talk in private with Jojo."

Edinam left and Boseman moved into Jojo's personal space.

"My friend," the inspector said, "tell me what happened. What time did you arrive here? Was it in the afternoon? Or early evening?"

For the first time, Jojo detected a hint of alcohol on Boseman's breath.

"It was eight-twenty this evening, sir. I'm telling the truth."

"Were you harboring some grudge against her? Maybe you wanted to have sex with her and she refused? You can tell me, it's okay. These things happen all the time. Sometimes a very fierce argument results in a tragedy. I understand that."

Jojo shook his head. He was firm. "Inspector Boseman, I came to find the body the way you see it now. I didn't kill her."

One of the constables approached and whispered into Boseman's ear. The inspector nodded and turned back to Jojo as the constable left.

"I've been informed that the victim is Henrietta Blay, the one who sings that song—I don't remember the name. So, what did you have to do with her? Are you a gay?"

"No, sir," Jojo said resolutely. "I am not."

Boseman stared again, and Jojo found he couldn't meet the inspector's gaze.

"Okay, let's go back. Walk ahead of me."

When they returned to the others, Boseman had Jojo sit on the ground.

"Please, sir," one of the constables addressed Boseman, "no one in CSI is available."

Boseman cheupsed and muttered something only he could hear. "Okay, call the station, tell them to send a pickup truck and we'll wrap the body in a bedsheet or something and take it to the police mortuary."

"Sir," Jojo said, "please try to process the crime scene properly so that the culprit can be apprehended—"

Boseman whipped around. "You say what?" he yelled. "That I should process the crime scene. Is that what you said? *Kwasea!* Do you think I'm a small boy? Who at all do you think you are?"

"I work for a detective agency—"

"I don't care who you work for. Shut your mouth, you stupid boy! What impudence!"

Hot now, Boseman ordered the constables to take Jojo away. "Handcuff him and take him to CID to charge him. 'I should process the crime scene,' my *nyass*. Talking foolishness while he knows he is the one who killed the woman. *Hurry up!* Take him away before I slap him. *Kwasea!*"

The constables hastily yanked Jojo up and handcuffed him.

"Please," Jojo said to Boseman, "I didn't kill her."

"Where is the weapon?" the inspector shouted in his face. "Is it a knife or machete or what? Where did you hide it?"

"*I didn't kill her!*"

Boseman slapped Jojo across the face, and one of his fingernails caught the corner of Jojo's left eye, leaving it bleeding.

"Take him away!" the inspector yelled again furiously.

CHAPTER TWENTY

AT MORNING BRIEFING, EMMA felt outside of her body, as if her inner self had departed and left an empty shell behind. She couldn't recall feeling so depressed in a long time.

She jumped as she realized Sowah was addressing her. "Sorry, sir?"

"You were miles away somewhere. I was asking where you are with the ICF people."

"I had a meeting with Madam Gertrude to start enrolling in the Ambassador program."

"How did it go?"

"She's an extremist, boss," Emma said with concern. "I got her to confess that she's okay with gay people being stoned or beaten to death."

"Seriously?" Gideon said, aghast.

With deep distaste, Sowah blew out his breath. "Insanity," he muttered. "It raises the possibility that she and maybe someone else in that organization wouldn't have a problem butchering a Marcelo Tetteh to death."

"Exactly, sir."

"Keep working on her. See if you can get her to confide in you and reveal more."

"Sure, boss."

Sowah looked at Manu. "How are you getting on?"

"I'm meeting Chief Nii Lante II this afternoon."

Sowah nodded. "Good work. I feel like things are moving in the right direction."

As he sat at his desk to begin the day's work, he received a call from Detective Chief Inspector Boateng.

"Morning, Yemo," Boateng said.

"Hey, big DCI Boateng! It's been a while."

"Yes, I hope you're well; but listen, Jojo was arrested last night. I'm at the CID charge office where he's being detained."

"*What?*"

"Have you heard the news that Henrietta Blay, the trans female artist, has been murdered?"

"*No!?*"

"She was Jojo's friend. When he went to visit her last night, he found her dead. The inspector on the scene arrested Jojo on suspicion of murder."

"Oh, God." Sowah let out a small gasp. "Have they charged him?"

"I think they want to, but they're hoping he'll confess first."

"Are you still at the CO?"

"Yes."

"Tell him not to say another word to anyone until I get our company lawyer over there."

"Yes, I did tell him that, and I'll let him know the lawyer's on his way."

"Thank you."

Sowah put in a call to Julius Heman-Ackah, who listened to Sowah's account and said curtly, "Okay, this is Ghana Police nonsense. We must get Jojo out of there. Can you meet me at CID in an hour?"

SOWAH ARRIVED FIRST and joined Boateng to enter the CO. Officers and armed guards stood at the long L-shaped counter. Behind them, arrestees packed the two noisy jail cells beyond capacity.

"Do you see him?" Boateng asked.

"No, I don't," Sowah replied, worried.

"The cell farthest from us."

"Oh, yes," Sowah said with relief as he spotted Jojo pressed up against the bars. Sowah smiled, gave him a power salute, and signaled to him to hold on.

The door opened again and Julius Heman-Ackah walked in dressed in a fitted, navy-blue three-piece suit. In a resonant voice that seemed to emerge from the heart of his hefty, six-foot-two frame, he said good morning to Sowah and Boateng, both of whom he'd known for decades. He dispensed with pleasantries and got to the point. "Have you spoken to him?" he asked Sowah.

"I haven't, but DCI Boateng has."

"Let me talk with the charge officer. One moment."

The charge officer at the counter's far end was entering information into a large ledger. Heman-Ackah knew him by name. "How are you, Inspector Poku?"

"Hey, boss man! I'm good, and you?"

"Very well, thank you. I need to speak with my client, Jojo Ayitey."

"No problem." Poku turned and yelled, "Jojo Ayitey! Show yourself."

"Yes, sir!" he responded from the cell, raising his voice above the clamor. "I'm here."

"Bring him out," Poku ordered one of the jail attendants, who wielded a giant key to unlock the cell door. Appearing dejected and subdued, Jojo emerged. Sowah felt for him as the attendant escorted him to the counter.

"How are you doing, Jojo?" Sowah asked, almost tenderly.

"I'm good, boss," he replied sadly.

"This is our lawyer, Mr. Heman-Ackah." Sowah gestured.

"Good morning, sir."

"Don't worry, eh?" Heman-Ackah said. "We'll get you released shortly." His voice and confident manner were extraordinarily reassuring.

Overnight, the corner of Jojo's left eye had become swollen and bloodshot.

"What happened?" Sowah asked in alarm.

"The officer who arrested me. He slapped me."

"For what reason?" Sowah asked sharply, his eyes narrowing in anger.

"I told him to preserve the crime scene and he got annoyed."

Sowah looked at Heman-Ackah. "This is criminal."

"What's the officer's name?" Heman-Ackah asked Jojo.

"Inspector Jeremiah Boseman."

"Is he here in the room?"

"No, sir."

"May I take a pic of the injury, Jojo?"

"Yes, sir."

With his phone, the lawyer snapped several photos from different angles and summoned Inspector Poku. "Do you know Inspector Jeremiah Boseman?"

"Yes, I know him well."

With fingertips, Heman-Ackah turned Jojo's head toward the inspector. "This is what he did to my client last night. Do you see that, Inspector Poku?"

"Inspector Boseman said he had to defend himself when the boy attacked him."

"Number one," Heman-Ackah said, "my client, Jojo Ayitey, is not a boy; he is a grown man. Number two, he did *not* attack anyone. Inspector Boseman is lying. He slapped Mr. Ayitey across the face in an unprovoked and unnecessary act of aggression."

"I'm sorry, sir," Poku said firmly. "This should not have happened."

"No, it shouldn't have," Heman-Ackah said. "But it's something the Director-General must know about."

The inspector's eyes widened in alarm as Heman-Ackah took out his phone. The present DG of CID, Commissioner Ohene, was one of a rare breed of men in power fighting against corruption, and he was known for swiftly firing officers of any rank for infractions.

Heman-Ackah waited only a few seconds before Ohene picked up the call.

"How are you, sir?" Heman-Ackah said heartily. "I'm doing well, thank you, but all is not well here in the charge office."

Heman-Ackah detailed what had taken place, and then sent the images of Jojo's face with closeups of the left eye. "Inspector Boseman assaulted my client in an unprovoked attack. Wanton police brutality, Mr. Director-General. Not what we want to see in our police force, I'm sure you'll agree. As it stands, there are no legal grounds to hold my client for a minute longer. I will leave it up to Mr. Ayitey, but we may file charges against the inspector."

After a pause, Heman-Ackah held the phone out to Poku. "The Director-General wishes to speak to you."

Poku nervously put the phone to his ear. "Yes, sir?"

The conversation didn't last long. Poku returned the phone. "We will release Mr. Ayitey at once," he said.

JOJO AND THE boss returned to the office well into the afternoon as the other investigators anxiously waited. By this

time, they knew what had transpired, and a pall had blan-
keted the agency. None of them, especially Emma, would
have wished this double trauma on Jojo. They cheered and
clapped for him to get his spirits up as he entered the room,
to which he responded with a rueful smile. The next issue
was the side of his left eye. Sowah found a first aid kit that
had been around for a while but was still in reasonable
shape. Emma cleaned the scratch and applied a little anti-
septic ointment.

"Thanks, Emma," Jojo said softly.

After that, Jojo launched into his story. His colleagues
and the boss listened intently to his tale, from the horrific
discovery of Henrietta's body to Boseman's assault to being
thrown ignominiously into a crammed, foul jail cell. Emma
noticed how Jojo cleverly told the group from the beginning
that he and Henrietta had been friends for years, preemp-
tively warding off potential queries about his relationship
with her.

Emma listened with her head down, trying to stop the
tears threatening to spill over. She didn't want to make a
display of herself, so she held it all in. Jojo's ordeal magni-
fied the shock of Henrietta's brutal death. Emma's thoughts
sharpened in her grief. Was Henrietta's murder connected
to those of Marcelo Tetteh and Abraham Quao?

Emma thought about the juju pebbles they had found at
Marcelo's crime scene. "Jojo," she said, "I know it's tough to
relive this, but besides Henrietta's body and the blood, did
you see anything else?" She didn't want to lead him on.

"She was in the bathroom," Jojo said, his voice quivering
faintly. "Apart from the usual bathroom stuff, I didn't notice
anything special."

"No weapon?" Sowah said. "Like a machete or knife? Or
an ax?"

That was a discerning question, Emma reflected. In asking it, Sowah showed he was still open to the idea of a link to the other two killings and was looking for patterns.

Jojo frowned, trying to think back. "No, sir," he said finally. "I'm sure of it."

"What about a pile of about six smooth pebbles somewhere around the body?" Emma asked.

Jojo hadn't heard about this finding at the scene of Marcelo's murder, so he was puzzled. "Pebbles? Meaning?"

Emma explained and showed Jojo the images on her phone.

He shook his head. "I never noticed anything like that, but it's possible I missed it."

Sowah's phone rang. "Yes, DCI Boateng, Jojo's back with us at the office. He's a little shaken."

The others looked at each other, wondering what was going on.

"Aha," Sowah said. "Congratulations. Yes, you're correct. Henrietta and Marcelo Tetteh were friends. I'll have Emma call to fill you in."

When Sowah hung up, he told the group, "Boateng's been assigned the Henrietta Blay case."

The response was unanimously positive.

"Emma," Sowah said, "call him back as soon as possible and brief him about Henrietta Blay and Marcelo. It might put him on the right path."

"I will," Emma replied, "but there's another call I want to make first."

She turned to Jojo. "Do you have the phone number for Henrietta's mom, Georgina?"

Jojo nodded. "I do. I'll send it to you now.

Emma called Georgina to express her condolences. "How are you holding up, madam?"

"I'm not sure," she answered, her voice tremulous and feeble. "I feel numb."

"Yes," Emma said, remembering the day she lost her father to a sudden death. For months after that, she was so muddled, she barely functioned. "Please, have you been to Henrietta's house?"

"I will have to very soon, but I haven't yet gathered my strength."

"Would it help if I picked you up and we go together?"

"Oh, thank you, Emma!" Her voice had regained some of its vitality. "I would so appreciate that. Now that Henrietta has gone, I have no one—"

That was what broke the dam. Georgina let out a choked cry and began to sob. Emma wanted to offer comforting words, but it would have been impossible without setting off her own weeping. She gulped her tears back and waited.

"Sorry," Georgina whispered after she had collected herself.

"It's all right," Emma said. "Let me come and pick you up and we'll go together. I think you'll gain strength from it."

"God bless you."

CHAPTER TWENTY-ONE

EMMA AND GEORGINA ARRIVED at Henrietta's home an hour later. They knocked and waited.

"Who is it?" a woman's voice called out from inside.

"Is that you, Florence? It's Georgie."

Locks and keys rattled, and the door opened. Florence was an angular woman halfway between dressed and not. She wore a faded, roseate housedress with one side slipping off her right shoulder, and her hair was in curlers. Her face softened and then crumpled as she saw Georgina. "Oh, my dear! I am sorry, eh? So sorry."

They embraced, crying for a while until Florence stepped back, grasped Georgina by the shoulders, and wiped the tears off her face. "Don't worry, eh?" she said firmly. "Everything will be all right. Your beloved daughter has gone to a better place where people will not harass her. And the people who did this to her here on earth? May God strike them down!"

"Oh, sorry, I forgot!" Georgina said, turning to Emma. "Florence, please meet Emma, a good friend to Henrietta and me."

Florence gave Emma a warm smile. "It's nice to meet you. We are cleaning up."

"How is that going, please?" Emma asked courteously.

Florence turned down the corners of her mouth. "Hmm, is not easy, sistah. Georgie, are you sure you can bear to come in? It's serious, o!"

"I must face it," Georgina said. "No matter how much it hurts, I must face it."

Emma nodded and put her arm around Georgina's shoulders. "Let's go together."

At the bathroom doorway, Georgina stopped and stared while Emma prepared to catch her should she faint. Two male workers were mopping the floor, including the shower cubicle. So far, they had done a creditable job getting rid of the blood, one of the toughest biological substances to clean up completely. Multiple streaks remained, especially on the walls. Emma noticed cast-off drops of blood on the ceiling, a result of wielding the weapon back and forth in a wide arc. It spoke of abject violence, and for an instant, a terrible image infiltrated Emma's mind. She shook it off.

"Where was she?" Georgina asked Florence.

"On the floor of the shower."

"Did you see her? Did she suffer badly?"

Florence's expression twisted with pain, rendering her nonverbal response. "Sorry, Georgie."

Georgina turned away and sat heavily on the bed behind them. She stared numbly at the floor. Emma quietly took a seat beside her.

"I know who did this," Georgina said.

Emma snapped to attention. "Who?"

"Henrietta's Uncle Richie. My brother. We don't speak to each other, but I heard about what happened on Sunday. That was the second time he had kidnapped Henrietta to take her to Pastor Timothy for deliverance. Richie has said more than once that 'Henrietta killed Henry the man, and now someone should kill Henrietta the woman.' It's him. I *know* it's Richie. He hated my daughter and everything she stood for."

Emma studied Georgina for a moment. "So, what are you going to do?"

"We shall see. One way or another, Richie will confess. Mark my words."

It sounded ominous, but Emma didn't press any further. She overheard the day workers complaining to Florence that the shower wasn't draining quickly enough. *Blood?* Emma thought, returning to the bathroom. One of the workers was sweeping bloody water into the open shower drain, waiting at intervals for the level to drop.

"What's causing it to be so slow?" Emma asked.

The guy shrugged. What did he care? He wasn't a plumber.

"Please," Emma said, "may I take a look?"

Without waiting for a reply, she leaned over the drainpipe and beamed her flashlight in. "What's that?" she asked.

"What?" asked Florence.

"Something's blocking the flow, but I can't see what."

She stood back to allow Florence to take a look.

"I don't think it's anything special," Florence said. "We often get blockages like this."

"Can you call a plumber?"

Florence shot her an alarmed expression. "Do you know how much a plumber costs? Are you going to pay for it?"

She had a point. "Okay, then," Emma said. "Wait a moment, okay? Don't send any more water down the drain."

Emma darted out of the bathroom, leaving the other four looking at each other nonplussed.

Still on the bed with arms folded and head down, Georgina looked up at Emma. "What's happening?"

"Please come with me to the kitchen, Madam Georgina. Where did Henrietta keep her spoons?"

"Spoons?" Georgina echoed in puzzlement. "I'll show you."

Georgina pulled open a middle drawer next to the stove.

Emma examined the collection: soup ladles, large and medium tablespoons, and teaspoons.

"What do you need them for?" Georgina asked curiously.

"I need one that passes below the blockage."

Emma rummaged through the flatware. The teaspoons were too small, the soup ladles too large, and the table-spoons the wrong shape. She pulled the drawer open all the way and fished around in the back where her own utensils usually ended up. She found what she had hoped for: a per-fect soup spoon.

"Here," she said to Georgina. "This is good. Now, we need a long stick and some string."

Emma grabbed a broom leaning against the wall in a cor-ner while Georgina looked through several chaotic drawers and found a length of twine. "Is this okay?"

"We're going to find out," Emma said.

They returned to the bedroom where Georgina held the spoon in place at the top of the broom handle as Emma secured it tightly with the twine. A puzzled Florence looked on. The workers were chatting and taking a break.

"One problem," Emma muttered. The heavy broom brush would make manipulating the shaft awkward.

After an effort, she got it loose and spun it off.

"Okay, let's try. Madam Florence, please hold the light for me."

While Florence trained the beam into the drainpipe, Emma held on to the broom shaft and inched the spoon along the pipe wall to bypass the obstruction.

She pulled back gently, and at least a portion of the object began to rise with the spoon. If it fell away, it could be lost forever down the drain.

"I got it," she gasped.

"What is it?" Florence asked.

"A pebble," Emma said. "I think there are more."

Over the next ten minutes, Emma, her forehead pouring with the sweat of effort and concentration, recovered four more blood-stained pebbles and lost one.

"Emma, what's the meaning of these stones?" Georgina asked, her forehead creased in puzzlement.

"I'll tell you later." Her instincts told her to keep the juju theory under wraps for now.

But Florence must have already caught the sense of something bizarre. Knotting her brow, she took a couple of steps back muttering, "This is bad. Very bad."

"I don't understand how those stones got there," Georgina said.

"I know what happened," Emma said. "The person who murdered your daughter put the pebbles near her body next to the drain. When Jojo got here, he didn't notice the pebbles and accidentally knocked them into the drain as he tried to lift Henrietta's body. So, when the police got here, they didn't see anything."

She took multiple photographs of the pebbles, just as she had done at Marcelo's site. Now, she was convinced. His death and Henrietta's were connected. The question was whether it was the same killer or a group of vigilantes doing their best to exterminate LGBTQ people.

CHAPTER TWENTY-TWO

As Emma was wrangling the drainpipe pebbles, Manu arrived at the La *Mantse* compound at his appointment time. The guard, different from the first one Manu had met, escorted him past Madam Dolly's office to the central part of the palace and knocked at the front. Moments later, a small, wizened man opened the door.

"Morning," he said. "Please, you can follow me."

The small man led him through a vestibule, its walls decorated with *adinkra* symbols, and through another door. They were now at the entryway of the chief's chamber. Taking the chaperone's lead, Manu slipped off his shoes.

The chaperone called out, "*Agoo!*" requesting permission to enter. On the reply, the two men entered. The chief was seated on his throne some ten meters away. Resplendent in a traditional Ghanaian toga in brilliant shades of purple, yellow, and burnt orange, Chief Nii Lante was a big man with a build suggestive of physical strength and softness. A crown of silken antelope hide sat on his clean-shaven head, and he wore a heavy beaded necklace.

A man in his sixties stood to the chief's left. He wore his toga up to mid-chest, where it was folded over several times. Manu assumed that was the *otsiame*, the "linguist," or spokesperson to the chief. On the right, at a lower elevation than the chief's throne, sat three village elders in white togas.

First order of business: Manu presented the La *Mantse* with gifts indirectly through the *otsiame*: one bottle of schnapps, one of gin, and some cash in a discreet envelope. After shaking hands with the town elders right to left, Manu took his designated seat several meters in front of Nii Lante and the others.

"Please introduce yourself," the *otsiame* said.

"My name is Walter Manu. I want to thank His Majesty for granting me this audience."

The *otsiame* passed the message on to Nii Lante, who nodded and welcomed him, again indirectly through the linguist.

"What mission brings you to the La *Mantse* today?"

"Please, I work at the Sowah Private Investigators Agency," Manu said. "One Mr. Godfrey Tetteh has asked us to investigate the murder of his son, Marcelo. We are investigating from several angles, but we know that Marcelo was born and raised in La. We've also been told that Marcelo was not popular in La because of his gay activism. We seek his majesty's guidance as to what the situation was regarding Marcelo and La's citizens."

Through the *otsiame*, Nii Lante said, "Thank you for that information, and I commend you and your agency for taking on this investigation of the death of Marcelo Tetteh. We had problems with that boy, Marcelo. You know, Mr. Manu, our society is very conservative, so when he began agitating for rights for these LGBTQ people, the community backlash was powerful. I summoned Marcelo's father, whom I know well, and told him about the issue. He promised to stop his son from continuing in the same way. I understand he strongly chastised Marcelo and disowned him."

One of the town elders spoke up. "We don't harbor ill feelings toward the boy personally, but this homosexuality nonsense is too much. It is not part of Ghana's culture or the La people. It must be struck down as an abomination."

Manu felt the same way, but he tucked that aside for now. He waited a few beats to be sure that neither the chief nor the town elders had more to add before continuing. "I wish to ask His Majesty and the elders if there was anyone in the town who had particularly disliked Marcelo."

"Many, many people," a town elder said with a bitter smile, "but it's no secret that the macho brothers were the ones who threatened Marcelo's life. Many people heard them say it."

Manu's ears perked up. "Please, you say, the macho brothers?"

"They are two—Addo and Adjei Adamah. People hire them for heavy physical work, which means different things for different people. We know that sometimes they do vendetta work for people."

"Please, vendetta work?"

"You see, Ghana has become violent," the elder continued almost dispassionately, "because from the police to the courts, you may never see justice for a crime committed against your person. So, if you need justice or revenge, there are macho-men like Addo and Adjei who are happy to carry it out on your behalf. Such is the case with the Adamah brothers."

Manu suddenly felt chilled. Brutal truth so bluntly stated.

Nii Lante spoke up. "We don't like people such as Addo and Adjei here, nor do we like someone preaching that God loves homosexuals as much as he loves normal people. Yet still, we don't approve of killing anyone for any reason."

"Please, Your Majesty, is there any indication that the two brothers might have been involved in the death of Marcelo?" Manu asked.

"The rumors are the only indication," the chief said, "and rumors are often wrong. I don't have any facts to share with you. You are the investigator, so you must speak to them in person. You may tell the brothers that Chief Nii Lante has authorized you to discuss it with them. You're obviously a respectful man, so there will be no trouble."

Using the chief's name could smooth out a bumpy road with the brothers, and Manu was glad for the bonus.

"Please, may I know where I might find the brothers?"

"You can try the La Man Chop Bar," one of the elders said. "They like to go there."

Manu thanked them profusely, shook hands again with the chief with a slight bow and then with the town elders. As Manu emerged from the palace, he felt relief that this had not been as painful as he had feared.

A small crowd stood outside the palace, waiting to see the chief next. Two white men, one graying and the other much younger, were conversing with a Ghanaian man in a light-blue suit and tie, behind whom was an entourage of four men and two women. The *oburonis*' bland white shirt and tie with dark slacks gave them away as members of the Church of Jesus Christ of the Latter-Day Saints. Manu was curious about the pending meeting, but he continued to the guard's sentry box to sign himself out.

WITH INSIDE AND outside seating, the La Man Chop Bar was buzzing with patrons. Every table was taken. Manu's salivary glands spurted from the aroma of cooking food. He went inside and caught the eye of a maître d' of sorts.

"Yes?"

"I'm looking for two brothers," Manu said. "Addo and Adjei Adamah. Do you know them?"

The maître d' pointed to the rear of the bar, where Manu

found a door opening onto a less-crowded patio. At one of the half-dozen tables, two enormous men were guzzling Star beer and chatting. *Must be them*, Manu thought.

They looked up as Manu approached.

"Good afternoon," he said.

They both gave him a brief raise of the eyebrows and an upward flick of the head as if a verbal response would have been too much work.

"Are you Addo and Adjei?"

The slightly bigger one said, "I'm Adjei. That's Addo. And you are who?"

"My name is Walter Manu. Chief Nii Lante II told me to talk to you."

"Is that so," Adjei said with little interest.

"What is your mission?" Addo asked.

"I work for an investigation agency. We're trying to find out what happened to Marcelo Tetteh."

The brothers exchanged a glance. They couldn't have been more than two years apart, and their coarse, flat features were almost identical.

"You mean like for a news website, or what?" Addo asked.

"No, it's not for the public. Private."

"Eh-heh," Addo said dully. "Okay—have a seat."

"Thank you." Manu sat opposite them. "Chief Nii Lante told me Marcelo was causing problems in La town."

"We don't like that gay shit around here," Addo said brusquely.

"Did you warn him about it?" Manu asked.

"Yes," Adjei replied, pouring himself more beer.

"I mean, the two of you personally warned him?" Manu clarified.

"Yes," the brothers said at the same time.

"But he didn't mind you?"

"He kept coming back here. We told him to stop."

"Why you, if I may ask?" Manu said.

The brothers looked at each other, smiled, and flexed their biceps.

"That's why," Addo said, laughing. "People ask us to take care of business."

Manu grinned. "You're scaring me, o!"

The brothers' mirth told Manu he was striking the right chord with them. Addo signaled to a circulating waiter and asked him for a plate of yam chips.

"So, did you teach him a lesson?" Manu continued casually.

They shrugged. "Somehow," Adjei said.

"Meaning?"

"But why do you want to know?" Addo asked, displaying the first real signs of wariness.

"Oh, you don't worry, my brother," Manu said reassuringly. "Whatever happened, this is between you and me."

"Hmm," Addo said. "But what do you know about us?"

"Almost nothing, but it's more Marcelo I'm concentrating on. I mean, did someone in La town want to kill him?"

"Many people," Adjei said, pausing for the yam chips, hot sauce, and ketchup.

"Yeah," Addo said, popping a chip in his mouth. "You are invited."

"Thank you," Manu said with a smile. The invitation to share a meal was a Ghanaian convention. He persisted. "Do you know anyone who wanted to kill Marcelo?"

"Of course," Addo said, as if it were a given.

"Can you give me any names?"

The brothers both shook their heads.

"Not possible," Adjei said firmly. "When we do jobs for people, it's confidential."

Manu's pulse picked up. *They do jobs.* "Contract jobs?"

"My brother," Adjei said, deadpan, "I don't have to tell you because you know already. When someone has done something wrong, you can't depend on the police to get the guy, because he only has to pay them some small cash to leave him alone."

"That's true," Manu said. "But I mean, did someone ask you to handle Marcelo?"

"What do you mean, 'handle'?" Adjei said.

"Warn him, hurt him, kill him—however you want to call it."

"If we told you 'yes,'" Addo said, "then what?"

"Then nothing," Manu said, flipping up his palms.

They paused. "Some guys in the town came to us asking if we could kill Marcelo," Addo said at last.

"Who were those guys?" Manu said.

"Agh!" Adjei said in irritation. "Didn't we just tell you we don't give names?"

The brothers' almost-empty glasses gave Manu an idea. "More beer—as much as you like," he said. "Just I need some information from you."

They nodded approval. "Okay. But you didn't hear it from us."

Manu summoned the waiter: another round of beers for the brothers and a Sprite for himself. No drinking on the job, although he could do with a beer.

"So when those guys came to you to ask you to kill Marcelo, what did you tell them?"

"We told them we can beat him well, but not kill him," Addo said.

"And then?"

"And then nothing," Adjei said. "We never got a chance to beat him up. Someone killed him first."

"Really. You didn't?"

Adjei cheupsed impatiently. "Isn't that what I just said? We never touched the guy."

"What about Abraham Quao?"

"Who?" the brothers said in unison.

"Abraham Quao."

They shook their heads. "We don't know anyone with that name."

Establishing a link between the murders of Marcelo and Abraham wasn't proving any easier for Manu.

"Then, you see," Addo began, "a certain minister contacted us yesterday. He asked us if we could do a job."

"What was that job?"

"To kill that Henrietta Blay."

Manu's mind was spinning. *Henrietta?* "Let me understand this," he said. "Was the minister asking you to kill Henrietta for him or for someone else?"

"For someone else," Addo said, "but he didn't tell us who the person was."

"And what did you reply to the minister?"

"What he was going to pay us was a joke, so we told him to bring more money first. And then yesterday, someone killed Henrietta before we could do anything—same way it happened with Marcelo."

"Who do you think is doing these killings?" Manu asked.

Adjei shrugged. "No idea please. If you find out who asked the minister to get Henrietta killed, then you will know."

"But you're sure you don't know," Manu pressed.

The brothers looked at each other. "We told you everything we know, boss. More beer, please."

CHAPTER TWENTY-THREE

THE SEATS THAT HAD been empty while Manu had visited with Nii Lante II were now filled with town officials and invited dignitaries. Gertrude sat in the back row, making herself barely noticeable. Simon Thomas greeted the chief with a reverent bow, continuing in the obligatory right-to-left sequence to shake hands with the five town elders present on the chief's right-hand side.

Christopher Cortland followed, doing the same, and behind him, Peter Ansah and his entourage, not all of whom were needed for the meeting, but then what's an MP without their following?

Thomas sat next to Ansah facing the chief. The *otsiame* made introductory comments and invited Ansah to speak first.

"Chief Nii Lante," he began, "we are happy to meet with you today, Your Majesty. We come here with respect and are honored to be in your presence. My mission today is as I indicated in my official letter. I bring you Mr. Simon Thomas, president of the Africa West region of the Church of Jesus Christ of Latter-Day Saints, and Mr. Christopher Cortland, CEO and founder of the Christian group International Congress of Families. These two gentlemen bring good tidings to you and your subjects, Chief Nii Lante."

He paused for the *otsiame* to convey the message to the

chief in decorative and lyrical Ga, which was far more interesting than the dry, English version.

"We are aware, Chief Nii Lante," Ansah continued, "of
the strides your community has made and its resulting
achievements, but we do know that one of the concerns to
which you are most dedicated is the state of the youth. Many
are unemployed or may be uneducated, and as we all know,
an idle mind is the devil's playground, which is why many of
our young ones are falling prey to the temptations of drugs
and profligate, self-destructive behavior. In this context, we
acknowledge what you have so often said, that the youth of
La and the surrounding towns would benefit greatly from a
community and training center. And now, with your permission, Simon Thomas would like to say a few words."

The attendees clapped and Ansah took his seat as
Thomas stood up to speak. "Your Majesty, Chief Nii Lante,
what an honor to meet with you today! We haven't seen each
other in almost a year, and I hope we can make the visits
more frequent—as His Majesty's time permits.

"Since my arrival in Ghana in my capacity of the Africa
West president, I have seen how deeply you care about the
people of your town and the efforts you've made to improve
conditions. But, as our dear friend Peter has remarked
upon, La needs more facilities for real change. For this
reason and the close association between Your Majesty and
the Church of Jesus Christ of Latter-Day Saints, we propose
building a state-of-the-art community center, where people
can get together for recreation and learning. In this way, we
can reduce crimes of lust and passion by providing healthy
outlets for all that youthful energy."

Now Chief Nii Lante II spoke up in erudite English—after
all, being a chief wasn't his only job. In his other life, he was
a Classics professor at the University of Ghana. "Thank you

very much for your visit and this very welcome news," he said. "I look forward to planning the facility with you and starting a new future for our town and communities."

"Your Majesty," Thomas continued, "we at the LDS know that God loves all his children, and so we continue to work for Him to bring his message to all. As has been the custom, our missionaries will continue to preach his word as representatives of Jesus Christ, sharing His gospel with the world and bringing new followers into our Latter-Day Saints family."

"I too, Mr. Thomas," Nii Lante said, "praise you for bringing the Word to us, and I always appreciate your missionaries when I see them at work."

"Thank you so much."

Ansah spoke to the *otsiame*. "With His Majesty's permission, I would now like to give the floor to Mr. Christopher Cortland to speak."

Christopher made all the necessary reverent pleasantries before launching into his speech: "Your Majesty, the International Congress of Families stands squarely in support of what Mr. Simon Thomas has said. We, too, care about the youth of Ghana, and they are the ones on whom we primarily depend for our work. Just like the LDS has missionaries, the ICF has ambassadors who spread the word of Jesus to the community. An essential component of that message is the concept of proper sexual rights and strong Ghanaian family values, and in fact, that is the title of the new bill Mr. Ansah has introduced to parliament that is awaiting debate by the body.

"I know, Your Majesty, that you are a devout Christian and a follower of Christ. In your wisdom, you are aware that a movement exists that threatens to destroy our cherished and traditional godly family of a man, his wife, and his children. That is what the LGBTQ people are trying to do with their blasphemous quest for same-sex marriage, which is truly an abomination in the sight of God."

The small crowd burst into exaggerated applause.

Christopher beamed, and gave a small bow. He glanced at Gertrude, who was smiling in strong approval.

"Last, Chief Nii Lante, Your Majesty," Christopher said, "the ICF will pay particular attention to the wonderful citizens of your town. They deserve the very best."

CHAPTER TWENTY-FOUR

EMMA RECEIVED A CALL from her mother twenty minutes to briefing time Thursday morning.

"Is something wrong?" Emma asked.

"No, nothing. Why?"

"I thought we agreed to avoid calls during the workday, Mama."

"That's why I'm catching you just before you start."

Emma was about to say, "That makes no sense," but she dropped it.

"How's everything, dear?" Akosua asked.

"Good," Emma said curtly. "Just working our case."

"Ah, that's good. How's Courage?"

This was the inevitable question Emma hadn't wanted to hear. "Fine."

"You don't sound your usual self. You sure nothing is wrong?"

"Positive."

"Well, anyway, give him my regards."

"Mama, we're about to start the meeting. I'll call later on, okay?"

"All right, dear. Have a great day."

Emma acknowledged she wasn't in a good mood. She was unsettled, off track. Nagging like a malicious tsetse fly was what had transpired between her and Courage. Speak of the devil, her phone rang and the screen said *Courage*.

Emma answered, wondering why she hadn't merely ignored his call.

"Just wanted to hear you," he said, his voice wobbling. "I miss you a lot, Emma."

She felt anger about what Courage had done, and anger that she missed him.

"Can we get together and just talk sometime?" he asked.

She sighed, feeling empty and wretched. "I don't know, Courage. I'm bewildered right now. And anyway, why are you calling me at this time of the morning when you know I'm just about to start work?"

"I know, I know; it's not a good time. Sorry. I just . . ."

"I'll call you later." Emma hung up. She'd sounded surly, and she hated being this way.

Beverly had just arrived and was setting up for the day. "Good morning!" she called out to Emma.

"Morning," she replied, faking cheerfulness.

The rest of the crew began filing in—Jojo and Gideon arguing about soccer teams, and then Manu, who was miraculously on time.

At eight sharp, Sowah emerged from his office with a spring in his step, his gout attack gone.

"Morning, all. Let's get started. Manu first. What happened with Chief Nii Lante II?"

Manu related the story, continuing with his meeting with the Adamah brothers.

"I was stupid enough to hope they would confess they'd killed Marcelo," he said ruefully. "I should have known better. To be honest, Addo and Adjei may be thugs, but I don't see that they committed any or even one of the murders. For instance, they had no idea who Abraham Quao was."

"Maybe they're lying?" Jojo suggested.

"Could be," Manu agreed, "but with their body language

and the way they answered my question both of them at exactly the same time . . . I don't think so."

"All the same," Sowah said, "what they told you about the church minister is a potential lead. We need to find out who this minister is. In addition, it seems a *third* party was involved—someone who contacted the minister, right? So, who was that?"

"Could it be someone in the ICF?" Emma suggested. "Maybe Cortland himself, or someone on his staff?"

"We need to work on that, Emma," Sowah said. "When will you meet with the ICF people next?"

"This afternoon," she said. "With Kwabena Mamfe. And, sir, I have an important update."

"Ah, yes? Fill us in."

"I called Henrietta's mother to express my sympathy yesterday. She hadn't been to her daughter's home since the murder, and she was terrified of facing it alone. I offered to go with her."

"Good of you," Sowah said. "Continue."

Emma narrated the sequence of events leading up to retrieving the pebbles from the drainpipe.

Sowah looked stunned. "What? You say you—"

"Hold on," Manu asked in disbelief. "The same kind of pebbles we saw at Marcelo's crime scene?"

"Yes," Emma said, removing a paper bag from her backpack. "Here they are."

She opened the top of the bag and everyone rushed to peer inside.

"*Wow!*" Jojo exclaimed.

"Okay, okay," Sowah said, "settle down, everyone. Let's discuss what this means. Well, first, let me ask you, Emma, what do *you* think?"

She cleared her throat, not wanting to make too grandiose

a statement. "I think they connect Marcelo's and Henrietta's murders, but we still don't know about Quao's, and we can't say that the murderers are the same person or persons in all those cases."

Manu, Gideon, and Jojo agreed.

"Can we build a profile of the killer or killers?" Sowah suggested. "These are beach pebbles, I guess you can call them. Is it someone connected with the sea in some way? A fisherman?"

"A surfer?" Jojo suggested. He got a couple of funny looks. "Guys *do* surf in Ghana, or didn't you know that?"

"That's true," Gideon conceded, laughing.

"What about a fish seller who gets her fish fresh with the morning catch?" Emma said. "Maybe she has a gay son or lesbian daughter and hates it so much she sends men out to kill gay people."

The others made skeptical noises. "A bit far-fetched, don't you think?" Manu said.

"You thought the pebbles were far-fetched," Emma said, returning the ball, and then regretting it because she had sounded snarky.

"All right, all right," Sowah said. "Let's all keep thinking about it. Meanwhile, Emma, what are you going to do with these?"

"I'll take them to Dr. Jauregui after we're done here," Emma said. "She can arrange to have the DNA analyzed. I also need to alert her to be sure she does Henrietta's autopsy."

"One other thing," Sowah said. "Don't forget to include DCI Boateng. This is very important. We *cannot* steal his case, do you understand?"

Emma got out her phone to call Dr. Jauregui and caught her just as she was preparing to start a new autopsy.

"Hold on," the doctor said. She called out to one of her staff to ask if Henrietta Blay was on the books for the morning. After a pause, the answer came back in the affirmative.

"Then assign it to me, please," Jauregui instructed her staff before returning to the phone. "I've got it, Emma. Are you coming down?"

"Yes, and I have something to show you."

EMMA ARRIVED AT the police mortuary before 10 A.M. and joined Dr. Jauregui in the changing room to suit up.

"Sadly, you're back here so soon, and under these circumstances," Jauregui said.

"Henrietta became my friend, Doctor," Emma said, putting her arms through her PPE sleeves. "I never expected this to happen, but maybe I shouldn't have been surprised, given Ghana's political climate."

"I don't understand it," Jauregui said glumly. "Tell me the story of this victim, Emma."

She gave the doctor a quick rundown of Henrietta's story. "I had no idea this was the woman who sings that catchy song," Jauregui said.

"Her body was on the floor of the shower cubicle," Emma continued. "A lot of blood all over the floor, the walls, even the ceiling."

"Any other clues?"

"Yes, that's what I'll show you after the autopsy." With a grin, Emma lifted the pebble-containing paper bag.

"Oh, I can hardly wait!" Jauregui exclaimed in curiosity and excitement, and Emma detected her smile behind the surgical mask. "I think they're ready for us, so let's go. Bring the bag with you, please. Especially if it's a diamond necklace."

They laughed at Jauregui's quip as they entered the autopsy room. Another pathologist was working on a corpse at the far end of the room. As accustomed as Emma was growing to the mortuary, she still flinched when she heard the bang of a corpse on a metal gurney. The morgue attendant handled the cadavers with abandon. True, a corpse had no feeling, but it was cringe-inducing. Henrietta's body was on the table closest to Emma and Jauregui. Henrietta's body wasn't in as advanced a stage of decomposition as Abraham's had been, but it was bad enough. Death had disfigured her, and again, just like she'd found with Abraham, one person or more had dealt Henrietta multiple deep slash wounds from head to toe. As Jauregui examined the body, Emma stood at the side of the table overwhelmed with sadness and outrage.

"Are you okay?" Jauregui asked, looking up.

Emma shook herself. "Yes, Doctor."

"Let me show you something."

Emma went around to Jauregui's side on the body's left.

"Look at these lacerations, oriented in multiple directions and very deep. They appear to be made by a machete. I measure them up to ten centimeters, the deepest in the thigh. Some of the bones—arms, legs, ribs—have been broken. She has defense wounds on both forearms. You see here on the right? Henrietta raised her arm to her face to protect herself and this was probably how she got this particular laceration you see about midway along the forearm. Then, both hands also have defensive wounds throughout the palm and the finger webs.

"Now, let's go to her right side. The same deep lacerations, but not as deep as on her left side. I measure their depth to a maximum of seven centimeters." Jauregui paused to ask one of the attendants to flip the body over, which he did adeptly. "Look at the wound pattern here. There's a mixture of wound depths—some deeper than others."

"The same pattern as Marcelo's?" Emma asked.

"Similar," Jauregui said, "so, as with his case, I'm suggesting there are two assailants, but one is significantly stronger than the other. The stronger one, probably right-handed, slashed Henrietta's flesh on her right side, facing her. His cuts are deeper than the ones on the left side from the weaker killer. That's why there's a mixture of deeper and more superficial cuts." Jauregui took a breath, then shook her head decisively. "Brutal. It's a shame. Now, what did you have to show me?"

Emma retrieved the paper bag from the side counter. "Pebbles."

Jauregui peered in. "Ah! These resemble what you found at Marcelo's murder scene, right?"

Emma nodded. "So now, we're establishing a pattern of injuries with the juju pebbles."

"You're thinking the same killers in both cases?"

"I am, yes. And possibly Quao as well, since he was so closely tied to Marcelo. Could DNA testing on the pebbles help?"

"To link the murders to the murderer?" Jauregui was doubtful. "Only if somehow the killer left trace amounts of their DNA at the separate crime scenes—semen, blood, or saliva."

Emma nodded, feeling deflated.

"You're welcome to stay for the complete autopsy," the doctor said, "but I don't know how you feel about that."

"I think I've reached my limit for today," Emma said, with a nod of regret at Henrietta's body. "But if you find something important, please let us know. Thank you, Doctor."

OUTSIDE, EMMA CLOSED her eyes and leaned against a pillar of the building, relieved to be away from the morgue but still experiencing feelings of grief and anger.

"Emma!"

She opened her eyes. DCI Boateng was ambling toward her. Then she realized she had forgotten to call him as Sowah had requested.

"Inspector? Are you here for Henrietta's postmortem?"

"Yeah," he said, attempting to tuck his wayward shirttails back into his generous waistline. "Has the doctor done it already?"

"She's working on it now," Emma told him. "You can still catch her."

"Okay. What's new on the case?"

"We think there were two attackers," Emma said. "We also found the same kind of juju pebbles close to Henrietta's body that we saw with Marcelo."

"Oh!" Boateng said. "Where did you find them exactly?"

"In the shower drain," Emma said. "But you should hurry, Chief Inspector. Don't miss the autopsy."

CHAPTER TWENTY-FIVE

Gertrude opened her hotel room door to Emma's knock.

"Hi, Ruby! Kwabena just texted me to say he'll be down in a minute. How've you been?"

"Very well, thank you. Yourself?"

"Just finishing off some details for the ambassadorship, and once Kwabena's here, we can start."

Kwabena entered a few minutes later.

"Morning, beautiful ladies," he said, all smiles.

Gertrude beamed. "Ah, Kwabena. Always the gentleman."

He pulled up a chair as Gertrude stood up to walk to the writing board propped on an easel. "Ruby, what I'm going to do for you is show you how we are organized and where you'll fit in."

Gertrude wrote *ICF* in large letters at the top of the board and underlined the acronym twice. "Here we are at the top, the parent company founded by my brother, Christopher Cortland, CEO, whom you've met, of course. I'm second-in-command." Gertrude began a block diagram to show the ICF hierarchy. "Next is the Board of Directors composed of religious leaders not only from the United States, but from African countries. For example, here in Ghana, Pastor JB Timothy is on our board."

That struck a chord in Emma as she recalled what the Adamahs had told Manu: a church minister had asked the brothers to kill Henrietta. Could Pastor Timothy be that minister?

"The primary mission of the ICF is to serve God and promote family values all over the world as God would have it," Gertrude continued. "The true family starts with holy matrimony between a man and his wife, and from there it can bloom in God's sight. But as you know, the true family has been under attack by liberals who approve of the LGBTQ agenda. So you may be wondering how we can fight against these threats. The answer is simple. With our allies: the clergy, the government, and the chiefs. And now, we're adding another weapon, and that's where you come in, Ruby."

"Yes, I am excited to help, Madam Gertrude."

Gertrude exchanged a smile with Kwabena. "I'm very pleased you're here, Ruby. You're going to start in the town of La, where the ICF is coordinating with the LDS to build a new community center. Now, Kwabena will have you as his apprentice for a few days, and then you'll begin your personal journey bringing the good news to so many. How does that sound?"

"Wonderful, madam."

"Now, I'll leave you with Kwabena, Ruby, so he can coach you on the most powerful Bible passages we use, and how we interpret them to the people. Paloma should be joining you in a little while. I'd like her to get a short video clip of the coaching to put on our website."

That raised an alarm in Emma's mind. If the video was shared on ICF's Facebook page, it could blow her cover if someone recognized her.

Before Gertrude reached the door, Paloma burst in and stood there for a moment with a black tote bag in one hand. For a second, she looked terrified, and then her face crumpled and she began to cry.

Kwabena sprang from his seat and went to her. "What's wrong, baby? What happened?"

Paloma responded, but her message was unintelligible as she sobbed.

"Say again, baby?"

"Henrietta's dead!"

"Henrietta? Henrietta who?"

"*Blay*, Henrietta Blay! She's been murdered."

"Oh!" Kwabena exclaimed. "Did you know Henrietta?"

"Yes, yes, I did."

Kwabena put his arms around Paloma. "I'm sorry for the bad news. You never told me you knew her."

Paloma wiped her tears with the back of her hand. "We met at an event a couple of years ago when I was in Ghana, before I met you. We became friends."

"And you knew she was an LGBTQ activist?"

Paloma nodded as she moved out of Kwabena's embrace and pulled herself together. "Yes, I did. She was also a nice person, Kwabena. You don't have to take that tone."

"Okay," Kwabena muttered. "Sorry."

"We empathize with your loss," Gertrude said stiffly. "What happened to Henrietta?"

"They say she was hacked to death," Paloma said with a shudder.

"Do you want to postpone this to another time, then?" Gertrude asked.

Paloma shook her head. "We'll go ahead as planned. It will help me take my mind off things."

"Thank you, dear. And again, my condolences."

Gertrude left. Paloma began to set up the camera equipment from the tote bag. For a moment, she stopped, lost in a daze.

"Are you okay, Paloma?" Emma asked. "I'm so sorry."

Paloma shook herself. "Thanks. I'm fine—almost done here."

"Did you bring your Bible?" Kwabena asked Emma.

"Yes." She removed it from her backpack.

In the almost forty-five minutes that ensued, Kwabena coached Emma on the most-quoted Bible passages, how to start a conversation as an Angel Ambassador, how to prepare people to accept Jesus as their savior, and how to talk about the sinfulness of homosexuality. Emma engaged as a sincere, eager, and wide-eyed participant.

At the conclusion, Paloma was pleased. "I've got some super footage. The two of you were great."

Kwabena had to depart, leaving the two women alone. Paloma packed up her equipment and invited Emma to join her at the hotel café. They found a snug corner where they could talk in private. Paloma ordered a latte, while Emma, who had never developed a liking for coffee, had black tea with milk and sugar. They both munched on bruschetta.

"I'm sorry about your friend Henrietta," Emma said. "Tell me more about her."

"Have you ever heard of her, Ruby?" Paloma asked.

Emma avoided responding directly. "You said she was an LGBTQ activist?"

"Yes, and I didn't relate the whole story to Kwabena or Gerty because I could tell they were getting their knickers in a twist. I met Henrietta at a secret LGBTQ event where she performed. It was marvelous. She was transitioning to female and needed moral support. I cheered her on and tried to keep her spirits up, even after I'd returned to the UK. So, we've been in touch all along."

"Now I understand your grief," Emma said

"She had plans and ideas for both her artistry and

activism," Paloma said, sadly and spiritedly. "Those two almost always intersect."

"But people don't understand that," Emma said. "Did Kwabena ever express any opinions about Henrietta?"

Paloma shook her head. "He always kept silent if the subject came up, at least in my presence, but I found out what he thought about any LGBTQ topic once he joined the ICF. That marked a change from the jazz lover he had been to this religious guy."

"I wonder why that happened in the interim," Emma said.

"Kwabena suffered an awful loss," Paloma said. "His sister died in a plane crash on a flight to Kumasi. From that point, Kwabena began searching for something to alleviate the pain. I don't know who suggested ICF to him or if he just googled it or what have you, but that's where he ended up."

"But . . ." Emma paused to frame her question appropriately. "But you aren't much in favor of ICF—or am I wrong? So where does that leave you?"

"In an awkward position," Paloma said, her discomfort clear. "I like Kwabena, and I've helped him get through some of his darkest days, but this stuff he's involved himself with is getting too extreme for my taste. For a while, I thought he would come out of this religious phase, but I don't think that's going to happen anytime soon. To be honest, I think he's trying to slowly indoctrinate me." She heaved a sigh and shook her head. "I'm not the indoctrination type."

"So then, what's your role in ICF in Accra?"

"Kwabena told Gerty I was a videographer and asked if I could do some work for them. I think he's hoping some of this stuff will rub off on me."

"Ahh, I see." Emma hesitated. "Speaking of the video . . ."

"What's up?" Paloma asked.

"I'm not that comfortable with my being in it."

"Oh!" Paloma was taken aback. "The way Gerty described it, you were happy to do a video."

Emma frowned and smiled at the same time. "I don't think that's correct. She never asked me."

"That's rather unprofessional, I must say," Paloma said. "Of course—if you don't want to appear on the internet, you shouldn't be forced to. Don't worry, I'll take care of it."

"Thank you."

Paloma smiled. "I'm glad I met you! You're so cool."

"Wow, thanks. And likewise."

"There's something else I need to let you know," Paloma began, but a phone notification interrupted. "It's Kwabena. He wants me to come upstairs. Can we meet up again soon to talk?"

"Would love to."

CHAPTER TWENTY-SIX

AT MORNING BRIEFING, THE group discussed Georgina's accusation that Uncle Richie had killed her Henrietta.

"For certain, we need to gather more intel on Richie," Sowah said. "Emma, talk to his sister some more, see what you can unearth."

"Sure, boss."

"We also still need to get into Pastor JB's dealings and how they may be connected to Marcelo's, Abraham's, and Henrietta's murders. Ideas, Manu?"

"I could talk to him," he said uncertainly. "Maybe after his church service this Sunday?"

"I'll come along," Emma said quickly.

Sowah nodded. "The two of you, come up with a plan." He stood up. "I'm off to Takoradi this afternoon for the weekend with the wife. Call if you need me."

EMMA HAD BEEN going over an idea in her mind. She went down the hall to Sowah's office and knocked on the door, which was open.

"Boss? Do you have a moment before you leave?"

He looked up. "Sure, Emma; come in. What's up? You can shut the door."

She sat on the crimson sofa, which had just been reupholstered in pleather after showing its age. "Sir, I think Jojo's exclusion from the case as an investigator makes sense, but what if he were a witness or informer?"

Sowah nodded. "I still think bias might affect his judgment."

"But look at the quality of the person, boss. Jojo's one of the smartest and sincerest people I've had the pleasure of knowing, and as an investigator, he's aware of the possibility of that bias and will avoid it."

Sowah thought about it for a moment. "Okay. We'll try bringing him in carefully."

"Thank you, sir. Can I call him? Because I need to ask him certain questions and maybe you have some of your own."

Sowah glanced at his watch. "Okay, let's conference. I have a little time."

Emma texted Jojo, who had been making himself scarce at the morning meetings. He joined them in the office after a few minutes.

"Even though you excluded yourself from the investigation," Sowah said to him, "Emma has pointed out that we may be missing the benefit of your knowledge. So, yes, you won't be an investigator, but no, we shouldn't exclude you completely. I think it's my mistake, and I apologize."

Jojo's face lit up. "Thank you, sir." Then, he was bashful. "It's no harm done."

"Okay," Sowah said. "Emma, give us a summary of where we are at this point."

"Manu and I have been working from different angles with the question in our minds of who would want to kill Marcelo Tetteh and Henrietta Blay. It looks like a hate crime, but is it random or is it targeting LGTBQ leaders and influencers? Is it the same people committing the crime, or different? We think it could be the same people because of a strange thing we found at the scene of both Marcelo and Henrietta. A pile of grayish, whitish pebbles, five or six in number."

"The very smooth ones you can find at the beach?" Jojo said.

"Yes," Emma said. "Do you know anything about them?"

"Not a lot, but my grandma used to collect them and put them around the house, saying they represented the sea gods and would protect us from evil spirits. She stacked the pebbles, like four or five, where you think evil spirits are or might attack, then you keep one pebble on yourself for protection outside home."

"Interesting," Sowah said. "Was your grandma a Ga?"

"Yes, sir."

"Have you heard of such a thing, sir?" Emma asked Sowah, who was also Ga.

"To be honest, no," Sowah said, "but belief in the supernatural isn't monolithic. It takes many forms. In the mind of a murderer, the victim's ghost may be vengeful and restless. Maybe they think the pebbles could discourage the ghost from escaping the crime scene to cause mayhem."

"So," Emma said decisively, "we're looking for a man with a machete and a pebble."

Sowah and Jojo burst out laughing.

"Good one," Jojo said.

"But seriously, thanks for your insight, Jojo," Sowah said. "Maybe it means the killer lives close to the beach and has easy access, which would fit the Adamah brothers."

"Are we missing anything?" Emma asked.

"Yes," Jojo said. "The guys at Ego's. You met Ebenezer, but I think you should follow up."

"What do you suggest?"

"Well, Ego's is short-staffed at the moment. We should check if they need someone to fill in. And if so . . ."

Emma looked at Sowah. "And if so, boss, time for me to go undercover at Ego's? I could try to get close to Ebenezer."

"Finish up with Pastor Timothy this Sunday, and we'll tackle Ego's next week. Okay guys; that's all for now."

EMMA ARRIVED SUNDAY evening at JB Timothy's church on Spintex Road thirty minutes before the start of the seven o'clock service. She didn't see Manu, but then she wasn't expecting him to be there that early, never mind on time. A crowd mingled outside the building. Its exterior was predominantly white with accents of beige and brown stone. Emma had passed by on occasion, but this was the first time she had been up so close. Floodlights on the massive, circular building made it incandescent and larger than life. A central dome with a golden cross sat on top like a crown. Illuminated in red, the name INTERNATIONAL CALVARY CHURCH stretched across the dome's base.

It had occurred to Emma that questions might arise if a chance ICF member spotted her at the service. She was decked out in a long, curly auburn wig and thick-rimmed glasses, one of her favorite disguises. She walked past a well-maintained garden of lush grass and flowering bushes, noticing at the same time the tall, ornate fence enclosing the entire area. She continued to the entrance to the church, where a set of broad, gracefully arched wooden doors were each flanked by a slender bell tower.

Entering the building, Emma was impressed and surprised by its vast size. Vibrant colors defined the walls and high-domed ceiling. The octagonal nave comprised hundreds of pews in stadium arrangement, funneling from the periphery to the church floor, ending several meters from the broad stage. A TV cameraman was setting up on the left, and a tech was doing a final sound check on the three stage microphones, one next to an electric piano. Two overhead jumbo screens tilted toward the pews. The choir filed in to take their seats.

Twenty minutes to showtime, the congregation grew quickly. Emma went outside again to check her phone to see if Manu had texted. No such luck. She stayed unobtrusively to the side watching the stream of people, some dressed to kill, while others wore ordinary attire.

At six-forty-nine, Manu called.

"Sorry, I can't make it there," he told Emma. "My boy is sick, so we're taking him to the hospital to be checked."

"Not too serious, I hope?"

"The fever is high; we're worried it's malaria. Are you at the church?"

"Yeah, I've been here about twenty minutes."

"I should have called you earlier—I apologize."

"No worries."

"We're leaving for the hospital now; talk soon."

Emma joined the congregation rapidly filling the church to capacity. This kind of crowd in as large a structure wasn't the type of worship Emma was familiar with. Albeit inactive now, she was a member of the Anglican Church, relatively stiff and staid compared to charismatic churches like this one. Emma marveled at how just one pastor could cultivate such a massive and devoted following.

She sat at the end of one of the pews about halfway down to the floor. Cued by soft sounds from the piano, the choir began to sing "Jesus, I Walk with You" as a deacon introduced JB Timothy, who came bounding up the three steps to the stage, waving ardently at the cheering and clapping congregation.

In a quavering tone that was the hallmark of some religious melodies, Pastor Timothy sang along slightly over the choir. When the song ended, he announced he would begin his international Tour of Redemption in two days, and would be away from Accra for three weeks.

We don't have three weeks, Emma thought. If they were to probe JB's possible involvement with the murders, it had to be tonight.

Pastor Timothy began his sermon, moving back and forth across the stage with a microphone in hand. He spoke about the wickedness of the heart, the Ghanaian heart. Now, it was only money that mattered, he said. People had forgotten about service to God and country and were succumbing to Satan, turning to unnatural lusts and a life of sin involving depraved sexual acts.

Switching to Twi, Pastor Timothy raised his voice: "And some of you have come here tonight with that same Satan in your hearts. You are *in God's house*, yet you harbor Satan within you?"

He lifted his hand and pointed to the congregation in a sweeping fashion. "I know who you are already—every single one of you. Oh, you think I don't know?" He momentarily lowered his voice to a whisper. "I *know*. You must not dwell in this house with *demons!*"

A rustle went through the congregation and then a loud, grating scream erupted somewhere on Emma's left near the stage. People craned their necks or stood up to see. Dressed entirely in white, a woman in the middle of one of the pews was in a state of half collapse. Three people supported her as they made their way awkwardly to the stage, where the woman sank to the ground uttering intermittent high-pitched shrieks.

"What's wrong with you?" Pastor Timothy said calmly. He switched again to Twi. "Why have you come here?"

One of the assistants put a mic in front of her so everyone could hear her when she said in a deep growl, "I was sent into her by a curse."

The woman writhed on the floor and became bizarrely arched and tetanic.

Pastor Timothy suddenly lunged at the woman, shouting, "Come out! *Force yourself out!* In the name of Christ, I say, come out of herrrrr."

For several minutes longer, Pastor Timothy spoke to the demon, persuasive in one breath, and condemnatory in the next. With one final scream, the woman sat up disheveled and sweating, looking around as if disoriented and confused.

Pastor Timothy rested his hand on the crown of her head. "You are free now. Go in Christ, and sin no more."

Two of the pastor's assistants picked her up to help her to the side to recover.

Then, like a wave, congregants in several different states of demonic possession came forward until a multitude of people were on the stage rolling, writhing, grimacing, shouting, squealing, and falling backward. Emma noticed that there was always a church attendant to catch them. The ushers and family members of the possessed attended to almost everyone, whether standing or fallen. With so many subjects, Pastor Timothy could no longer attend to them individually. Now he launched a mass deliverance of them all.

Emma made a decision. She counted down from five and stood up, weeping hysterically, and ran past the pews to the stage. As she mounted, an usher approached, ready to catch her when she fell under the power of God's word, but Emma deftly avoided him and made a beeline for Pastor Timothy. Taking him and everyone else by surprise, she wrapped her arms around his shoulders. He staggered back as two ushers rushed to pull Emma off. But she held fast, long enough to say in the pastor's ear, "I love you, make love to me."

Emma became deadweight as the assistants tugged her away, and as she sank to the floor, she began to thrash around, screaming, "*He's trying to know me!*"

The ushers knelt beside her to restrain her and prevent her from getting up. Pastor Timothy advanced, stopping about two feet from Emma. Into the mic, he asked her, "Who is trying to know you?"

An usher trotted around to Emma and held another mic in front of her. "*Him!*" she moaned. "Satan!"

"Satan is within you?"

Emma moaned and let her head fall forward. "Yes yes yes."

"What is Satan telling you?"

"That he will know me tonight . . ."

"What do you mean, 'know' you?"

"He wants to become one flesh with me!" Emma shrieked.

"Meaning his flesh will enter you?"

"Yes yes yes yes! He wants me to bear a demon child."

Pastor Timothy came closer to Emma and prayed over her. Then he invoked God's power to command Satan out, but Satan refused, and for ten exhausting minutes, JB Timothy battled with the demon. They were equally matched, but in the end, the pastor conquered and Emma lay at peace.

Pastor Timothy didn't release her with the words "Go with God, and sin no more," as he usually did. Instead, two ushers lifted her up and quickly took her behind a screen at the back left corner of the stage with a small vestibule. They crossed to one of three doors. Inside a room beyond it was a desk with a Bible atop, a couple of chairs, and a sofa.

The ushers shut the door behind them and spoke in low voices.

"Put her on the couch," said one. "Get the water for her."
The other shook Emma. "*Hey!* Wake up, eh? *Hey!*"

She opened her eyes slowly. "Mm?"

"Drink some water." He brought the bottle tip toward her lips. "Ah, *drink!* Stupid girl."

Each time the bottle got within a few centimeters of Emma's mouth, she flopped her head in the other direction.

"Hold her!"

Her head in the usher's grasp, Emma couldn't move, but as he pushed the bottle to her, she began to retch violently. The men both jumped away to avoid being sprayed with vomit. Nothing came up, but they were done with her.

"Stupid girl!" one said in fury. "Just lie her down, it's okay—leave her like that and we'll inform Pastor Timothy."

They left the room and Emma sprang to life. First, she looked quickly through the drawers of Pastor Timothy's desk—a Bible, sermon notes, letters from other pastors and church officials. She smirked when she saw a glossy pamphlet advertising massive homes for sale in the expensive parts of Lagos, Nigeria. *So much for humility.*

In the last drawer, something caught her eye: a printout of an email to JB Timothy from Gertrude Cortland. *Madam Gerty?* Emma took out her phone and snapped a photo, then shut the drawer as she heard footsteps and voices approaching. Quickly, she resumed her position on the couch.

"That's her, please," one usher said.

"Okay, yes, that's fine," came Pastor Timothy's voice. "Here's a little something for your trouble."

"Thank you, sir."

"God bless you, sir."

Pastor Timothy shut the door and locked it. Emma heard the sounds of his clothes dropping to the floor. Peeking through her eyelids, Emma saw he was naked from the waist down.

"Making like you had a demon," he said with a snort as he sat next to her. "I know why you were up there, eh? I know. It's because you want this. That's why you're here."

Emma moaned.

He unbuttoned the top of her jeans. "Push your legs up. Now, that's what I'm talking about."

As he straddled Emma, he froze and let out a stifled cry. She had closed her fist around his testicles.

"Get off me," she snapped.

Pastor Timothy wheezed in agony as she tugged on his scrotal sac. "Please . . ." he gasped, flipping over to the side.

"How many women have you done this to?"

"No," he croaked, "I never did that before."

Emma increased the pressure until he gave a squeak and went rigid again.

"Some women," he said. "Not many, please . . ."

"What about Henrietta? You raped her."

"No, no . . . I never penetrated—"

"So you think that's not rape?" Emma twisted ninety degrees.

JB screeched. "No please. I'm very sorry."

"Why did you try to deliver Henrietta?"

"Richie told me—"

"Henrietta's uncle?"

"Yes please."

"So you have to obey him? Is he your boss, or what?"

Timothy let out a long groan. "Please, *abeg*. We're just friends, okay? Please, who are you?"

"Tell me one more thing and I'll release you. If you lie, I swear I'll crush your balls. Who killed Henrietta?"

"I . . . I don't know," he whispered, hyperventilating.

"*You* did it. Why did you kill her?"

"Please, no." He contorted and began to snivel. "I didn't—please, talk to Richie. He's the one who said he would kill his niece if she didn't stop being trans."

"Did *he* kill her?"

"I don't know. Maybe . . ."

"After you tried to deliver Henrietta and failed, is that when he decided to kill her?"

"Please, I don't know. I haven't talked to him in some time."

"How do you know Gertrude?"

"Madam Gertrude? She's a friend. Business associate."

"What kind of business?"

"Church business, please."

"Are you the minister who wanted the Adamah brothers to butcher Marcelo, Abraham Quao, and Henrietta?"

"Not me who wanted it . . . somebody else."

"Who? Tell me now."

"It was . . . please, Madam Gertrude called me to ask if I knew someone who could kill Henrietta. I said, no."

"Liar," Emma said, amping up the pressure. "What did you tell her?"

Pastor Timothy yowled and contorted in pain. "Please, I told her about the Adamahs—how they do those kinds of jobs."

"You're supposed to be a man of God, and you shared such dangerous information? *Why?*"

Spent, the pastor wept. "She said she would pay me for it."

"Even worse," Emma scoffed. "You're *sick*, Pastor Timothy. And so you contacted the Adamahs on her behalf?"

"Yes please."

"Did the Adamahs kill Henrietta? Answer me!"

"I don't know." Pastor Timothy gasped raggedly. "*Abeg*, I'm telling the truth."

Emma released him and he curled into a fetal posture. "Please," he moaned, "who are you?"

"Your worst nightmare," she said.

Before leaving the room, she gave herself two ample pumps of the hand sanitizer on Pastor Timothy's desk.

CHAPTER TWENTY-SEVEN

ON MONDAY MORNING, EMMA feared Boss Sowah would disapprove of her potentially risky actions the night before.

As Sowah walked in, he noticed someone was missing. "Where's Jojo?"

"I guess he's running late, boss," Emma said. "I'll text him to see where he is."

"Okay. How did the church visit go?"

Emma answered quickly. "Manu's boy was sick, so he wasn't able to go."

"Sorry, boss," Manu said. "The wife and I had to take him to the hospital."

Sowah nodded. "Of course. The first obligation is family. So, Emma, what did you do?"

"I found out the pastor's going on an international tour for three weeks. We don't have that kind of time, so I decided I would try to see him after the service."

"Were you able to?" Sowah asked.

"Yes, sir. In his office."

"Really!" Sowah exclaimed, intrigued.

"Must have used her female charms," Gideon blurted.

Everyone laughed, but Emma was thankful that Gideon had just saved her from having to give the dirty details.

"How did JB behave?" Sowah asked. "Did he comport himself?"

"We had a small disagreement at first," Emma said cryptically, "but he settled down."

"Okay," Sowah said, letting it go at that. "Did you find out anything useful?"

"At first the pastor denied having anything to do with the death of either Marcelo or Henrietta," Emma said, "but I found out he does know Madam Gertrude, and she did call him about eliminating Henrietta. After some persuasion, Pastor Timothy suggested Addo and Adjei and did Gertrude the favor of calling the brothers."

A murmur buzzed through the room and Sowah's eyebrows shot up. "That strongly implicates Gertrude."

"And the pastor isn't innocent either. Take a look, sir," Emma said, scrolling briefly through her phone.

She handed it to Sowah, who read out the message. "'Hello, JB, I attached the plan we discussed.' Gertrude Cortland sent it. What plan? It shows there was an attachment. Did you see it?"

"No," Emma said. "I didn't have a lot of time."

"Agh," Sowah said in some exasperation. "It feels like we were so close."

"But how did you see this?" Manu asked her.

"While Pastor Timothy wasn't in the room, I checked his desk drawers."

With a little smile, Sowah gave a slight shake of his head, but Emma knew he wasn't displeased with the information.

"I think we're headed in the right direction," he said, "but we still have bits and pieces we need to fit together."

Another jigsaw reference, Emma thought. It would have pleased Mama.

"We need to follow the Gertrude lead," Sowah said soberly to Emma. "Focus on her, okay?"

"Yes, sir."

"I'm meeting with Marcelo's father after lunch," Sowah said, "and I'd like you and Manu to be there."

"Okay, sir," Manu said.

"Did you hear from Jojo?" Sowah asked Emma.

She checked her phone. "No, he hasn't texted back. It's strange."

GODFREY WAS A slight man with moth-eaten hair on a balding pate. He was deadly serious, with two deep vertical frown lines between his eyebrows. He looked nothing like his son, Emma reflected.

This was his first time meeting Emma and Manu. They sat in front of Sowah's desk in a square formation.

"So, how far?" he asked the group.

"We've found out a few things, Mr. Tetteh," Sowah said, "but we still have work to do. Did Marcelo ever mention the names of Festus or Ebenezer, his coworkers at Ego's?"

Godfrey shook his head. "No. Why do you ask?"

"Perhaps there was bad blood between them and your son."

"What I recall is once, after I had allowed Marcelo to return home, and a few weeks before his death, I did overhear him arguing with someone on the phone, but not Festus or Ebenezer."

"Any idea who?" Sowah asked.

"The only name I heard was 'Jojo.'" Tetteh shrugged. "I don't know who Jojo is."

Emma flinched, and her stomach plunged. *Jojo?* That wasn't what she had wanted to hear.

CHAPTER TWENTY-EIGHT

JOJO HAD SPENT SUNDAY night with a high school friend, Ofori, who was also gay but with whom Jojo had a strictly platonic relationship. Up late playing video games, they had both crashed later than they should have. Jojo had planned to get up at 5:00 A.M. to go home for a shower and change of clothes, but he overslept.

"Ah, *shit*," he muttered, scrambling off the cramped sofa that had served poorly as a bed. He pulled on his clothes and shoes. Ofori was still asleep, and Jojo didn't bother to wake him on his way out.

Jojo emerged onto the relatively quiet residential street with its rutted, unpaved surface. Three young men sat chatting idly at an empty vendor stall on the opposite sidewalk.

As Jojo walked past them, he gave them a good-morning nod, which they returned. Ten paces along, Jojo turned as one of the men called out to him—the fat one. One of the other two was of average build, while the third was lanky and wiry. They all wore loose T-shirts and long shorts.

"Yes?" Jojo said.

"Oh, we just want to ask you something."

"What's that?"

"You can come a little closer. Are you afraid?"

"I'm not afraid," Jojo said, retracing a few more of his steps, "but I'm late for work."

"Where do you work?"

"Asylum Down area," Jojo responded, thinking, *None of your business.* "*Chaley,* I need to go."

"Where are you coming from?" the skinny one asked.

"What do you mean?"

"Did you go to see Ofori, that gay guy?"

Jojo turned away without replying. He had no time for this. As he walked, he realized the three men were following him.

"Are you a gay?" one of them called out.

Jojo initially ignored them, but when he looked back briefly, he saw how close they were. Instinctively, he walked faster and then broke out into a run, but the skinny guy grabbed Jojo's shirt and pulled him back.

"Look," Jojo said fiercely, switching to Ga. "Leave me alone."

The fat one smacked Jojo on the side of his head.

"*Hey!*" Jojo shouted. "Get your hands off me!"

"Are you a woman?" the fat guy taunted.

Jojo let loose a full complement of the most offensive of Ga insults.

The fat guy landed a punch straight to Jojo's nose. He tried to swing back in retaliation but stumbled. Two of them pulled Jojo by his shirt and he fell to one knee.

"You're a gay," the thin one said. "We know you're one of them. You walk like a woman."

The fat guy spat on Jojo and slapped him across the face.

"*Kwasea!*" the other one said.

Swinging punches, the three men swarmed Jojo as he tried to fend them off, but he was beginning to succumb to the attacks.

A man came out of the front yard of the nearest house yelling, "Hey! What's going on?"

"He's a gay," the fat guy said, laughing. "He fucks that guy Ofori."

"Is that so!" the fourth man exclaimed. "Agh! Beat him well. Wait, I'm coming."

He rushed back into his yard and returned with a cane. As the other three kicked and punched Jojo, the newcomer called out foul names and whipped him wherever the cane found a spot. "Don't bring your nasty gayism here!" he shouted.

Jojo screamed and struggled.

"Get up, *get up*," the fat guy said.

Jojo scrambled to his feet, swaying, but the fourth assailant punched him in the face, opening a cut over his left eye. Jojo jumped back, and they grabbed at him but got mostly his shirt. Jojo wriggled and twisted, and the shirt came off, setting him free. He ran like he never had, not daring to look back. The four men didn't give chase, but their laughter and name-calling echoed in Jojo's ears.

At the next cross street, he slowed to a walk to get back his breath. Passersby shot him looks of alarm but quickly averted their eyes. Jojo realized his face was streaming blood. Shirtless and bloodied, he imagined he was quite a sight.

A woman setting up her housewares kiosk at the roadside looked at Jojo with concern. She grabbed a washcloth from her stock and approached him.

"Sorry, brother," she said in sympathy. "Here."

"Thank you, sister," he said, wiping his face and looking at the towel to see how much blood there was. A lot.

"Here too," the woman said, indicating his chest.

Jojo mopped that up as well. "Thank you, madam," he said.

"Oh, don't mention," she said, returning to her work.

Checking his pockets, Jojo realized he had lost his phone in the altercation, which infuriated him further, but he still had his wallet. He tried flagging a taxi, but the first two went by when the drivers saw their would-be passenger's state. The third stopped, apparently not bothered. Jojo haggled with him over the price and gingerly got in the rear seat. He ached all over, and it hurt to breathe. After a few minutes, the taxi driver asked Jojo what had happened to him.

"It's nothing," Jojo said. He hadn't come close to processing what had just occurred. He was still at a numb stage of disbelief. He paid his fare at the end of the ride home and walked slowly to the room he shared with two roommates, who were at work.

In the bathroom, Jojo stared at his reflection in horror. Tender to even a light touch of his fingers, his left eye was ballooning fast, threatening to close completely. Blood had caked around his cut lip and underneath his nose. The knuckles of his right hand were puffy and tender, as were the ribs on his left side.

He sat on the bed without moving, staring at the floor. Soon, bloody tears plopped on the floor between his feet. Marcelo, dead. Henrietta, dead. *They might have killed me if I hadn't escaped.*

Was there any point to all this? Why was there only fear in life and no more joy? What had turned people's hearts into cold stone?

Jojo felt hopeless. He hated life; he hated himself for being gay. He felt alienated from the agency team, knowing the boss had only half-heartedly restored him to the case under Emma's pressure. He didn't want to live anymore. *No one will miss me for more than a couple of days.* Could he hang himself? No rope. He could use his sleeping cloth—roll it tight and then make a secure knot. But how would he hang? *How do people even hang themselves?* he wondered.

Then it hit Jojo. *Bathroom.* The window was high and strongly barred. The metal would hold. He removed his sleeping cloth from his bed, and, numbly, rolled it tightly up lengthwise. In almost a fugue state, he fashioned the noose. The other end he secured to the bathroom window bars, pulling against it with all his strength to be sure it would hold.

He stood on a bucket turned upside down and put the noose over his head, shutting his eyes tight, his heart thumping madly. A split second before he booted over the bucket, he heard knocking at the front door and two people calling out his name. In that instant, he changed his mind. *I want to live.*

But it was too late. The bucket went swiveling away. The moment the cloth rope tightened its suffocating grip on Jojo's neck, his head went forward and his heels hit the wall convulsively.

EMMA AND GIDEON had arrived at Jojo's place to look for him.

"Where could he be?" Gideon said as he knocked and tried the door. It was locked. "*Jojo?*"

Emma echoed with her own call, but no response came. "Let's go around the side," she suggested.

The house was constructed with sullen yellow stucco. A machete leaned against a large trash container of weeds. Someone must have been trimming the narrow grass verge beside the building's border fence.

A barred window with mosquito netting was high up on the wall. Emma and Gideon heard faint thudding from inside. They looked at each other.

"What's that?" Emma said.

"Jojo!" Gideon called out. "Are you there?"

He tried to jump up to the window but could reach the sill only with his fingertips.

"*Here!*" Emma said, running to the trash receptacle. "Use this."

She dragged it over and turned it upside down, holding it steady while Gideon climbed atop.

"Oh, *shit!*"

"What?" Emma said, alarmed. "What's wrong?"

"He's hanging—"

"*Hanging?*"

"We need to cut him down," Gideon said, hyperventilating. He looked around. "Bring that machete."

Emma dashed for it and returned.

"Get up here with me," Gideon said. He held out his hand and helped Emma up. There was hardly room for the two of them, but they managed. The hanging cloth had been threaded through a tear in the mosquito netting, which Gideon ripped apart. "I'm going to reach in and pull him up," he told Emma, breathing heavily. "And you cut the cloth with the machete."

"Okay."

They could only just see the top of Jojo's shoulders and head, which had lolled forward. Gideon squeezed his bulky forearms into two different spaces between the metal bars. He reached down, grabbed Jojo under his arms, and pulled him up to relieve the pressure.

"Can you cut the cloth away? Be careful you don't hurt him."

Emma sawed at the knot as close to Jojo as she could without harm. It seemed to take forever before the ligature finally snapped.

Gideon was still holding on. "Jojo!" he shouted, his voice cracking. "*Jojo!*"

Emma reached down to squeeze his shoulder. "Jojo, *please.*" She started to weep. "Oh, God, he's gone."

Then, Jojo coughed.

"Jojo!" Emma screamed. "Jojo, can you hear me?"

Jojo gasped.

"I can't hold him much longer," Gideon gasped. "But if I just drop him . . ."

"Emma?" Jojo whispered.

She let out a scream of joy. "Jojo, you can hear me . . . thank you, God."

"Jojo," Gideon called out. "I don't want to drop you, but I won't last much longer. If I drop you to the ground, can you stand?"

"I can stand," Jojo said in a raspy voice. "You know, it's tough to kill a Ga boy."

CHAPTER TWENTY-NINE

EMMA ASSESSED THE DAMAGE to Jojo's face and neck in the bathroom as he told them about the attack.

"Jojo, you should really go to the hospital," Gideon said.

"And wait fourteen hours for a doctor to tell me I should go home and rest?" Jojo cheupsed. "No. Forget it."

"Look what they've done to your beautiful face," Emma said, shaking her head. "I'm really worried about your eye. It's as big as a ball now."

"I just need to put ice on it."

"Do you have ice?" Emma asked.

Jojo gave her a side eye with the good one. "You're not serious, are you? We have a tiny fridge with space for only two balls of *kenkey*."

Gideon rolled his eyes. "You Ga people and your *kenkey*." He stood up. "I'll go out for ice."

"Get something from the pharmacy for the wounds too," Emma said. "And some water."

After Gideon had left, Jojo and Emma went to the bedroom and sat on the bed.

Emma studied him, worried. "Are you sure you're okay, Jojo?"

"I feel bad."

"About?"

He shrugged disconsolately. "Everything. Marcelo and Henrietta; my arrest; the attack . . . And I feel stupid for what just happened. I'm glad you and Gideon got here in time."

"I am too. And overjoyed you're safe." She tucked her hand in his. "Promise me something."

"What's that?"

"When you're feeling bad, call me, okay? Anytime, day or night. I care too much about you to lose you, and so does everyone else. You're smart and a great investigator. You're funny and beautiful inside and out. We love you, Jojo. You hear me?"

Head bowed, Jojo nodded. "Okay."

"I would give you a kiss on your cheek if your face wasn't so messed up."

They giggled.

"Don't make me laugh," Jojo protested with a groan. "It hurts."

"But I heard laughter is the best medicine," Emma said, trying to keep a straight face.

Gideon returned with ice, a six-pack of bottled water, and a first aid kit, which Emma went through to find a wound cleanser and antibiotic ointment.

"Ow!" Jojo said, as she began cleaning.

"Sorry."

Still in the dark about how this catastrophe had come about, Gideon gingerly took a seat on a rickety chair. "Jojo, what happened? Why did they target you? I'm still confused."

Emma looked at Jojo, wondering what he would say. He heaved a sigh. "Gideon, there's something you don't know about me. I'm gay."

"Yes." Gideon was dispassionate. "And? I always suspected it, so it comes as no surprise."

But that was a shock to Jojo, whose eyebrows shot up. "But how? How did you suspect it?"

Gideon snorted and laughed. "Jojo, I've been in the street with you. I see where your eyes go. I'm a detective too, you know."

"Oh, shit," Jojo said with a sheepish laugh. "I didn't realize it was so obvious. So, it doesn't bother you?"

Gideon cheupsed. "Why should it? I don't worry about such things. I have a family to care for and that's enough."

"So . . . what should we do about Manu?" Jojo said. "I should tell him too?"

"There's no 'should,'" Emma said. "It's what you want to do and when you want to do it."

Jojo nodded. "Okay. I'll tell him, but not until I feel the time is right."

"I must get back to the office," Gideon said. "Do you need anything else, Jojo?"

"I'm good. And Emma, if you need to go too, that's fine."

"I'm not leaving you here by yourself," she said firmly.

"One of my roommates will be back soon."

"Well, then I'll stay until then."

Jojo chortled. "Okay, boss."

Gideon left.

"Any new developments in the case?" Jojo asked Emma.

Emma paused to choose her words carefully. "Marcelo's father came to the office this morning. He told us something I must ask you about. It's not that I doubt you, and I know your answer will be truthful. It's only that the question must be settled."

"Go ahead."

"A few weeks before Marcelo's murder, his father overheard him arguing on the phone with someone called Jojo. Was that you, and if so, what was going on?"

Jojo nodded. "Yes, it was me. It was like the WhatsApp messages the night he was murdered. He wanted us to get back together, but I was done. It was over, but Marcelo couldn't accept it. He was angry, and I was getting tired of him constantly calling to worry me, and so, we were shouting at each other. That's how we Ga people talk, anyway—loud." Jojo allowed himself a smile. "That was all. I never hated Marcelo, nor was I jealous of him, and so, for the record, no, I did not kill him."

"That's all I needed," Emma said quietly. "I won't ask you again, and anyone who brings up any suspicions about you to me—well, woe betide them."

"*Ei!*" Jojo exclaimed in mock terror.

Someone jiggled the key in the door and pushed it open.

"My roomie," Jojo said.

The roommate stopped, stared, and said, "Well, I hope the other guy looks worse."

WITH JOJO'S TRAUMA still top of mind, Emma met with Christopher in a reserved conference room early that afternoon. Kwabena was supposed to have been there but hadn't shown up yet. After the meeting, he and Emma would set off to La to start the ambassadorship.

"We'll continue when Kwabena arrives," Christopher said, "but I want to go over the most critical elements of the work we'll be doing. Chief Nii Lante will set up a large tent, where we'll announce the new community center with Simon Thomas, the LDS elder. We'll use the same tent for events in which all the family can participate—games for the kids and workshops for the adults to discuss the challenges the town has, the obstacles in the way of family life, and possible solutions. We also want to partner with the local social welfare workers to tackle difficult topics like teen pregnancy.

"Sundays, we will offer Bible study classes that emphasize

the importance of family values. For example, we'll have classes on reproduction and abstention from sex before marriage because sex should be for procreation only. We have to emphasize what Genesis says—and I'm sure you know this passage—'That is why a man leaves his father and mother and is united to his wife, and they become one flesh.'"

"Please," Emma said, "are we expected to talk about how to resist the sin of homosexuality?"

"There's no need to attack anyone or anything in your own words," Christopher said, "because the Word of God tells us all we need to know. Leviticus 20:13: 'If a man lies with a man as with a woman, they have both committed an abomination. They must surely be put to death; their blood is upon them.'"

"We should say that part?" Emma asked innocently. "The part about putting them to death?"

He smiled kindly at Emma. "It's what the Word of God says. You read a verse to its completion, even if it's difficult."

"I see. Could that be why they've been killing homosexuals around town, sir?"

Christopher looked befuddled. "What? Who's *they*?"

"You know—how they killed Marcelo Tetteh and Henrietta."

Christopher's mien changed abruptly. "What the hell are you talking about?"

"Marcelo was the man who—"

"I know who Marcelo was," Christopher snapped, "but why do you bring up that topic here? What does it have to do with me or our work?"

He was irked and defensive. "All I'm asking," Emma persisted gently, "is have you heard of any vigilantes going after gay people because of what it says in the Bible?"

Christopher sat back in his chair. "Ruby, what's going on here? What's with the questions?"

Before Emma could respond, Kwabena burst into the room ten minutes late. Emma sensed there was something off. He didn't appear to be his usual relaxed self.

"Sorry I'm late, Chris," he said, taking a seat.

"Not a problem. We discussed the work you and Emma will do in La as Angel Ambassadors. I was about to say we must empower these people by channeling their energy into the community. We could create a volunteer force of people with carpentry skills—the young Adamah brothers, for example."

It surprised Emma that Cortland know about the Adamah brothers.

"I also thought of counseling services for families, especially women," Christopher continued.

"Brilliant idea," Emma said, giving Christopher more credit than she had expected.

After another twenty minutes, Christopher ended the meeting. "Good luck today in La," he said.

"Thank you," Emma and Kwabena chorused.

"Oh, Kwabena?" Christopher said. "Can I speak to you a moment?"

"Sure," he said, retracing his steps.

Emma left, but instead of walking away, she put her ear to the crack in the door.

Christopher spoke in a low voice to Kwabena. "She asked me a bunch of suspicious questions. Run a background check in case she's not who we think she is. The last thing we need is an undercover journalist."

"I'll take care of it, sir," Kwabena said. As he opened the door to leave, Emma jumped away and fled around the corner with seconds to spare.

Fifty minutes earlier

AT 1:46, DIANA opened her hotel door to let Kwabena in. She was already half naked as he lifted her up and threw her on the bed. She let out a guttural squeal of pleasure.

"What time are you meeting him?" she asked.

"I have only fifteen minutes," he said, unzipping himself and pushing his pants halfway down his thighs.

"Where's Paloma?" Diana asked.

"She isn't with me today. Shut up and stop asking questions. Get on all fours. Hurry up."

AT 2:05, GERTRUDE exited the hotel elevator on Diana's floor. They were going to lunch and had agreed to meet at Diana's room to go down together. At the instant Gertrude was making a right turn into the carpeted corridor, she saw Kwabena emerge from Diana's room, tucking his shirt in as the door closed behind him.

Gertrude pulled back quickly. Certain Kwabena hadn't spotted her, she escaped to the corridor on the other side of the elevators and ducked into an emergency exit, waiting until she heard the *ding* of the elevator. She resumed her walk to Diana's room.

"Hi, Gerty!"

"Hello, Diana."

"Come in—I just need to slip on some shoes."

Gertrude stopped in the center of the suite to face Diana. "What do you think you're doing?"

Diana had one shoe on. "Huh?"

"How long have you been messing around with Kwabena?"

Diana went pale. "Who said that? I'm not doing anything with him."

Gertrude shook her head. "Stop it. I saw him stepping out of this room two minutes ago. I'm pretty sure you weren't having tea and crumpets."

Now Diana had turned a deep red. She began to say something but shut her mouth.

"It's one thing to drool over these Ghanaian guys," Gertrude continued. "It's something else to be whoring around with them. I won't say anything to Christopher, but you need to stop."

Diana continued her blank stare.

"How many of them have you been doing this with?" Gertrude asked, contempt laced into her tone.

"No one else besides Kwabena," Diana said softly. "Even if I was, I wouldn't tell you."

"What is this thing you have for these damn Africans? Their big penises, or what?"

"Wow, stereotype much?" Diana said coldly. "That's a pretty fucking crass thing to say, Gerty. And I don't think *you* should be lecturing me about whoring around."

Gertrude frowned. "What do you mean?"

"Oh, so you conveniently forgot about your affair with the mayor of Youngstown years ago? That's why you moved to Columbus, isn't it? Or the parties and orgies you had with your bisexual ex-husband? Give me a break, Gerty. Save your sanctimonious lecture for someone else."

"Christopher told you?"

"I don't need to answer that question," Diana said. "You and Christopher both think you're better than me, but you don't know what I'm capable of. You think I'm just a pretty face."

"Don't flatter yourself," Gertrude sneered.

"Get out," Diana said. "*Get out.*"

Gertrude stood up. "I hadn't planned on staying."

"Okay, sure. Go sulk in your room, you *bitch*."

Breathing heavily with ire, Gertrude left with her blood boiling.

WHEN EMMA GOT to the hotel lobby, she saw an obviously angry Gertrude stride toward the meeting room, then wrench the door open, letting it slam behind her.

Emma returned, slowly easing the door slightly open.

"Why did you tell her, Chris?" Gertrude said furiously.

"Tell who what?" Chris asked innocently.

"Your *wife*. You told her about my personal business with Jonas?" Gerty said, her voice rising.

"It just came out, I'm sorry, I didn't mean—"

Through the narrow space, Emma watched Gertrude slap her brother's face. He jumped out of his chair and turned to the wall, shoulders hunched and heaving. *Crying?*

"You really love her so much you'd betray me like that, Chris? You're pathetic."

She left the room so quickly, Emma didn't have time to escape, so she spun around to face the opposite direction until Gertrude was halfway across the lobby. Emma need not have worried. Gertrude was truly blind with fury.

CHAPTER THIRTY

ON A STAGE UNDER a large tent, Kwabena and George took turns touting the International Congress of Families Angel Ambassador program to the citizens of La. Competing with religious music blaring from a speaker, they spoke in Ga, the mother tongue of 99 percent of the audience wandering in and out of the tent or listening for a moment before moving on.

Side tables displayed glossy flyers of a beautiful Ghanaian family of a mom, a dad, one boy, and one girl standing together in a loving circle and looking upward at the camera with brilliant smiles, lustrous hair, and glowing skin—the very picture of health and happiness. Above the image, the words *International Congress of Families* curved like an arc in red lettering. The flip side of the sheet was filled with praise for Ghanaians and the Ghanaian family, God, and religion. *Jesus loves the Ghanaian family*, it said, followed by Bible quotes referencing family.

> *But if anyone does not provide for his relatives, and especially for members of his household, he has denied the faith and is worse than an unbeliever.*
> **1 Timothy 5:8**

> *Let each one of you love his wife as himself, and let the wife see that she respects her husband.*
> **Ephesians 5:33**

Honor your father and your mother, that your days may be long in the land that the Lord your God is giving you.

Exodus 20:12

Beneath the quotes was a photo of Christopher Cortland delivering one of his speeches in a huge auditorium.

George joined Emma after a while, asking how she was doing.

"Everything is cool," she said.

"Have people been asking questions?"

"Yes, quite a few," Emma said.

A small, diffident man in his fifties dressed in a *batakari* came up to them as if on cue. "Good afternoon."

"What can we do for you?" George said.

"I feel bad," the man said. "I don't know the Bible as well as I'm sure you do, but I'm troubled by this verse from Luke's gospel saying that if someone divorces and then remarries, then the man has committed adultery. I'm one of those people—divorced and remarried. So, am I going to hell because of that?"

"Oh, no!" George said with a kind smile. He looked at Emma. "Can you handle this one?"

Put on the spot, Emma's face went hot. She recalled the Bible verse, but not how to explain it.

"You know, in biblical times," Emma said, feeling her way through, "women had limited rights, and divorce could leave them in a bad situation. So, we can say that this teaching protects women from hardship."

"Also," George added, "Jesus provided an exception for divorce in cases where an unbelieving spouse abandons the believing spouse."

The man's face lit up. "Ah, good. That was my case—my ex-wife was not a believer."

"There you go!" George said, grinning. "So, don't worry, you're good."

The man went off happy.

Emma looked at George anxiously. "How did I do? Was it okay?"

"You did well," George replied with an approving nod. "It wasn't an easy question."

Something caught Emma's eye. Two muscular men bearing a strong resemblance approached the tent. *Must be the Adamah brothers.* Even if Emma hadn't had their photo for reference, she could have identified them. On the way to the tent, Addo and Adjei stopped a couple of times to talk to people. Once there, they looked around, briefly read the pamphlets, and then sauntered off.

"Excuse me," Emma said to George.

She slipped away and followed the brothers at a distance, curious to know what they were up to. The two men, walking almost in sync, soon made a left and disappeared behind a reddish brick building. Emma picked up the pace to keep them within sight. After the turn, she saw Addo and Adjei walking along a narrow, shaded passage, a shallow gutter of murky, trickling water at their feet. Emma tread quietly after them.

The brothers emerged into the burning sunshine again and crossed a dusty square of land to more houses, one of which they entered through a battered screen door.

Between Emma and the house, many people moved back and forth attending to their lives. Emma didn't want to arouse anyone's suspicions while she waited for the Adamahs to reemerge, that is, *if* they reemerged. She would give them five minutes and then she had to get back to the event. George and Kwabena were probably already missing her.

Addo and Adjei appeared before their time was up, each carrying a large tote bag and a machete. Barefoot and dressed in muscle T-shirts, they walked toward the beach, swinging the machetes at their sides.

Emma could hear the faint roar of waves from Labadi Beach. She held back for a moment and resumed shadowing the Adamahs. They descended a steep winding path to the beach as gracefully as gazelles. Emma wasn't quite that agile, slipping and sliding most of the way down.

At low tide, the ocean's waves were soft and hesitant coming ashore. The sound of surfers and other beachgoers enjoying themselves faded away as Addo and Adjei entered a thicket of hardy, gnarly trees and bushes with plants underfoot. Emma paused behind a clump of vegetation—luckily so, because Addo glanced behind him once.

Where are they going?

In a slow arc, they were moving away from the beach. When they reached a clearing with a cluster of palm trees laden with coconuts, Emma stopped where she was. The view she had of them could have been better, but she didn't want to risk getting closer.

The brothers jostled playfully, calling each other the worst names they could think of. Their mother tongue had some of the best.

"Today, we're going to time it," Addo said.

"Okay."

"Ready . . . go!"

Emma didn't understand what was happening until she saw Adjei leap onto the palm tree closest to them and then, climbing like a frog, he shot up to the tree's fronds overhead.

"Wooo!" he yelled, looking down at Addo. "How much?"

"Sixteen seconds."

"Ha! I beat your record from last week."

"If you know what's good for you, you'll shut up because I'm going to destroy you!"

Adjei picked six coconuts and tossed them to his brother before climbing down.

Back together, the brothers each picked up a coconut to expertly chop through the outer coat and shell, reaching the delectable inner white flesh cocooning the milk. They tilted their heads back, draining their coconuts in record time.

Well, Emma had her answer, and it was anticlimactic. They were using the machetes to chop up coconuts, not for anything nefarious.

As Emma turned to sneak away, she stepped on a twig, which snapped audibly.

"*Heh!*" she heard one of the brothers shout. "Who's there?"

Emma began to run, tripping over creeper undergrowth. She had lost her way, but she hoped she was moving in the direction of the beach. More or less correct, she emerged into the open air several meters from the water. Out of breath, she didn't hear anyone behind her and thought she was safe.

But, from the corner of her left eye, she saw Addo and Adjei coming toward her. They had evidently taken a different path but arrived at essentially the same place at the same time.

Emma thought fast. Ahead of her, walking barefoot and shirtless along the water's edge, was a middle-aged man in beach shorts.

Emma called out, "Honey!" and waved at him. He turned as she ran up to him.

"Pretend we're a couple," Emma said in a low, urgent

voice to the nonplussed man. "Hold my hand and walk with me. *Walk!* Look forward. I'll explain later."

So, hand in hand with a gentleman she knew nothing about, Emma escaped an encounter with the Adamah brothers.

CHAPTER THIRTY-ONE

PALOMA STAYED AT A B&B in Cantonments near El Wak Stadium. Kwabena often spent the night with her, and she occasionally accompanied him to meet with Christopher or Gertrude.

This morning was different and special as ICF-Ghana opened its new Ring Road East headquarters, an ultramodern building with plush offices, meeting rooms, and a communications center. The Cortlands, George, and Kwabena hosted a select group of people who were critical to their mission: Simon Thomas from LDS; First Lady Abigail Nartey with her assistant; Peter Ansah, his wife Flora, and *her* entourage; MP wives; the archbishops of the Roman Catholic and Charismatic International Churches, the head of the Ghana National Chiefs Association, and the Chief Imam, the highest-ranking Islamic leader.

In the largest meeting room with a view of the perfect lawn outside, guests helped themselves to snacks and soft drinks as they waited for Christopher to speak. After officially welcoming the crowd, he spoke of "sinister forces threatening the existence of the Ghanaian family."

Standing next to Kwabena, Paloma wondered what qualified Cortland to speak authoritatively about the Ghanaian family in front of a group of Ghanaians. What did *he* know?

As Cortland spoke, Diana stood to the side beaming at him and holding a glass of sparkling water. Paloma wondered what Diana and Christopher's story was. Was she really that fawning of him, or was that just for public consumption? Sometimes, Diana seemed a little absent, as if she would rather lounge at the side of a pool with an umbrella drink.

"But the power of Christ is great," Cortland said, finishing his speech. "Can I get an amen?"

The audience responded and clapped enthusiastically, including Kwabena. Paloma, feeling impatient and irritated, did not.

By the time some of the other VIPs had run through their expansive comments, Paloma was more than ready to leave. She leaned to whisper in Kwabena's ear. "I'm not feeling so good. I think I'll go home to lie down for a bit."

"What's wrong?" he whispered back.

"Just a stomach thing, I think."

"Do you want me to come with you?"

"I'll be fine. Drop by this this afternoon."

"Okay."

PALOMA SPENT SOME time thinking about her relationship with Kwabena and if it had any real meaning. She realized she had lost her enthusiasm for it and was becoming depressed.

On impulse, she called Emma. "I was hoping to see you at the function."

"Sorry, I couldn't make it. How did it go?"

"That's what I wanted to talk about. People were getting up, speaking with lofty words I don't think they deserve to use, given their mindset. I mean, seriously? Sheepish Ghanaians sitting there listening to this white guy teach them about Ghanaian families. It's absurd, don't you think?"

"I agree."

"And now all this religious stuff has turned Kwabena into

a sheep. He doesn't even think for himself anymore. Well, except for the sex."

The women cracked up simultaneously.

"That was good," Emma said, suddenly thinking about Courage. He had been in and out of her mind.

"Where are you now?" Paloma asked.

"I'm at a club called Ego's. Have you been there before?"

"Yes, a couple of times. It's quite nice. What are you doing there? Partying?"

Emma snorted. "No, I'm trying to get a job here. Paloma, we could possibly get some clues as to what happened to Henrietta."

"How do you mean?"

"Henrietta used to spend time at Ego's, and Marcelo was working here. I think their murders may be connected, and I'm trying to find out if anyone here knows anything."

It was about time to tell Paloma the truth. Emma felt she had gained enough of her trust, and vice versa. "I have a confession to make. I'm really a private investigator working for an agency, and my true name is Emma, Emma Djan."

"Ohh," Paloma said. "Now I understand all your pointed questions. Look, more power to you. I'm actually glad you're investigating that, and I'm all in. So, what's the story with Henrietta and, who did you say? Wait . . . is that why you've been coming to IFC events?"

"Yes, we think members of IFC might be involved."

"Really!" Paloma sounded shocked. "How do you know?"

"Before I explain everything, I need to be sure you'll keep anything that we discuss confidential."

"No problem. You can trust me."

"Okay, so Gerty asked Pastor Timothy if he knew how to have Henrietta murdered," Emma explained.

"Oh, my God." Paloma drew in her breath sharply. "Are you serious?"

"Did you hear anything, anything at all, that would suggest Gerty hated Henrietta Blay, or that Gerty wanted to contract one or more people to kill Henrietta?"

Paloma paused to think a moment. "No, I don't think I ever heard anything of the sort."

"Did Henrietta ever mention her Uncle Richie to you?"

"Mm, she did once, now that I think about it. When she was talking about her family, she said Richie was her least favorite member and that he was bonkers and a bit of a brute."

"Did she say he had threatened her life?"

Paloma shook her head. "No."

"All right, thanks. I need to go now—they're going to tell me if I got the job or not."

EMMA'S ATTEMPT TO infiltrate Ego's had succeeded.

"You'll start part-time, and we'll see how you do," Festus told her in his office. "Just cleaning work in the evening."

"Thank you, sir," Emma said.

"No, call me Festus. By the way, I never had the chance to express my condolences for Abraham's death."

"Thanks. I was heartbroken."

"Have the police started an investigation?"

"They say they have, but we haven't heard any news."

"Sorry to say this, but they're not serious."

"But maybe we could figure it out? I mean, did he have any enemies?"

Festus grunted. "Not that I know of. What are you thinking?"

"Well, was something going on among the three—Marcelo, Ebenezer, and Abraham?"

"Hm, that one," Festus said lightly, "you'll have to ask Ebenezer. I don't know anything about it."

"Okay," Emma said, certain he was lying.

Festus looked at her quizzically. "But Ebenezer had nothing to do with Abraham's death, if that's what you're driving at. He's not that kind of person."

"I hear you, boss. Sorry for poking my nose into other people's business."

"Okay. So anyway, come back this evening around six. Tonight is a light night, no dancing, so we'll be on the ground floor and it will be a good start for you."

KWABENA GOT TO Paloma's place just before five that evening. He snuggled up to her in bed. "Are you feeling better?" he asked her, giving her a kiss.

"Yes, much, thank you. I think it was something I ate."

"Do you want me to get you some soup, or something like that?"

"No, that's okay, baby, thank you."

"What did you think about the opening this morning?"

"It was fine," Paloma said, noncommittally. She turned to look at him more directly. "What's your honest opinion of the Cortlands?"

"Why do you ask?"

"No special reason," she said, resting her head on his chest. "Just curious."

"Chris Cortland is a very good person," Kwabena asserted, "and so is his wife, Diana. They are very caring."

"Mm."

He looked down at her. "What does that mean?"

"I just think sometimes you're a little too accepting of them. Kwabena, be careful with white people. They play nice, but they stab you in the back the minute you turn around."

Kwabena grunted. "Ghanaians are expert at that too, so I don't see any difference."

"But, at least it's *your* people in *your* homeland. The British, Europeans, Americans, and now, the Chinese have no right to meddle in African affairs."

"You're British yourself, aren't you?" Kwabena scoffed.

"*Half*," Paloma corrected him fiercely. "I have African blood in me."

"Christopher and Diana aren't meddling," Kwabena said. "They're doing good. In the end, everyone is an individual and you accept them as they are."

"Except gay people, that is."

"But that's different."

"How is that even remotely different? You just said, 'Everyone is an individual and you accept them as they are.' Isn't that what you said?"

"But the gays are sinners, and they're threatening our marriage traditions."

"I see. So if you and I were married and there are two guys next door also married, they'll make our marriage fall apart? Do I have that right, or am I missing something?"

"No, not exactly like that. I mean . . . well, I can't explain it."

"I can explain it. Christopher Cortland came along and told you this, and now you believe it too."

"Let's talk about something else," Kwabena said tensely.

"Okay, then. What about Gertrude? What do you think of her?"

Kwabena moved Paloma off his chest and sat up against the headboard. "I don't want to discuss this topic anymore," he said crossly.

"I'm sorry, Kwabena. I shouldn't have been so harsh."

Kwabena grunted resentfully. "I'm going for a shower," he said, swinging over to sit at the edge of the bed.

WHILE KWABENA WAS in the bathroom, his phone rang in the bedroom. Paloma furtively looked at the screen. It was Diana Cortland calling. Paloma wondered why. Kwabena's points of contact had always been Christopher and his sister, not Diana. For a moment, Paloma felt suspicion nagging, but she dismissed it.

CHAPTER THIRTY-TWO

BEFORE REPORTING FOR WORK at Ego's, Emma paid a visit to Mrs. Blay, who lived in a modest cottage in Achimota.

"I'm happy to see you!" Georgina said. "Thank you for coming."

"I wanted to see how you are doing."

"Well, you know," she said, "I'm managing the best I can, but sometimes I feel so *angry*." Georgina clenched her fist. "What they did to my baby . . ."

Emma let some moments pass as Georgina stared grimly at the floor.

"Would you like something to drink?" Georgina asked, looking up.

"Just water, thank you, Mrs. Blay."

Georgina went to her kitchen and returned with a bottle of water and a glass with ice. "How has your investigation been going?" she asked.

"That was what I came to discuss with you. We want a fuller picture of your brother, Richie. Have you spoken to him recently?"

Georgina shook her head firmly. "We are not speaking."

"Ever since Henrietta's death, or before that?"

"For the last six months after he first tried to get JB Timothy to cast out her so-called demons."

"How did it happen?"

"Richie attended Pastor Timothy's church. I went to a

different one. Henrietta sometimes went too, but in disguise to be safe. Then, Richie invited us to join him at a daytime Sunday service with JB Timothy. I persuaded Henrietta to go with me. I felt some spiritual renewal couldn't hurt.

"So, we went, and after some time, churchgoers went up to Pastor Timothy on the stage to receive his blessing. Richie said we three should go down. I said okay; Henrietta was hesitant about it, but in the end she joined us, and we knelt in front of the stage. When the pastor got to us, he said to Henrietta, 'Come, so I can cast out the demons in you.' We were confused. What was going on? And then Richie grabbed Henrietta by the arm and began to pull her onto the stage. They struggled. I wanted to stop Richie, but two of the church attendants blocked my way.

"Before I knew it, they were holding her down on the ground. Henrietta was screaming—not because she had any demons, o! Because she didn't want to be there and she was a fighter. Then Pastor Timothy tried to perform a deliverance on her. When it was all over, she was exhausted, and they took her somewhere in the back to recover."

Timothy's MO, Emma thought, clamping her jaw tight in anger. *He may have raped her then too.*

"I wanted to go check how she was," Georgina continued, "but they wouldn't allow me. I was furious. I even attacked Richie and would have beat him with my fists were it not for people intervening."

"How long did it take for Henrietta to come out?"

"An hour after the service was over. I was outside the church waiting."

"That must have been a terrible for you."

"It was, and when Henrietta came out, I knew they had drugged her with something. I wanted to take her to the hospital, but she wouldn't agree, so I brought her here to stay the night. In the morning, she was okay."

"Did Richie ever call you after all that?"

Georgina nodded. "Once. The next day, he called to ask of Henrietta. I screamed at him and hung up. We never spoke again. I never expected he would try such a thing on my girl again, but he did—that Sunday before she died."

"Did she ever tell you your brother directly threatened her life?"

"No, but I still believe he killed her. After the second failure at deliverance, I learned Richie became crazy. You know, when Henrietta was growing up and she showed feminine traits, Richie used to call her names—*trumu trumu*, *Kojo Besia*, and all of those nasty things."

"Did *you* ever feel bad about Henrietta's status?"

"Only fear that she would be targeted. But Henrietta herself? No. If you love someone, you love them. Full stop."

"Yes, truly," Emma said, and again, she thought of Courage. He had made a big mistake, but, . . . She brought herself back. "Have you ever heard of Adjei and Addo Adamah, either from Richie or anyone else?"

Georgina pursed her lips. "Doesn't ring a bell, no. Why?"

"We think they could have been the two men who helped Richie kidnap Henrietta."

"Oh, I see." Georgina stared ahead vacantly for a few moments. "Listen, would you like me to help you find out who those men were?"

Emma brightened. "Yes! How would you do it?"

"First step is to get my brother here."

IT WAS A long two hours before Richie showed up. Georgina had badgered him until he relented. Emma stationed herself behind the half-open bedroom door adjacent to the sitting room. The siblings spoke in low tones initially; even from her concealed spot, Emma felt the tension between them.

"So," Richie said rigidly, "what do you want from me?"

"I've been suffering, Richie," Georgina said. "I still can't sleep, and I think about Henrietta every day."

"Sorry," he said impassively.

"That's all? 'Sorry'?"

"I don't know what you want me to say."

"You tortured Henrietta practically all your life, and now she's dead. You remember you once said you'd rather kill or die if a family member was gay?"

Richie grunted. "I was just talking. It didn't mean anything."

"You're my brother," Georgina said, "and I know we've grown apart over the years. Can we stop fighting now?"

Softening him, Emma thought. *Good.*

Richie heaved a sigh, and Emma heard his chair creak as he shifted position. "It's up to you, Georgie."

"It's up to *both of us*."

"Okay." Long silence. "Okay, then, let's make peace."

"Thank you. Look, at the end of the day, I care about you; you *are* my little brother. So, I'm concerned about the company you keep. Richie, who are the men you came with to take Henrietta away?"

"You don't know them."

"Are they Pastor Timothy's bodyguards?"

"No."

"Then who are they?"

"Why do you want to know?"

"Have we made peace or not?" Georgina snapped. "Already, you're putting on that hostile tone. Why?"

"Sorry, sorry. Okay, they're some guys from La—Adjei and Addo. They do odd jobs—labor, and all that."

So now we know. Adjei and Addo had helped Richie kidnap Henrietta. The question now was, did they also kill her?

As if Emma's thoughts had transmitted to her, Georgina said, "Richie, tell me the truth. Did you have them kill Henrietta?"

"Heh?"

"I said, *Did they kill Henrietta for you?*"

"My sister, I'm telling you, *no.*"

"Could someone else have asked the brothers to kill her?"

"That I can't tell."

"Could it be Pastor Timothy?"

"What?" Richie said, sounding appalled. "He's a man of God, Georgie."

"Come on, now." She laughed in derision. "He's no man of God, and you know it like I know it."

Richie grunted. "No, no, no. I can't accept that."

"Then, I'm asking it another way," Georgina resumed. "Did he *want* to have Henrietta killed?"

"I never heard anything like that. I don't think so."

"Do you know that when they took Henrietta to the back rooms of the church, they drugged her?" Georgina asked.

"Why would they do that?"

"Figure it out yourself. Why else does a man drug a woman?"

"Oh, God," Richie muttered, sounding exasperated. "I can't see him doing such a thing."

Men, Emma thought. *They'll side with each other no matter what.*

"I need you to ask Pastor Timothy if he knows anything about Henrietta's murder," Georgina said.

"I'm not going to ask him that."

"Why not? Isn't he your best friend? If you can't ask him the question, it isn't much of a friendship."

"He would never admit it, even if it was true."

"It's not so much what he answers, but *how*."

Richie sighed heavily again. "Okay, I will ask him."

Another weighty silence until Georgina spoke up. "Do you want to stay for dinner?"

"Oh, no, thank you, sis."

WHEN RICHIE HAD left, Emma came out of hiding.

"Did that help?" Georgina asked her.

"Yes, it did. I thank you for setting that up, Mrs. Blay."

"Don't mention it. If you need anything more, just let me know. I want you to catch the monster who killed my daughter."

Leaving Georgina's place, Emma thought, *Addo and Adjei Adamah are high on our list, now.* But then, so was Gertrude. And Pastor Timothy? Hard to say. Could a man as slithery a con artist as him also be a murderer?

CHAPTER THIRTY-THREE

As Festus had predicted, Ego's wasn't that busy on a non-holiday weeknight. Still, Emma had enough work. As the club stood at the side of an unpaved road, customers tracked in mud or dust depending on the season, rainy or dry. She needed to mop the entrance quickly and efficiently. Then the bathrooms could be problematic. The floor by the washbasins was always wet and muddy between customers. The toilets could be a challenge. In the Ladies', the sign clearly said *Don't flush sanitary napkins or paper towels*, which apparently made women do just that. In the Gents', the men's aim was notoriously bad. After wondering multiple times why this was a phenomenon, Emma realized her best bet was to become serenely detached.

Two hours into her shift, Ebenezer appeared. "Are you okay?"

"Yes please," Emma said.

"I started like you," he said with a smile. "Festus will make you a waiter soon, I'm sure. You'll be right for that job. I'll talk to him and we can train you."

"Thanks. Is Festus here this evening?"

"He's upstairs working, but he'll come down later. You'll have a break soon—I'll let you know."

He went off somewhere, leaving Emma wondering how she could have a more serious talk with him. *After work?*

As promised, Ebenezer returned an hour later to release

Emma for a breather of thirty minutes. Emma sat unobtrusively in a corner outside the staff room watching the restaurant buzz. Because Ego's handled takeout food as well, motorcycle delivery boys constantly came in to pick up orders.

A staircase on Emma's right went up to the second floor, access restricted by a chain and a STAFF ONLY sign. Ebenezer went by Emma and stepped over the barrier to head upstairs. She had an impulse to follow him but decided to wait. After seven minutes, Ebenezer hadn't reappeared. She made her move. Making sure no one was watching, she cautiously headed upstairs.

Unlike on her first visit to Ego's with Manu, now the space was set up with chairs and tables around the dance floor. It was pitch dark except for a slit of light from the bottom of Festus's office. Emma was torn. Creeping to the door was risky, but she had to do it. Trotting silently across the floor, she pressed her ear against Festus's door and heard murmurs she couldn't decipher initially. Then it became clear what was going on from the low moans, heavy breathing, and rhythmic thumping.

Taking liberties at the workplace, Emma thought disapprovingly, but then it could very well have been the only location they could have sexual relations in secret. How long had this affair been playing out? Whether it predated Abraham's arrival at Ego's or came afterward might indicate who had developed jealous feelings when—and at whom they were directed.

The thumping stopped. The two men were quiet inside the room except for a few exchanged words. Emma imagined they were putting themselves back together after their furtive tryst, and she turned to hurry back to the stairway. But at that moment, Festus's door opened and a flood of light spilled out. Jolted, Emma pulled back into the shadows. She would never make it across without being spotted.

In desperation, she tried the door to the left of Festus's office. Thank God it was open. She slipped in and pushed the door up to the jamb just short of closing it all the way. She held her breath until she heard Ebenezer's and Festus's voices receding, followed by the sound of their footsteps going down stairs.

She didn't turn on the light in the room. Instead, she switched on her phone flashlight and looked around. It was a junk-filled storeroom: an old printer, outdated computers and keyboards, broken tables and chairs, a box of old chargers and tangled cables, some nails and hammers on a shelf, mops, buckets, and brooms. And then Emma saw something in the corner farthest from her—a flat, two-foot-long object wrapped in plastic.

She held her phone in her mouth as she unwrapped the item, almost sure she knew what it was. *A machete.* She laid it flat on the ground. The handle was worn, and the blade was partially rusted along the edge. But could some of those brown spots be old blood? Possibly. Emma couldn't be sure, but she needed to find out one way or the other.

In her back pocket, she had a clean rag, which she folded in two and ran along the edge of the blade enough to transfer some of the stains onto the material. She wrapped the machete up again, and replaced it. Her time was running short. She got up hurriedly and made for the door, but she heard footsteps approaching from behind it.

Shit.

If either Festus or Ebenezer found her here, she would be in trouble and out of a job. Emma slid into the narrow space between a stack of cardboard boxes and the wall behind it. She held her breath as the light in the room came on. Someone entered and rummaged around. Emma didn't dare peep. After a few more minutes, whoever had come in left, switching off the light and slamming the door behind them.

Breathing again, Emma crept out warily and switched on her flashlight again. She put her ear to the door to ensure she heard nothing further. Before she left, she took a final sweep of the room with her flashlight and realized something. The machete was gone. Whoever had entered the room had removed it.

Emma hurried back downstairs, freezing as she saw Ebenezer walking away from her toward the restrooms. She hoped he hadn't missed her. She descended the remaining steps and went back to her bucket and mop.

"Where were you?"

Emma looked up at Ebenezer's voice.

"I was looking for you," he said sharply.

"Oh, I'm sorry," Emma said sheepishly. "My mother called me so I stepped out to answer." That *could* have been true, so she forgave herself for the lie.

"Look," Ebenezer said, "you handle your private business on your own time, not while you're at work here, do you understand?"

"Yes please. Sorry for the trouble."

"Don't let it happen again."

"Yes please. I won't."

Ebenezer grunted while scrutinizing her as if trying to gauge how sincere she really was.

"Please, is Mr. Festus still here?" Emma asked.

"He's left for the day. He's the manager, so he can do whatever he wants."

Had Festus taken the machete with him?

"Why, do you need something?" Ebenezer asked her.

Emma felt uncomfortable as he stared at her. "Nothing special," she said. "I can ask him tomorrow."

Ebenezer jerked his thumb over his shoulder. "Someone spilled a drink near the bar."

"No problem," Emma said. "I'll take care of it."

As she went toward the spillage, she wondered how long she could keep this "job" up. Her every muscle was aching.

AT THE END of the night, Emma mopped for the last time after flipping the chairs upside down on the tables. She was exhausted. Ebenezer and the bartender were at the register, balancing the account.

Emma tackled the restrooms next, leaving them spotless. As she emerged, Ebenezer came up. "Good job, Ruby," he said, surprising Emma with his friendly tone in contrast to the earlier exchange. "How do you feel?"

"A little tired," Emma said honestly, "but all is well. Thank you. I hope I will become as good as Abraham. I'm sure he was very good at his work."

Ebenezer smiled. "He was."

"You must miss him," Emma said, wringing out a wet rag.

"We all do."

"Please, remind me about why he left for his hometown; did he say someone was threatening him?"

"Not as such."

"But everything was fine with him here?" Emma asked cautiously. "I mean, no problems?" Ebenezer frowned at her quizzically, so she quickly added. "It's nothing—was just asking."

"We didn't have any problems. What are you thinking?"

"Just that . . . well, sometimes I lie awake at night wondering what really happened to Abraham. I loved him, but I hope he never did anything to make you angry."

Ebenezer smiled, or tried. "No."

"That's good, then. I mean . . . did he or Marcelo somehow betray you?" Emma felt her heart thumping. She was venturing into sensitive territory.

"Betray me!" Ebenezer scowled. "What the hell are you talking about?" He stared at her. "Oh-ho, now I see. You came here to get information about us? You think we had something to do with Abraham's and Marcelo's deaths?"

"Oh, no!" Emma said, feigning shock. "Nothing of the kind."

"Hm," Ebenezer grunted. "Finish up. I'll have to talk to Festus about you. I'm not sure if he'll want you back here."

CHAPTER THIRTY-FOUR

At morning briefing, Emma related Uncle Richie's admission that Adjei and Addo had helped Richie in Henrietta's kidnapping.

"That was a fruitful visit," Sowah said, but he looked a little frustrated. "We have to nail this thing down. Adjei and Addo, the pastor, and Gertrude Cortland. Manu, please go back to question the Adamahs—I'll give you spending money for the beers—and try to get them to confess if they really had more to do with Henrietta's death."

"All right, boss."

"Emma, how did you do last night at Ego's?"

She told the group how events had unfolded, and revealed the intimate relationship between Festus and Ebenezer.

"Wait," Manu said, disconcerted. "You say you overheard Festus and Ebenezer in the office and that they were . . ."

"Having sex," Emma said, not sure what the puzzlement was about.

"Eesh," Manu muttered. "Two men . . ." He shuddered visibly.

Emma exchanged a glance with Gideon and rolled her eyes.

She moved on to the machete. The reaction was mixed. Gideon thought it was significant, Manu dismissed it as a red herring, and the boss was neutral.

"Anyway," Emma said, "I scraped some of the rust on the

blade. Maybe the forensic lab can test it for blood and DNA. I'll get it to Dr. Jauregui."

Finally, Emma related her last conversation with Ebenezer.

"You definitely touched a nerve there," Sowah said. "Think you went a little too far?"

Suddenly despondent, Emma nodded. "Too far, too fast. I'm sorry, boss. I blew it. I should have taken more time, and I'm not sure Festus will have me back after Ebenezer reports me."

"What were you trying to get at?" Sowah asked.

Emma bit her bottom lip. "Let's imagine the scenario. Ebenezer, Abraham, and Festus were in love. When Abraham started work at Ego's in January this year, suppose he got infatuated with Festus and seduced him before he started dating Marcelo. Ebenezer was so furious and jealous, so he killed Abraham. Marcelo accuses Ebenezer of committing the crime. Ebenezer gets angry—and kills Marcelo too."

"I don't think so," Manu said. "Here's a better version. Abraham and Marcelo are platonic but both fall for Festus, but Marcelo gets there first. When Abraham finds out Marcelo is seeing Festus, Abraham kills Marcelo out of jealousy. Then Festus kills Abraham to avenge Marcelo's death."

"What about the fact that Festus has a wife and kid?" Sowah asked. "That's a potential blackmail situation. For example, Festus and Marcelo could have been in love, but when Abraham arrived at Ego's, he fell in love with Festus, as you suggested, Emma. Abraham needed to eliminate the competition, so he kills Marcelo. Meanwhile, Abraham had secret photos of Festus and Marcelo together in a compromising position and tried to blackmail Festus. Festus decided he wouldn't put up with that, and so he kills Abraham."

"This is getting confusing," Sowah said, rubbing the back of his head. "Let's diagram it." He stepped to the marker board. "Here is Manu's theory—actually, why don't you come up to diagram your theories? Put your names at the top. Manu, you first."

Manu sketched his, followed by Emma and Sowah.

Manu's	Emma's	Sowah's
Abraham, Marcelo ⊘ Festus	Ebenezer + Festus in love Abraham arrives, seduces Festus Ebenezer kills	Abraham, Marcelo ⊘ Festus
Abraham kills Marcelo (jealousy)	Abraham (jealousy and fury)	Abraham kills Marcelo (jealousy);
Festus kills Abraham (revenge)	Marcelo accuses Ebenezer of crime Ebenezer kills Marcelo (fear and anger)	Abraham blackmails Festus with sex vid/pic of Festus+Marcelo Festus kills Abraham

"Gideon?" Sowah said. "What do you have?"

"Nothing, sir. I'm confused. And anyway, if we're thinking Henrietta's murder might be connected to the other two, how or where does she fit into all this?"

Sowah winced and blew out his breath. "We're nowhere."

"And another thing," Emma said gloomily, "Dr. Jauregui theorizes two killers."

"True," Sowah said, dropping the marker at the base of the easel. His frustration was evident. "Maybe we're on the wrong track. Emma, anything more from the ICF side?"

"No, but I'll be going to see Paloma this afternoon. She texted me earlier."

"All right, good," Sowah said. "Let's adjourn now. Manu—get back to the Adamahs, and Emma, come with me."

She followed him to his office and shut the door, wondering what was up.

"I wanted to show my support for Jojo and so I've called him into the office in a couple of hours. How is his face now?"

"He sent me a photo today. It isn't too bad."

"I'm glad," Sowah said.

"Me too, boss. Thank you."

"I'd like you to be here for that meeting, if possible."

"Yes, sir. I can meet Paloma after that."

At that moment, Christopher Cortland was holding a meeting of his own—family, not business. His two closest women, his sister and his wife, were butting heads, and it needed to stop. He held the gathering on "neutral" territory—at one of the just-finished and unassigned offices in the brand-new ICF building.

He had deliberately arranged three identical chairs in an equilateral formation to signify that he, Gertrude, and Diana were equal. The silence in the room as they took their seats was as stiff as Christopher's starched shirt and the hostility between the two women as thick as groundnut soup.

"Diana, Gerty," he began, "we've gotta talk this out now and air our grievances because we can't go on this way.

Think of it as a truth and reconciliation session. I'm not a judge; I'm merely a participant. Because I love you both dearly, and because you're so vital to my life, we should all be at peace with each other and not let this fester.

"I'm going to start off by confessing my own transgression. Now, Gerty, it is true that I spoke of you unbefittingly to Diana. It was many years ago when you were going through a lot with your ex-husband, Jonas, and before the long, painful divorce. Diana was as concerned about it as she could be, and because she needed some context to understand the full picture, I told her some aspects of your life. But to be clear, I laid it at Jonas's feet. I believe he *did* drag you into all that debauchery. Since then, Gerty, you've changed for the better, and it's a beautiful thing. And although I don't say it enough, I owe you a debt of gratitude.

"Diana, I've hurt you terribly, and I'm sorry. Sometimes I resented your taking refuge with Gerty, but now I'm thankful you've had that outlet. I, too, have demons. Perhaps I should go to one of those Ghanaian deliverance services."

His attempt at a joke invoked only the feeblest of smiles from the women, but it did soften the landing somewhat.

"I'm sorry as well, Gerty," Diana said. "I struck out in anger and brought up something that needn't have been said at all. As Chris says, that's all in the past now. Of course, you're part of our family, and the kids love you. I think—well, I *know*—that I have a chip on my shoulder about how you and Chris have such a close relationship. I feel cast aside. All I ask is for more inclusion. Maybe I could add something to your speeches, Chris, even if it's after Gerty has taken a look. I *am* capable. I *can* get things done, and I can prove it."

"I realize I've made it seem like I don't value your input,"

Christopher said, "and going forward, you can certainly participate more in crafting my speeches. Gerty?"

"Well," she began, "I know I'm bossy and at times even—"

"Vindictive," Diana said.

Gerty flinched. "In what way am I vindictive?"

"Do you remember you once called me just a pretty face?"

Christopher looked from one woman to the other in some confusion.

"I do," Gertrude said, "but that was in the heat of an argument—"

"I've never said anything as hurtful as that to you," Diana asserted.

"Even when you called me as ugly as sin? That's what my father called me; so, excuse me if I'm a little sensitive about it."

"That was a joke, Gerty. Do you have *no* sense of humor? Jesus Christ."

"So we're taking the Lord's name in vain now?" Gertrude said.

"Spare me the sanctimonious lecture," Diana returned.

"Calm down, Gerty," Christopher said quietly.

"Why should I? Why, Chris? Just shut up."

Christopher did, but his jaw was working with tension.

"There you go!" Diana cried to him, pointing a finger. "There it is. She's the only person you *really* listen to. Oh, no, she won't get any flak from you. You really think she's quite the shit, don't you? One day, she's gonna find she has *nothing* on me."

"I haven't the foggiest notion what the fuck you're talking about, Lady Di," Gerty said in an awful attempt at a British accent.

"Did you just call me 'Lady Di'?" Diana said, a smile creeping to her lips.

Gerty snorted with suppressed mirth, after which neither Christopher nor Gerty could keep a straight face.

When the laughter subsided, Christopher proudly reflected that his "Truth and Reconciliation Commission" had been a success.

CHAPTER THIRTY-FIVE

PALOMA WAS OUT GETTING her nails and hair done while Kwabena enjoyed a relaxed morning at her Airbnb. Still, he had work items to take care of. One was a background check on Ruby as Christopher had requested. Kwabena searched as much social media as he could, but came up with nothing. Who was Ruby Mensah?

He went to his Facebook page to admire photos of Paloma and him together. They made a beautiful couple.

Kwabena went to Messenger to catch up with his unanswered communications. The latest was from someone he didn't know with a screen name of "Bad Tidings."

Do you know the terrible reality of your relationship with "P"? Check out this article. This isn't fake—see for yourself. She should be punished for this.

There was a link. Kwabena was wary of such unknown sources, but the specific reference to "P," presumably for "Paloma," intrigued him, as did the phrase "terrible reality." So, even as he debated the wisdom of clicking, he did. That took him to a five-year-old article from the *Daily Mail*, UK.

Trans Woman Scandal Rocks Miss London Contest
Contestant Paloma Smith-Hughes Revealed Transgender
By Samantha Wilkinson

Kwabena frowned. What was this about? He read on.

In a shocking revelation, one of the top contestants in this year's Miss London beauty pageant, Paloma Smith-Hughes, is a transgender woman. Although the Miss London pageant rules do permit the participation of transgender contestants, they require full disclosure of the contestant's gender identity during the application process. Ms. Smith-Hughes failed to reveal this information before joining the competition, which has led to this scandal.

Paloma Smith-Hughes, a 24-year-old aspiring actress, quickly became a fan favourite due to her charm, poise, and undeniable beauty. As the competition progressed, rumours began to circulate about her gender identity, ultimately culminating in a leak of personal information that confirmed she is transgender.

In response to the controversy, the Miss London Organisation has released a statement:

'We are disappointed to learn that Paloma Smith-Hughes did not disclose her transgender status during the application process, as required by our rules. We celebrate and support the transgender community, and our decision to include transgender women in our competition is a testament to our commitment to inclusivity. However, we must also ensure that all contestants adhere to the rules and guidelines set forth in order to maintain a fair competition for all participants.'

Paloma Smith-Hughes has yet to make a public statement regarding the scandal, but her fans and supporters have taken to social media to express their disappointment and concern. While some are sympathetic and believe that Paloma's gender identity should not impact her chances of winning the crown, others argue that her failure to disclose this information constitutes dishonesty and should lead to her disqualification.

At the bottom of the article was a photo of Paloma Smith-Hughes. *Kwabena's* Paloma. He froze and stared at it in disbelief. No. *That can't be her.* His blood turned to ice and then to fire. He latched on to a morsel of hope: it could still be a bogus article. *Anyone can falsify anything online these days.* Kwabena took the next obvious step and searched for "Paloma Smith-Hughes Miss London." And there, in black, white, and color, was one article after another about the scandal: *The Daily Telegraph, The Sun, The Evening Standard, The Daily Mirror, The Guardian*—all had some version of the story with different images of a lovely Paloma. Shattered, Kwabena scrolled through the search engine headings and the introductory first lines of each post. Then came the more sensational website posts with racist and misogynistic comments.

Paloma's birth name had been Paul, and she was born in the UK to a Ghanaian woman and well-to-do Englishman with aristocratic connections. Over four years, she had undergone gender-affirming surgery to the final, definitive procedure that created an anatomically correct vagina with functional, pleasurable sensation.

Kwabena got up and staggered to the bathroom. In the grip of revulsion and loathing, he bent over the toilet and threw up. He had been fucking a *man*. He felt as defiled as if he had been smeared with feces from head to toe. Feverishly, he wrenched off his clothes and got into the shower, which he ran fast and hot as he frantically lathered up his body. Whimpering, he scrubbed his penis, scrotum, and perineum aggressively and repeatedly, examining himself at intervals as though some blemish might materialize. Turning his face up to the stream of water, he let out a scream of torment.

WHEN PALOMA RETURNED, Kwabena was on the sofa staring at the floor and cracking his knuckles repeatedly.

"I'm back, babe," she said. When Kwabena didn't look up, she approached him, puzzled. "Kwabena? What's wrong? Are you okay?"

His facial muscles twitched randomly and spasmodically.

Paloma went down on a knee and looked up at him. "Kwabena? You're frightening me. What's going on?"

"That's what I'd like to know," he said softly, caressing her cheek. "What have you not told me?"

"How do you mean? There's nothing I haven't told you."

He woke his laptop and turned it to her face. "What is this, then?"

Paloma scanned a few lines and then blenched. "Oh, God," she whispered.

"No, you leave God out of this."

"I never wanted you to find out this way," Paloma stammered. "I was going to tell you—"

Kwabena squeezed her face between the fingers and thumb of his right hand. "Tell me what? *What?* That you're really a man, and I've been fucking a *man?*"

Paloma tried to push his hand away and get out of his grip. "Please," she gasped. "You're hurting me. We can talk about it."

He slapped her so hard she fell back and struck the back of her head on the coffee table.

"What are you doing?" she cried. "Stop—"

He grabbed her by the neck and pulled her up with his left hand while striking her repeatedly with the right. "You're a *man*. Why you want to be a woman, eh? What's wrong with you? What kind of madness, what kind of sickness is this?"

He stuffed his hand into Paloma's mouth and throat, forcing her head back and making her gag. Her eyes widened in panic, and then she bit him hard. He pulled away with a curse. Paloma rushed to the front door but only managed to unlock the latch before he caught up with her and snatched her back.

"Please, Kwabena," she pleaded. "I can explain everything to you."

A ragged, strangled sound escaped Kwabena's throat as if he was retching, and moisture welled up in his red, puffy eyes.

"You made me fuck you," he said in disbelief. "You made me fuck your . . . what is that you have there? A false vagina? And I put my dick inside you? You are a *freak*. You are disgusting."

Now Paloma's anger sparked like a night flare. "You weren't saying that when you were cuming in my vagina, telling me what a nice pussy I had, were you? I didn't *make* you do anything."

He lunged at her. She shrieked and ran to the bathroom for refuge, but she never had a chance. He pulled her out and dragged her along the floor to the kitchen. As she staggered up to escape, Kwabena grabbed a meat cleaver from the knife rack on the counter.

As PROMISED, JOJO arrived at the agency mid-morning.

"It's good to see you back," Sowah said, smiling.

"Thank you, boss," Jojo said, sitting on the red sofa.

"How are you feeling?"

"Much better."

"Your face looks good," Emma said.

"Yes, thank God I'm beginning to look normal again."

"First of all," Sowah said, "is there anything we can do for you? I would like to help you see a private counselor."

"Thanks, boss, but I think I'll be okay."

Sowah studied Jojo for a moment. "Please think about it. Sometimes we think we're okay when we're really not."

"The boss is right, Jojo," Emma said quietly. "We want you to recover fully."

Jojo hesitated. "Okay, if I need it, I'll let you know, sir."

"There's a lot to bring you up to speed on," Sowah said, "so I'll summarize the main points and Emma can add anything I forget."

The summary was long indeed. Sowah handed it over to Emma at points where she had her personal experiences to relate.

"So, as you can see," Sowah said in conclusion, "we've come far, but not far enough. We're at a crucial point. Did random vigilantes kill Marcelo, Abraham, and Henrietta? Because of what we know about the victims, their injuries, and the clues at their respective crime scenes, we think not. So, is there an individual or an organized group behind the killings dispatching vigilantes to murder LGBTQ people? We're coming at it from different angles, but there's one we haven't touched: Minister of Parliament, Peter Ansah. And that's where you come in, Jojo. He may not be the kingpin, but he might have knowledge to turn this around. Are you up for this?"

Jojo nodded. "I am, boss."

"Okay, we'll put our three heads together and strategize the best way to tackle Ansah," Sowah said.

ON HER WAY to see Paloma that afternoon, Emma texted her without receiving a confirmation, but she continued the trip because Paloma wasn't the kind of person who would fail to show up without letting Emma know.

Paloma's Airbnb was an ultra-modern cream and cappuccino home with dark glass windows. Emma texted again, and then rang the doorbell. No one came to the door. Emma peered through the narrow glass strip between the door and the wall but didn't see anyone. On a whim, she tried the door and to her surprise, found it unlocked.

"Paloma?" Emma called out. "Are you here?"

She saw something that made her heart stop. The house's spacious, open design allowed an unobstructed view of the kitchen from the living room, and there was a vast pool of red on the floor from behind the center aisle. As Emma approached, she trembled, knowing instinctively what horror she faced.

Emma cried out. There Paloma lay in a scarlet lake with deep gashes to her body and limbs, and a throat slit open wide. Emma's face crumpled as her legs gave way. She broke down weeping uncontrollably. Then she stopped abruptly and stood up, pulling herself together. The bloody weapon lay beside Paloma's body. Emma didn't go near either of them, and she took care not to tread in the blood.

She experienced a horripilation as she felt she was being watched. She looked to her left to find a dead man gazing upon her. Kwabena's body was hanging from the railing of the stairs. The double-stranded electrical cord ligature around his throat was angled upward at his jaw. His elongated neck had been disarticulated by the weight of his body at the end of the drop, and his head had flopped forward. Blood had splattered his face, body, and clothes.

Something monstrous had happened here. Emma's teeth chattered violently with shock. Even so, she noticed two phones on the kitchen center island. *Their phones? Must be.* Both were smashed to bits and smattered with blood. Had Kwabena wanted to erase all evidence of his connection and history with Paloma? Odd that he went through the trouble only to then kill himself in her apartment.

Emma took photos of the phones, then opened a cupboard to find a paper bag, which she slipped over her right hand to pick up the devices. Then, she turned the bag inside out to ensure the devices were well-cushioned to go into her backpack. Yes, she was stealing from the crime scene, which she should not do, and somewhere along the way, she would probably pay for it, but Emma couldn't allow the phones to get into the hands of the police. The way things didn't work at CID, the devices would vanish into the evidence room's chaos. Even if there was retrievable data on the phones, the police lacked the skills to find it. The safest move was to have Gideon, the IT genius, have a go.

Was someone else in the house? Emma ascended the stairs to where Kwabena had tied the cord halfway up the railing and baluster. She looked down at him and shuddered.

At the landing, Emma called out, "Hello? Is anyone here?"

There were two bedrooms upstairs with two full baths. They were empty, clean, and tidy. Emma called DCI Boateng's number, but he didn't pick up. Emma returned to the ground floor and steeled herself to approach Kwabena's body. Blood had splattered his hands and clothing. He seemed smaller than he had been alive.

Boateng called back.

"There's been a murder-suicide," Emma told him. "Yes, it is. Very bad. You have no idea."

CHAPTER THIRTY-SIX

"Where?" Boateng asked as he entered the house.

Leaning against a wall in the sitting room, Emma flicked her chin in the direction of the carnage.

"Oh, my Jesus Lord," Boateng muttered as he approached the bloodbath. "The worst I've ever seen. Who is she? Do you know her?"

"Paloma Smith-Hughes. We had a meeting this afternoon, but this awaited me instead. And that was her boyfriend." She pointed to the staircase.

Slack-jawed, Boateng stared at Kwabena's lifeless form. "*Awurade.* You know him too?"

"Kwabena Mamfe," Emma said. "He's an official at the International Congress of Families."

Boateng gave a knowing nod. "I've read about them. Why can't these *oburonis* leave Africa alone?"

"Exactly."

"Why did this happen? Do you have any idea?"

"Take a look," Emma said, walking to the laptop on the coffee table. "I believe Kwabena must have seen this."

She woke up the computer, and Boateng sat down with a groan to read the *Daily Mail* post.

He went through it twice before looking up at Emma. "Are you telling me that the woman on the floor dead isn't really a woman?"

"She was born male, yes, but Kwabena probably didn't

know Paloma was a trans woman until he stumbled on this online article. He must have gone crazy because he and Paloma were in a sexual relationship. And then he killed himself—maybe remorse, or he couldn't stand the reality."

Boateng grunted, shaking his head as he took out his phone to call CID. "Hello? Yes. Look, we need CSI to come down here at once in the van. *What?* It has broken down?" Boateng scowled in annoyance. "Okay, find one of the guys and tell them to get in an Uber with as much equipment as possible to process the crime scene. I'll pay for the transport."

Fuming, Boateng put his phone away. "You see how difficult my people make my life? This is why all my hair has turned gray." He cursed under his breath. "Emma, I need a statement from you as quickly as possible while the memory is fresh."

"I'll do it on my phone and forward it to you soon," Emma offered. "But I must get back to the agency now."

"GIDEON," EMMA SAID, rushing in. "I've got something for you."

He was staring at his laptop screen growling impatiently at a slow download. "What's up?"

Emma opened the paper bag and Gideon took a look.

"Two bloody, smashed phones," he said blandly. "From where?"

"I believe they belonged to Paloma and Kwabena. Kwabena murdered her and then hanged himself."

Gideon's eyebrows shot up. "Are you serious? When?"

"This morning," Emma said tersely. She had dealt with the emotions; now, it was time to get down to business. "Can we try to retrieve data from them?"

"I don't know," Gideon said, staring into the bag. "They look awful."

"Nothing is beyond your talent. I need to show them to Manu and the boss first, though. Are they around?"

"In his office."

Sowah's door was wide open, indicating they weren't discussing any sensitive topics.

"What do you have, Emma?" Sowah asked.

She sat down to describe the bloodbath she had just witnessed.

"My God," Manu said, shocked. "But how? Why did this happen?"

Emma shared the online article about Paloma to Manu's and Sowah's phones.

"I see," Manu muttered as he finished reading. "I must say, I don't condone murder, of course, but I can see how Kwabena could go mad with this. Imagine finding out that your woman is really a man. Oh, no. It's too much."

Emma agreed that it would be disturbing for someone like Kwabena. *Or Manu,* she thought. She told the two men about her removal of the two destroyed phones from the scene.

"Oh, no, Emma!" Sowah exclaimed in dismay.

She needed to stand her ground. "Boss, the phones may have crucial information to crack the case, but we can't trust the police with it, even if DCI Boateng is on the case. We're dedicated to Mr. Tetteh to solve the death of his son—"

"But how do you know this murder-suicide is pertinent to Marcelo's death?" Sowah demanded.

"Well . . ."

"Well, what?"

"The phones will prove that."

"*Emma.*" Sowah was clearly irritated. He sighed. "You can't operate on conjecture."

"I know, sir."

"So, where are the phones?"

"They're in here," Emma said, lifting up the paper bag to show the two men.

"So, I presume you'll give them to Gideon?" Sowah asked.

"Yes, sir. Or, what do you think?"

Sowah turned both palms up in resignation. "Well, the deed is done and now the phones are in our possession, so we might as well see what we can get out of them. But you need to let Boateng know what you've done."

"Okay, sir," Emma said willingly. "I'll do that."

"The way you *should* have done this was call me from the crime scene so we could put our heads together for the next step," Sowah said. "We could have worked something out with DCI Boateng. And we have our lawyer as a resource as well if we're not sure what to do. You get me?"

"Yes, sir."

Manu, who had been making himself as still and small as possible to stay neutral, spoke up. "Do the Cortlands and the other people in the ICF know what's happened to Kwabena and Paloma?"

"I'm not sure," Emma said, "but I'm going to see them now at their brand-new office."

"All right," Sowah said, "but be careful. And *please*, don't take anything from there without letting me know. I'm serious."

"Yes, boss. May I go now, sir?"

He dismissed Emma, and she returned to Gideon with the phones.

"Boss is okay with it?" he asked.

"Fifty-fifty."

"Ha!" Gideon grinned and gave a snort. "Okay, I'll start on this now."

ON THE WAY to the ICF office, Emma called DCI Boateng, as she had promised the boss.

"You can't do this!" Boateng yelled. "Tampering with evidence and hiding it from me? You bring the phones to me right now, do you hear?"

"Wait, DCI, *abeg*. It will be well. Gideon will work on pulling any available data. You would have done that, anyway, so—"

"*I* decide what to do on my cases, not you. You're smart, Emma, but sometimes, you get arrogant. You had no right to do this and I feel you've broken our trust."

Emma was silent for a moment. "I feel bad now. I didn't intend to undermine your authority, Boateng, and I'm sorry. If you still want the phones, I can talk to the boss, but Gideon has already started working on them."

Boateng released a raspy, exasperated breath. "You must share every single piece of information on the phones, is that clear?"

"Yes, sir. I promise."

Boateng hung up abruptly. *He's right*, Emma admitted. She could have handled this better. But was she really arrogant?

She had a stop to make before her final destination. The Uber driver waited for her while she dashed into the police mortuary with the specimen from the machete blade at Ego's. Dr. Jauregui wasn't in, so Emma left it with the senior attendant, extracting a firm promise from him that he wouldn't forget it or lose it.

ALTHOUGH THE BRAND-NEW ICF-Ghana still lacked a few pieces of furniture, it was serviceable, most of the lightly used computers and printers having arrived from ICF-USA. Christopher, Diana, and Gerty each had their own offices.

His was the first one on the right down the hallway from the lobby. Emma tapped on the open door. "Mr. Cortland?"

He looked up from his laptop. "Ruby! What's up? Come on in."

"I have some bad news," she said, after taking a seat in front of him.

"What's happened?"

"I'm sorry to tell you that Kwabena and Paloma are dead."

Christopher froze and blanched. "What?"

"I went to visit Paloma today and found her dead on her kitchen floor—slashed with a knife. Kwabena had hanged himself."

"No," Christopher whispered. His voice shaking, he called out to his wife and sister.

Responding to his urgent tone, both women hurried in.

"Kwabena and Paloma are dead," Christopher said.

Diana pulled in her breath sharply.

Gerty narrowed her eyes. "*Dead?* What d'you mean, dead?"

He looked at Emma.

"I found their bodies when I went to see Paloma," she said. "It looks like Kwabena killed her and then took his own life."

Diana sat down weakly. "But *why?*"

"How can we be sure this wasn't a double murder?" Gerty asked.

Emma found that odd. "That's unlikely. Especially in this context."

Emma shared a copy of the *Daily Mail* story on her phone with Gerty. She read it quickly without a word. Grim faced, she passed the phone to Christopher, who let out a gasp and rested his hand on his forehead with his eyes closed.

"What is it?" Diana asked. "What's going on?"

"Paloma was a trans woman," Christopher said.

"You've gotta be kidding me."

"I *knew* something wasn't quite right," Gertrude said.

"How so, Madam Gertrude?" Emma asked.

"Her height, for one thing," Gertrude said, trailing off.

Emma inwardly declared that nonsensical. Women could be tall.

Diana's face turned tomato-red, and she began to cry.

Christopher got up and went to her. "I know, honey," he said softly, his arms around her shoulders. "This is terrible."

"How are *you*, though?" Gertrude asked Emma.

"Still in shock. But I'll be okay."

"I'm sorry you had to see that," Gertrude said, her eyes softening.

Through her tears, Diana's grief switched to anger. "Why would Paloma deceive us like that? Most of all, she lied to Kwabena and betrayed him. This is why we preach against this so-called gender-affirming surgery. It's butchery and a crime. People who go through it and the doctors who perform it should be ashamed."

That Diana was more distressed over gender affirmation than Paloma's death irked Emma.

"It's okay," Christopher said softly, rubbing Diana's back comfortingly. "It's a lot to take in. Paloma knew how we feel about this issue and was scared to expose the truth."

He grabbed a handful of tissues from his desk, and Diana patted her eyes dry. "You're right. I'm sorry. I shouldn't have spoken ill of her now that she's dead. Poor woman. And Kwabena . . . he was a soldier for us, you know?"

Something must have struck Christopher at that moment, for he looked sharply at Emma. "Did you know about her? Him, or whatever?"

"I did not. I was as shocked you."

"Hm," Christopher said reflectively. "I can't approve of this transgender stuff, but no one should be killed for it."

Emma agreed with his stance. She glanced at Gertrude, who appeared disturbingly impassive compared to her sister-in-law.

"Want us to go back to the hotel for a lie down, honey?" Christopher asked Diana.

"I wanna go home, Chris. That's what I want."

"You mean—"

"Yes, *home* home," she said fiercely. "I've had enough of this fucked-up country."

That offended Emma and took her aback, and Diana's raw disgust clearly embarrassed Christopher, who turned deep red. "Okay," he stammered hastily. "Let's discuss it at the hotel, okay? Ruby, we'll call it a day. Listen, I'm deeply sorry about Paloma, because I know you had formed a friendship with her. Are you up to continuing the ambassadorship? With George? I'll understand if you need to take some time."

"Yes, I'll continue; thanks."

"You're a trooper. Can't thank you enough. Come on, honey. Let's get back."

As Emma left ICF, she called Sowah to update him although there wasn't much to add so soon after the gruesome discovery.

"If you want to take a few days off," Sowah said, "please do. This hasn't been easy."

"Thank you, sir," Emma said. "I'll see how I feel—maybe work from home tomorrow."

"That's fine."

As Emma got into the Uber for her return trip, she yearned to talk to Courage and realized just how much she missed him. Whenever Emma received a jolt like this, Courage would be there to listen on the phone or in person. He had a way of responding that was neither trite nor patronizing. He was simply there for her. Emma pressed a tissue to her eyes to stop the tears from getting any farther.

Once home, she sprawled across the bed feeling enervated, her thoughts wandering like a Sahara nomad. Again, she wondered why Gerty had made reference to a double murder. Even if that hadn't occurred, what did Gerty know that led her to think along those lines? Emma hadn't the remotest notion. Still in her street clothes, she fell fast asleep.

CHAPTER THIRTY-SEVEN

Takyi owned an eponymous uniform shop in Abossey Okai at the Obetsebi-Lamptey interchange. He had been there longer than most businesses in the neighborhood, expanding as needed but never moving. With a large sewing team on site, he supplied outfits and uniforms to companies' specifications, including the required logos. The agency had long used him for disguise attire, which is what Jojo needed now.

Takyi was a small man with a pronounced limp from childhood polio. The affected right leg was deformed, causing him pain by the end of a long day, but he never complained.

"Jojo, where have you been?" he said, grinning. "What's this I see here?" He playfully ruffled the light beard Jojo had grown over the previous six months.

Jojo laughed. "Something new."

"I like it," Takyi said with approval. "What can we do for you today?"

"Dark-blue outfit, top and bottom, labeled 'Global Delivery Services.'"

"Left or right chest?"

"Left, I guess. Above the pocket. What do you think?"

"Sure, and I'll put an extra one on both sleeves. You want the embroidery in gold? That will look the best."

"Okay, yes; that sounds great."

"When do you need it for?"

"As soon as possible. Can you do it this afternoon? Like, by four?"

Takyi laughed. "Jojo, you're killing me o! No problem. I'll have one of the ladies do one for you quick. Do you want to wait for it?"

"I can, yes."

"Come back with me to choose a logo."

Workers operated noisy sewing and embroidery machines in the back of the store. Jojo followed Takyi to his office to look through his designs. They chose a simple one for faster execution, and Takyi picked out a dark-blue button-down shirt to fit.

"Needs to be tighter," Jojo said. "How about a polo shirt instead?"

"Okay, but they're a little more expensive."

Jojo shrugged and laughed. "Not me paying for it."

The dark-blue polo was snug across Jojo's fine chest. Takyi took it to Dorcas, one of his workers, and Jojo watched the process from marking the placement of the logo, setting up the Hoopmaster Mighty Hoop station, inputting the design on the computer, and finally engaging the Ricoma embroidery machine, which worked at an astonishing pace and was done in minutes.

"Wow," Jojo said. "I'm impressed."

ONE OF THE agency's sources at the ministries had told Sowah that Peter Ansah typically kept late office hours, although like all government workers, his assistant left promptly at five in the afternoon. At 5:20, the ministry's security guard on the ground floor okayed Jojo, clad in his snug-fitting GDS outfit, to go up to Ansah's office.

In the nose-bridge of Jojo's sporty glasses was a concealed camera, which he now switched on with a small Bluetooth device in his pocket. After Jojo knocked twice, a couple of minutes passed without a response. Jojo worried that Ansah might have already left for the day. Jojo was deciding on his next steps when the office door opened.

Jojo hadn't realized how large Ansah was in real life. He wasn't Jojo's type, but the minister's light-brown eyes and sandy hair were spectacular. He stared at Jojo at first but then dropped his eyes to his chest and all the way down before returning to where they should have stayed in the first place.

"Yes?" he snapped, almost a bark.

"Good evening, sir. Please, I've come to pick up the package."

Ansah frowned. "What package are you talking about? I don't have any package to be collected."

"Please, I was told you have an urgent delivery needing a courier service. I'm from Global Deliv—"

"I can read," Ansah said. "Sorry, but you must have the wrong information."

But he was lingering, Jojo could tell. "Please, maybe your assistant put it somewhere and didn't inform you?" he suggested.

"Um . . . okay, come in. I'll check, but I don't think so."

Ansah looked behind his assistant's desk in the workspace before his office. "I don't see anything. Look, call your people to find out what the problem is, but I have work to do."

"What about this?" Jojo said, moving to a small box in a corner of the room.

"That's nothing—"

Jojo stepped back, losing his balance and falling against Ansah, who instinctively reached out so that he caught Jojo in his arms.

"Are you okay?"

Jojo turned and pressed against him. "Please—"

"Hey, *hey*! What are you doing?"

"Please, sir, let me worship you; I dream of you every night. I purposely asked the company if I could do the pickup so I could see you."

"What?" Ansah said, backing away. "No, what the hell are you saying? What do you mean you dream about me?"

"Yes please. Every night, I see you with me in my dreams."

"Hold on one second," Ansah whispered, trotting to the door to ensure it was locked. He returned. "Look, what's your name?"

"Cedrick, sir. Please, can I be with you? Most Honorable Peter Ansah."

Jojo's arms went around his ample waist, and the minister did nothing to stop him.

Ansah cleared his throat and wiped his moist forehead with the back of his hand.

"Okay, wait," Ansah said, voice shaking. "We can't do anything here. I can take you someplace this evening where it's safe."

THE AIRBNB ANSAH had been renting outside of Accra in Kasoa was cheap and far from prying eyes. The drawback was that traffic into and out of Kasoa didn't ever flow smoothly, it crawled. So, Ansah had burned gallons of gas inching forward in his SUV, and it was almost eight o'clock at night when he and Jojo finally made it to their destination.

It was a small, no-frills, one-room residence suited to Ansah's needs. The only business he conducted here was sexual in nature. Two young men, one obviously high, were waiting in the sitting room watching soccer on the wide-screen TV. They could not have been older than nineteen or twenty. Ansah poured gin for his guests and himself before lounging on the bed. Jojo accepted the glass, but didn't take a sip.

Ansah dwarfed the two young men. They sat on either

side of him and began foreplay. Sitting at the foot of the bed with his back to them, Jojo called Ansah's number,

"Wait," Ansah said, sitting up. "Let me answer this. Hello? *Hello!* Who is this?" No reply. Ansah carelessly tossed his phone onto the bed. Jojo scooped it up before it locked and went straight to the bathroom to pull up Ansah's WhatsApp chats. The content on Ansah's device shocked even Jojo, who was fairly desensitized: images of teenage boys of all shapes, colors, and sizes and graphic videos of "father-son" sex. Looking down, Jojo was capturing all the data with his spy camera.

"Ei, Cedrick!" Ansah called from the sitting room. "Where are you?"

"Please, I'm coming."

Jojo scrolled hurriedly through the chats. His thumb stopped at one name, and so did his heart. *Marcelo.*

Tues May 16

Marcelo Tetteh
Hi
8:32 PM

Peter Ansah
Who is this?
9:01 PM

Marcelo Tetteh
You know me well.
9:01 PM

Peter Ansah
I thought so. The gay activist?
9:02 PM

Marcelo Tetteh
Correct
9:03 PM

Peter Ansah
How did you get my cell nbr?
9:03 PM

Marcelo Tetteh
We have our own intel
9:04 PM

Peter Ansah
What do you want from me?
9:07 PM

Marcelo Tetteh
You must withdraw the anti-gay bill from
consideration.
9:08 PM

Peter Ansah
You know I'll never do that
9:10 PM

Marcelo Tetteh
What about if I told you I have an online leak
of you having sex with a young guy
9:12 PM

Peter Ansah
Ur bluffing
9:15 PM

Marcelo Tetteh
Am I? Then look at this
9:25 PM

A video followed, not the clearest, but adequate to show Ansah, unmistakable in size, having sexual intercourse with a boy of about sixteen.

Marcelo Tetteh
Satisfied?
9:27 PM

Peter Ansah
I'll pay you for your silence
9:30 PM

Marcelo Tetteh
**I don't want
your money. I want you to
squash the bill**
9:34 PM

Peter Ansah
**Let me talk to my colleagues,
ok? maybe we can dilute it**
9:35 PM

Marcelo Tetteh
**No, stop it completely
from coming to a vote**
9:35 PM

Peter Ansah
IT'S NOT AS EASY AS THAT
9:37 PM

Marcelo Tetteh
Easier than seeing this sex
video on social media
9:38 PM

Peter Ansah
You're dogshit.
I could have you killed.
9:40 PM

Marcelo Tetteh
Are you going to stop the bill or not?
10:02 PM

Peter Ansah
I'll get back. Meanwhile,
don't do anything stupid
10:04 PM

That was the last conversation, and only three days before Marcelo's murder. There it was in black and white: *I could have you killed.* He could have contracted the Adamah brothers.

Jojo looked for Adjei or Addo in the chats but found neither. That didn't rule his idea out, however. Jojo thought he had enough material and emerged from the bathroom with the minister's phone in his pocket and a mixture of fury and disgust.

Naked, Ansah was sitting up in bed casting around while his boys fawned over him.

"Where's my phone?" he said wildly. "Who has my phone?" He shot Jojo an accusatory look. "Did you take it with you to the bathroom?"

"No," Jojo said, ducking below the foot of the bed and pretending to retrieve the device from the floor. "Here it is. It fell down."

Still suspicious, Ansah snatched it from Jojo. "Who are you?" he asked coldly.

"I told you. Cedrick."

Ansah threw off the boys and began scrambling off the bed. "Did someone send you? Are you a spy from Marcelo's people?"

"No, sir," Jojo said.

"You better tell me!" Ansah shouted, leaping off the bed with surprising agility. He rushed to the closet in the corner, removed a large, serrated-edge knife, turned, and charged at Jojo like a bull.

CHAPTER THIRTY-EIGHT

IN THE MORNING, EMMA arrived at the agency to find Gideon in his small electronics room with circuit boards and other pieces of the two battered phones strewn across the workspace.

"How's it going?" Emma asked, poking her head in. "You're early."

"Morning." Gideon stood up for a good stretch. "I wanted a head start. The devices are truly wrecked. I left at almost midnight yesterday and returned at five this morning."

"Ao!" Emma said sympathetically. "You must be exhausted. How much longer do you think it will take?"

"I've got the UFS chip out of both the phones and cleaned them up, and the JTAG has detected the first one and it's reading that now. The data is coming in, as you can see on the computer screen, and hopefully it will be complete and not corrupted. It might be at least another four hours before I can start on the other one."

"Sounds good," Emma said dryly. "I have no idea what you just said, but I take your word."

"Do you want me to explain it?"

Emma chuckled. "No, thank you. Just carry on."

She checked emails. The boss wouldn't be in today, and since that meant no morning briefing, she texted Jojo to ask if he had infiltrated Peter Ansah's circle yet or when he planned to.

Emma's phone rang. "Madam Gertrude? Good morning!"

"Ruby, we're holding an impromptu gathering this morning to honor Kwabena and we'd like you to attend if you can."

"But of course I will," Emma said.

"Thank you. We'll begin in a couple of hours."

EMMA WAS ON her way to the ICF Center when Dr. Jauregui called. "The material on the machete blade is all rust," she said. "I took it to the Forensics Lab myself and watched them test it. No blood."

"Thanks for getting that done so quickly, Doctor," Emma said.

"Hope it helps. I'm afraid the news on the bloody pebbles isn't as good. Accra's DNA analyzer is down, so they're sending the material to the University of Cape Coast, which is backed up. So, it will be a while."

Emma heaved a frustrated sigh. The delays never ended. She reflected how earth-shaking it would have been if Marcelo's blood had been on that blade. It was *never* that easy.

EVERYONE AT THE ICF was in a somber mood, especially George Mason in particular. His friend Kwabena was gone in the most awful way. So was Paloma, whose story carried a double shock.

Christopher knew that one of the ways to recover from a shock was to talk it out. With refreshments to lighten the mood, Gerty, Diana, George, Emma, and Kwabena's friends and mentees spoke about happy times with Kwabena.

Emma joined Gertrude and George, who were deep in conversation.

"How are you feeling today, Ruby?" Gerty asked.

"I can't get the picture of Paloma and Kwabena out of my head," Emma said.

"I can understand. I'm so sorry you went through that."

George, who had glanced at his phone screen, suddenly drew in his breath. "Oh, no."

"What's wrong?" Gertrude asked.

"There's a video going around," he said, gaping. "It's Minister Peter Ansah."

"What is it?" Emma asked.

Next, Gertrude received the viral video and watched it with growing revulsion. "It's fake," she pronounced, putting her phone away without completing the entire sequence. "I'm not watching that filth."

"What's going on?" Emma asked George.

"I'm even embarrassed to show you," George said, looking shattered.

"Come on, now," Emma said. "Let me see."

He handed her his phone. "Ten thousand views already."

Emma was horrified as she watched Ansah in bed with males barely out of their teens. But it was the final segment of the dramatic video that panicked her. She knew Jojo had planned to use his spy camera to film. If so, it meant Ansah lunged at him with a knife. Was Jojo okay? Could he have been wounded in the attack?

Christopher approached from the other side of the room in shock. "Gerty?"

"I've seen it, Chris," she said. "I wish I hadn't."

"Not Peter," he whispered. "This is inconceivable."

"It's not real," Gertrude insisted. "They can manipulate any images now with AI."

"I hope that's true," Christopher said, looking doubtful nevertheless.

Emma was about to call to check on Jojo when she got a notification that another video had surfaced. It was yet another with Peter Ansah having sex with boys significantly underage. The picture quality wasn't as good as the first, but Ansah's distinctive appearance made it all but impossible to dispute his presence in the graphic scenes. Gertrude's claim now seemed less and less likely.

A new shock wave, even greater than the first, traveled through the room. Dazed, Christopher stood staring out of the window with Diana at his side.

Emma slipped away to the hallway along the Cortlands' offices. As Jojo's number rang, Emma's anxiety grew.

"Jojo?"

"Hey, Emma. Did you see the posted videos? *Viral!*"

"But are you okay? He was coming after you with a knife!"

"Yes, but I was too quick. I got out as he tried to knife me. It hit the door instead."

"I was worried sick." The tension in Emma's body dissipated, leaving her relieved but shaky.

"God bless you. We'll talk soon, okay?"

Emma began her return to the gathering but stopped halfway. She had gone through JB Timothy's papers and discovered a connection with Gertrude. Perhaps this was Emma's chance to go further along that track. With a glance down the hallway to ensure the coast was clear, she quietly tried the door. It opened.

Nervous about being caught, Emma went through the desk drawers, which still smelled of new wood. They were all practically empty except for office supplies.

Emma woke up the desktop Mac but it had switched to its screensaver and was password-protected. She went to a wood cabinet across the room and opened the uppermost drawer, which was empty except for a throwaway phone. In the second a folder labeled *LGBTQ* held articles about the homosexuals' threat to proper family life, reviews of different kinds of conversion therapy, and an article written by

Christopher Cortland called "God's Answer to the Plague Destroying Families."

And then, she saw something that momentarily took her breath away: multiple printed articles about Marcelo Tetteh, Henrietta Blay, and Dr. Newlove Mamattah. The first two were dead. The third, the doctor, was still alive. Was he next on someone's list, *Gertrude's* list?

The office door opened. Emma jumped.

George stood in the doorway staring at her. "What are you doing in here?"

Emma crouched on the floor, looking underneath the cabinet. "I've lost my necklace. I was in here with Madam Gertrude, so maybe it slipped off somewhere. I don't see it, though."

George frowned suspiciously. "I've been with Madam Gertrude all morning."

"No, not today," Emma said lightly. "It was on Wednesday. You know, at the opening."

George didn't appear convinced. "You should ask permission before entering anyone's office."

"You're right," Emma conceded. "Sorry about that, please. I didn't want to bother Madam Gertrude, that's all. Anyway, I'm leaving now."

But George didn't allow her to. "Wait a minute, Ruby."

Emma's heart sank. "Yes?"

"Before Kwabena died, he told me Mr. Cortland had some concerns that you've been asking questions. Like you're snooping around."

"Just natural curiosity," Emma said. "That's all."

George's demeanor was turning hostile. "Is Ruby Mensah your real name?"

"Of course. Why wouldn't it be?"

He narrowed his eyes. "You know what? Stay here a moment. I'll be right back. Don't move."

He shut the door and left. Emma opened it again quietly and watched George disappear down the hallway. She exited quickly in the opposite direction toward the washroom, her first impulse being to hide in the ladies'. But that wasn't good enough. She had to get out of there completely. She made a left, picking up the pace. The corridor came to a dead end. *Shit.*

She heard George's and Christopher's voices in the hallway around the corner to the right as they approached Gertrude's office.

"I think we need to question her," George said.

Desperate, Emma turned again. There was a small alcove off the corridor with an emergency exit. How had she missed it? She moved quickly, pushing open the door to burst into the sunshine. She continued at a steady trot and reached a rocky decline to a lower roadway. Before descending, Emma glanced behind her. From the open emergency exit, Christopher and George were watching her recede into the distance.

In the wrong kind of shoes, she slid down ungracefully to the road and booked an Uber at the same time Courage texted her hello. The next message was from Festus that Ego's would no longer need Emma's services. With that, her tussle with Boateng, and now her brush with George, she felt distinctly unpopular. *At least Courage still loves me*, she thought to her surprise as she piled into the Uber. Maybe it was time to return his love.

CHAPTER THIRTY-NINE

Hopes that the extracted phone data would be available by Friday's end didn't materialize. Reading the memory files had taken longer than even Gideon had expected, and a software glitch developed that further delayed the process. He and Emma decided to go into work the next day to make up for lost time.

Emma slept poorly and was glad when 5 A.M. arrived. She was eager to get to the agency. By the time she arrived, Gideon was already there.

"I've got good news and bad," he told her. "The good is that data from the first phone is complete, and I'm putting it on pen drives for you and Manu and the boss. The bad is that I couldn't get anything off the second one."

"I'm grateful either way," Emma said.

While she watched Gideon work, she related him her ICF adventures.

"Wow," he said at the end. "Emma, I don't think it's safe to go back there."

"I know," she conceded. "My undercover work isn't going well at all, and I feel like the investigation is falling apart."

"Why do you say that?"

She shrugged. "We have no answers, Gideon. All we have are questions, and at each turn, there's more of them."

"I know it may not look good right now," Gideon said, "but a break will come soon. You watch."

An hour later, he handed a pen drive to Emma. "The data's from Kwabena's phone," he told her.

She had just plugged in the drive when Manu came in.

"What are you doing here?" Emma said in surprise.

He smiled broadly. Dressed in casual clothes, Manu seemed more approachable. "I thought since you said you and Gideon were coming in," he said, pulling up a chair, "I should at least support you."

"That's very good of you, Manu," Emma said. "I appreciate that."

Gideon came out of his workroom. "*Ei!*" he said in mock astonishment. "The great Walter Manu is here!"

They shook hands, ending with the sharpest of terminal finger-thumb snaps.

"Let's check it out, guys," Emma said. "Gideon, better that you go through it and we observe."

They sat together and Gideon pulled up the main blocks of data, targeting Kwabena's WhatsApp messages. Many were from family and friends and had no particular significance. Then there were messages from Paloma, some banal and others romantic. Finally, they spotted something curious: messages from "HQ."

"Who or what is 'HQ'?" Emma asked.

"Headquarters?" Manu suggested. "ICF Headquarters?"

"Maybe."

"Well, let's find out," Gideon said, smiling. "Let's call HQ's number."

He dialed it with his phone's speaker on. The tone rang once and shut off.

Gideon grunted. "Either the number is obsolete or the spam blocker is set to receive only wanted calls."

They examined the exchanges between Kwabena and the mysterious HQ.

Thurs May 18

HQ
Is the plan for tomorrow
evening's event proceeding?
8:34 AM

Kwabena Mamfe
Yh, it will be well
8:36 AM

HQ
Okay, good. Can you let me
know when it's over?
8:37 AM

Kwabena Mamfe
Yh, I will
8:40 AM

Fri, May 19

Kwabena Mamfe
Event was really great, went smoothly
11:53 PM

HQ
Good to know, thanks so much.
And when is the next event?
12:06 AM

Kwabena Mamfe
**Not sure, working
on the location now**
12:07 AM

HQ
**Thanks, c u tomorrow?
There's time on the schedule 430 PM**
12:10 PM

Kwabena Mamfe
Cool, c u then
12:11 PM

"What 'next event' are they're talking about?" Manu said.

"I don't know," Emma said. She snapped her fingers. "Hold on. May nineteenth was the night Marcelo was killed."

"Oh, yes," Manu said. "I forgot. But . . . I'm not sure how that matters."

"What if this is coded language?" Emma said with growing excitement. "Is 'this evening's event' a secret way of saying Marcelo's murder?"

Manu snorted. "Come on, Emma."

"It's not so outlandish, is it?" she protested.

"All right, all right," Manu said to calm her down. "Let's go on."

Sat May 20

Kwabena Mamfe
We found the locationfor event
10:07 AM

HQ

Glad to hear that. When can we do it?

10:20 AM

Kwabena

Maybe tomorrow

10:21 AM

HQ

Perfect, and what about the delivery? Will it be ready?

10:25 AM

Kwabena

The Y-Thimot Company says by Sunday 28 May

10:31 AM

"What in the world is Y-Thimot Company?" Emma asked. "And why are these messages so strange? That's why I believe they're coded."

"You google it and I'll check ChatGPT," Gideon said. After a few seconds, he read what he had found. "'I don't have any specific information on a company named Y-Thimot.' That wasn't helpful at all. What do you have, Emma?"

"The closest thing I found is Yolande Thimot," Emma said, scrolling, "who works for Haitian Centers Council."

"Doesn't seem relevant," Gideon said with a grin.

"Okay, let's leave that for a while," Manu suggested. "What else do we have?"

Between the seventeenth and thirtieth of May, no conversations between Kwabena and HQ had been stored.

Tue May 30

HQ
Things ok 4 tonight?
8:22 AM

Kwabena
**Yes, you
have time today?**
8:37 AM

HQ
**Not positive but
I'll let you know**
8:50 AM

There was another gap without messages until June.

Wed June 7

HQ
**I love the rain
Harmattan is terrible**
8:37 AM

Kwabena
**Then you'll love Mon night
Harmattan will be over**
8:39 AM

The comments about the weather, Harmattan being the dry season when a fine dust blew in from the Sahara Desert, seemed banal banter. For now, Emma didn't know what to make of it. She consulted her notebook, studying it for a while before drawing out a timeline.

Thurs May 18 —Text HQ to Kwabena re "event"
Fri May 19—Marcelo killed (night) "Event great."

Sat May 20—Text Kwabena to HQ re "location" + "event maybe Sunday 21"

Sat 20-Sun21—Abraham murdered (Dr. Jauregui's ETD)

Tue May 30—Henrietta killed
Tue May 30—Text HQ→Kwabena re "things ok?"

"It looks like a pattern, right?" Emma asked Manu.

He was more cautious. "Maybe, or just coincidence. But I have an idea. Can we find the ICF schedule of events to see if any of them coincide with the dates in the texts?"

"Like how?"

"If there were special activities on those days, it might explain their discussions—like finding a location for events and so forth."

"Got it," Emma said.

They went to the ICF website and looked at their calendar of events.

"None scheduled for the nineteenth of May," Emma said. "Nothing on the twentieth . . . nor thirtieth."

"Well, that might mean something," Manu said, "but still, we should be careful because they could have ad hoc events that weren't on the schedule."

"Or," Emma said, "all the texts are encoded."

"Let's try ChatGPT again," Gideon suggested.

After a few seconds, Chat responded.

With such limited information, it's virtually impossible to accurately decipher the meaning of "Y-Thimot Company" within these coded messages. While it could mean anything, as previously explained, without further context, we cannot narrow down the possibilities.

However, here are some general steps you might take to further your understanding:

1. Research: Try doing a web search for the term "Y-Thimot Company."
2. Context: The smallest detail could illuminate the meaning.
3. Expert Help: Consider consulting with someone with expertise in cryptography or relevant fields.
4. Associations: Try to associate "Y-Thimot Company" with ordinary words, places, or acronyms. Is Thimot a name? Does Y refer to a place or is it symbolic?

"Know any cryptographic experts?" Emma asked Gideon with a smile.

"Here in Ghana?" Gideon snorted. "I don't think so."

After a moment, Emma said, "My mother."

"What about your mother?" Manu asked.

"She's loved jigsaws since she was a kid and does word games and crossword puzzles. She's outstanding, so who knows? Maybe she can figure it out."

"Worth a try," Gideon agreed.

"I'll call her now," Emma said.

"While you do that, I'll go to the washroom," Manu said.

Akosua picked up Emma's call at once. She always did. "Hello, my dear. How are you?"

"I'm good, Mama. How's everything with you? Did you see the doctor?"

"Yes, I did. He said my blood pressure's better but still high."

"It's because you're not regular with the pills, Mama."

"I know, I know. I'll make a better effort from now on."

"Okay, good," Emma said. "Listen, Mama, because you love brainteasers and word puzzles, can I send you some text messages we're trying to decipher? We think there might be encoded language. Let me know if you see any pattern or code words."

"Of course," Akosua said, her tone brightening. "I'd love to."

Manu returned. "How's your mom?" he asked as Emma hung up.

"She's good. I sent her the texts."

Akosua's reply text came about thirty minutes later.

Mama

Does the name TIMOTHY mean anything?

10:01 AM

Emma's eyebrows shot up.

Emma

Yes but how did you know that?

10:02 AM

Mama

Rearrange the letters of Y-Thimot, you get TIMOTHY.

10:03 AM

Emma

I'm impressed

10:04 AM

Mama

And who's TIMOTHY?

10:06 AM

Emma

Pastor JB Timothy—I think

10:07 AM

Mama

Oh, that guy.
Has he done something bad?

10:09 AM

Emma

Maybe.

10:11 AM

Mama

Wouldn't surprise me. He's a fakr
fake

10:13 AM

Akosua was religious, yes, but she wasn't stupid.

Mama

Can I call you?
I prefer that

10:14 AM

Emma didn't but she said yes.

"Then, where HQ says 'delivery,'" Akosua resumed, "that could mean 'deliverance,' since we're talking about JB."

"Yes, you're right! When did you get so clever?"

"Where do you think you get your brains?"

Emma joined her mother in laughter. "Mama, anything else you see?"

"Nothing except for the word 'event,' which I'm sure you can see must be code for some act or occasion."

"Yes, we're working on that now. Thanks, Mama!"

Emma hung up. "This might be the key, thanks to Mom," she said, after telling Manu and Gideon about Akosua's insights. "I feel like HQ, whoever that is, knows JB and asked him to find assassins to take care of Henrietta for good. JB knows and/or procured the man or men—probably two men—who killed Marcelo, Abraham, and Henrietta."

Manu was nodding slowly. "I'm beginning to feel convinced, Miss Emma."

"Thank you. What do you think we should do next?" she asked, returning the compliment by looking to him for guidance.

"I think we should ask DCI Boateng to assist," Manu said. "He needs to interview JB. We've gotten as much as we can out of the pastor."

"Nice idea," Emma said. "And you know what? I think it's time we treated the DCI to some beer and *chinchinga*."

CHAPTER FORTY

EMMA WAS A BUNDLE of nerves. Her heart palpitated, causing a fluttering sensation in her chest. After Courage had texted her again to beg to see her, she relented, but she knew it wouldn't be easy. She was torn in two—still angry with Courage, albeit much less than before, but missing him. It was unsettling.

At around 7 P.M., Courage came to her door. A downpour had just begun and he was wet, if not yet soaked.

She welcomed him with a stiff, "Come in. How are you?"

"I'm good, and you?" Courage looked at her more directly than she him.

"Have a seat," she said, gesturing to the sofa. She sat to his right. "How's work?"

He shrugged. "It's there. Nothing new, really. How's your case?"

"We might be getting somewhere."

"If you need any help, I'm available. I mean . . . yeah, just in case, you know."

Emma cleared her throat. She was squirming and thought it best to get to the point. "What did you want to talk about?"

"Emma, I can't live like this anymore. I'm dying inside, baby. Life without you is so empty and worthless. I can't reverse the stupid thing I've done, but nor can I change how I feel about you. I can't eat, can't sleep. It's hell."

Emma nodded. "I see you've lost some weight."

"I miss you so bad. Are you really done with me? Please don't say that. I know I've done you wrong and I feel dirty for it. By the way, I did all the checks and I'm fine. No diseases. I can show you the result."

"Well, that must have been a relief," Emma said, but even she could tell her tone was slightly mocking.

"I've learned my lesson."

She sighed heavily, staring at the floor with her face planted between her palms.

"Is there any chance?" Courage pleaded. "Did you miss me just a little bit?"

Emma leaned back. "Actually, quite a lot."

"*Seriously?*" He was thrilled. "You don't know how much I wanted to hear that. Emma, do you really want us to be apart?"

Silently, she shook her head.

"Is there any chance I could hug you?" His voice quivered.

"A very small chance."

He rushed to Emma and knelt, putting his arms around her waist and pulling her to him. Slowly her arms went around Courage's shoulders. He let out a choked noise and she realized he had begun to cry, which set her off as well. Soon, they were both blubbering like a couple of babies. His transgressions didn't matter much anymore.

Emma was the first to recover. "My makeup is ruined because of you," she said.

"Impossible," he retorted, looking up at her with red, puffy eyes. "You don't wear any."

They began to giggle.

"You're so silly," he said.

"Takes one to know one. Come on; get up."

Holding hands, they sat on the sofa and she leaned against him.

"So," he said, "we good?"

"We good. You hungry?"

"What a question."

AFTER DINNER OF *waakye*, fish, *gari*, and fried plantain, they cuddled on the sofa and watched some news as the sound of rain on the roof intensified. The anti-LGBTQ debate was heating up with the added complication of Peter Ansah's disgrace as a closeted homosexual.

"So," Emma said, "I don't think we've ever talked about this, but how do you feel about the whole topic?"

"Homosexuality and the anti-gay bill?"

"Yes."

"Look, obviously man-to-man love isn't my style," Courage said, "but what bothers me is how these gay guys are always going after children."

Emma shook her head. "Who told you that?"

"Well . . . I mean, I just heard that."

"Not true."

Courage lifted his head. "No?"

"That's a stereotype . . . probably invented by heterosexuals."

"Oh," Courage said, surprised. "Then I feel bad for believing it."

"Never too late to become informed."

As the rain intensified, Emma sat up abruptly. "Shit, I forgot the roof leaks."

Courage followed her as she dashed to the expanding puddle of water on the bedroom floor. Emma groaned.

"I'll get the bucket," Courage said. He knew where everything was. When he returned, Emma was mopping up.

"I've asked the landlady to fix it three times already," she grumbled.

Once the puddle had been taken care of, she and Courage

moved to the bedroom, not for sex, but for cuddling, teasing, and giggling like a couple of teenagers.

"This rain is serious," Emma said, peering out of the window. "I hope there won't be floods again."

"There will be in the usual places around town with all the clogged drains. Something else the politicians could work on instead of worrying about who's gay. Idiots."

"The rain doesn't arrive at the same time as when we were kids," Emma observed. "Remember how November to end of February was the Harmattan season, and June to around end of August was the rains? Now it rains and floods in November."

"It's a wonder the Harmattan hasn't switched to June and July."

Emma frowned. "Yes." She sat up and turned to Courage with her legs folded underneath her. "Would you talk about the dry Harmattan weather in June?"

He leaned on his elbow. "How d'you mean?"

Emma found her phone and explained. "These are texts between two people in our present case. 'HQ,' says, 'I love the rain, Harmattan is terrible,' and Kwabena answers, 'Harmattan *will be* done with.' But Harmattan ended in March this year, so why are they even referencing it?"

"I don't know, baby," Courage said.

"And what does it mean, 'Then you'll love Mon night. Harmattan will be over'? The idea makes no sense."

Courage yawned. "I'm getting sleepy. Babe, it's not the idea that's wrong; it's the 'Harmattan' that's out of context."

"Ah," Emma said slowly. "So, the *word* is incorrect, yet it's significant or indicates something crucial."

"I guess so."

"Oh, God. Courage." Emma sprang out of bed, phone in hand. "Oh. God."

"What, what?"

"Harmattan is code for Mamattah, Dr. Mamattah," Emma said. "The middle part of both words is 'matta' and they both have three syllables. The Monday they say Harmattan will be over is tonight. Get dressed. We have to move fast."

AT ALMOST 9 P.M., Courage, with Emma behind him on his motorbike, pulled up in front of Dr. Mamattah's house after a treacherous ride through Accra's slick, dark, flooded streets. Two lamps dimly illuminated the entrance, where a bored security guard sat huddled underneath a flimsy tarp.

"Good evening," Emma greeted him. "Please, is the doctor home?"

"Not yet please. Who are you?"

"A friend. My name is Emma and this is Courage. I've been trying to call him but there was no reply."

"Sometimes, he stays late at the office," the guard said, "so maybe he's there now, I don't know."

SOAKED BY THE downpour, Emma and Courage dismounted at the clinic entrance, a high cast-iron gate and a brass plate etched with the address *One Mamattah Place*. Emma wondered where the security guard was. This type of high-target business wouldn't normally be unguarded.

The gate was ajar, and through the space below and around it streamed a strong current of flood water. Courage cautiously poked his head in while Emma beamed her flashlight. The shadows of flowering shrubs filled the courtyard beyond. Emma slipped in sideways without touching the gate, signaling to Courage to stay put. The courtyard was sodden and muddy. Lights were on in two of the building's windows, but curtains obstructed the view inside.

Emma jumped and turned toward a movement she detected in her peripheral vision. Bound and gagged on the ground at the other side of the courtyard, a man struggled to break free. Emma approached cautiously, switched on her flashlight, and discovered the security guard she had wondered about. Blood streamed from the side of his head across his face. As Emma knelt to free him, she heard another sound and whipped around. Emerging through a door were two men, Dr. Mamattah in the front holding his hands up and a masked man behind him shoving him forward with the tip of a machete. Emma shrank behind a jasmine bush.

"Kneel there," the masked man ordered the doctor as they got to the middle of the yard.

Mamattah obeyed, his hands still up.

"Put your hands behind your back and bow your head."

Holding the machete at chest level, the masked man stood beside Mamattah. "Why do you help these gay people? Don't you know they're an abomination in the sight of God? Because you support them, that makes you an abomination too, and you should die the same way as them. The same way Marcelo, Abraham, and Henrietta died. Tonight, you will see your own blood as I leave you bleeding to death." Preparing to strike, the masked man raised the machete high.

"*Hey!*" Emma yelled.

The man whirled around at her voice. In that instant, the doctor saw his chance and leaped up to wrestle the machete away. The machete clattered to the ground as Mamattah fell with it. The masked man took off running to the rear entrance of the courtyard. Emma followed, but he had a long head start.

"Stop!" she shouted. "*Stop!*"

"Halt!" a male voice rang out above the stormy din.

Courage, illuminated by the streetlight, stood in the man's path with his rifle raised. The fleeing man tried to change direction. But Courage was advancing with his rifle tracking every move. The man dropped to his knees with hands up.

"Lie down," Courage ordered as he approached with his rifle still up. "Put your hands in front of you where I can see them."

He checked his pockets for weapons but found only a phone. "Who are you?"

Courage brought the man's arms behind him one after the other and zip-tied his wrists, before rolling him on his back. He was soaked through, including his black mask. Emma shined her flashlight and snatched the mask off. George blinked at her in the beam.

"I should have known," Emma said.

DURING THE TUSSLE with George, Dr. Mamattah sustained a machete laceration to his left forearm. While Courage guarded George in one of the clinic's treatment rooms and waited for a police vehicle to arrive, Emma helped Mamattah dress his own wound in the surgical suite next door.

"Thank you for saving me," he said to Emma sincerely as he began to bandage his arm. "I've no idea how you predicted this was to happen, but I'm grateful."

"I'm glad we got to you before it was too late, but Doc, I should have figured it out much earlier and spared you this trouble."

"Ah, but you deny yourself the credit you deserve, young lady," Mamattah said with a smile. "Let me get some clean, dry clothes for you to change into."

"That's okay, Dr. Mamattah. I'm good."

"No, I insist," he said, walking to a standing glass cabinet to get a pair of scrubs. "Here you are."

He left her alone to change and she joined Courage minutes later as he stood guard over the captive. George was seated on the floor with his head bowed.

"How are you feeling?" Emma asked, sitting on the examination table.

George shook his head and didn't respond.

"Why, George, *why* did you do this?"

Again, no response.

"It's been you and Kwabena all along, hasn't it? Together, you killed Marcelo, Abraham, and Henrietta."

"No," George whispered.

After signaling Emma to wait, Courage addressed George. "You don't have to say anything, but if you do, it could be used against you in court."

George began to shiver.

"Hold on a minute," Emma said, leaving the room to go next door, where Dr. Mamattah was on the phone.

"Hold on," he said into it, then looked up at Emma. "Everything okay?"

"Can I borrow some more scrubs?"

"Of course. Help yourself."

Emma returned to George with a scrub top. "I can see you're cold. Courage, can you release his wrists?"

He did that, enabling George to take off his wet shirt and replace it.

"Thank you," he said quietly, which intrigued Emma. George the murderer remained a gentleman.

"I knew you were a spy," he added resentfully. "Like, I should have locked you in Madam Gertrude's office on Friday."

"But we can be on the same side, now," Emma said. "I know someone directed you to kill Marcelo, Abraham, and Henrietta. I don't believe you and Kwabena acted alone. You aren't like that, I can tell. Someone manipulated you."

George avoided Emma's gaze.

"If you cooperate with us by sharing information," Courage said, "we can help you obtain leniency at trial."

As George fidgeted uncomfortably, Emma could see he was weighing his options, so she pressed him. "Things aren't looking good for you right now. Once Courage releases you to the police, they'll charge you alone with all the murders. The sentence is severe."

"Who was it, George?" Courage said. "Who made you do this?"

"I don't know," he said softly. "That's the truth."

"Look at these messages between Kwabena and HQ," Emma said, showing her phone screen to George. "Who is HQ?"

"I don't know."

"Come on, George," Emma said.

"It's true." He raised his head. "HQ sent us all the orders, but only to Kwabena, and he refused to reveal who it was. He was protecting them."

"Ah," Emma said. The jigsaw puzzle was beginning to come together. "You know, it would favor you to expose HQ."

George hesitated before nodding. "Yes."

"You can help us do that right now."

George's mood lightened and he looked up, interested. "What do you want me to do?"

"Courage, give me George's phone, please."

Emma wrote a message and sent it via Facebook.

Hello, it's George Mason, pls that girl Ruby who joined ICF ambassadors is really a private investigator spying on us, her real name is Emma, and she knows what's been going on because she has Kwabena's phone that he left behind at Paloma's house when he killed himself and pls hurry and get the phone from her because everything is on it—who you are, and what we've been doing. I have to get out of Accra tonight. Pls go to Emma's house rn before she goes to the police, I'll send her coordinates

THE RAIN HAD let up only barely by midnight as Emma waited in the darkness of her bedroom. She heard the front door open and faint footsteps approaching from the sitting room. A silhouetted, hooded figure crept into the bedroom, stepping silently up to the bed, where the blankets covered a human form. The intruder drew a long knife, lifted it high, and stabbed twice, grunting with the effort. Emma switched on the overhead light. Staggering back with a gasp, the invader whirled around and dropped the knife.

Emma emerged from behind the door. "Hello, Diana Cortland," she said. "I've been expecting you."

CHAPTER FORTY-ONE

Chest heaving from exertion and shock, the assailant gawped through the holes in the crudely made ski mask. "I'm not Diana," came a woman's voice.

"Yes, you are," Emma said. "Take the mask off."

She hesitated and then obeyed, but she also retrieved the knife from the floor. Her blond hair was tangled and wet, making it appear darker. Emma had never seen Diana makeup-free, and she seemed quite ordinary compared to her public presentation.

"You have a beautiful Facebook page," Emma said with a slight smile. "That's where I used George's phone to send you tonight's message."

Diana's expression turned bitter. "That spineless piece of shit came to you and spilled the beans, didn't he?"

"No. We caught George red-handed about to murder Dr. Mamattah."

"How did you know he was going to do that?"

"You revealed it in your text to Kwabena. 'You'll love Monday night, Harmattan will be over.' You couldn't come up with a better code word than 'Harmattan?' But 'HQ' was good; I'll give you that. Initially, we thought it was for 'headquarters,' but after following your online trail—Facebook, Wikipedia, and all that—for the second, third, and fourth times, it hit me."

Diana seemed intrigued. "What made you keep going back to read about me?"

"You recall when I brought the news of Paloma's and Kwabena's death? You reacted strongly and oddly against the fact that Paloma was trans, while depicting Kwabena as betrayed. It seemed unlike the Diana I'd so far known. Yes, you attempted to walk it back by apologizing for speaking ill of her, but what you said had already made an impression. Why had you gone on a tirade against Paloma? There could have been two reasons: either you hated her for being trans, or you were jealous of her as Kwabena's girlfriend, or both.

"Had I missed something? I returned to the HQ texts to Kwabena, and it finally clicked. Messages like 'Do you have time today?' could be code for sexual liaisons. Yet, the 'HQ' still threw me off. What did it mean? So, back to your Facebook again, and, finally, there it was: Homecoming Queen. Bishop Patterson High School, Columbus, Ohio."

Diana tried to scoff in contempt, but Emma could see she was becoming anxious and agitated. Her eyes circled the room and stopped at the bedside table where Emma's phone sat. Diana picked it up and examined it. "Are you recording this on your phone?"

Emma shook her head. "No, but you might have noticed a pair of glasses on the table behind me. It has a spy camera that has filmed everything up till this point."

"It's not going to matter," Diana said, beginning to move closer with the knife raised, "because you won't get out of here alive. I'll slit you from throat to belly, and at seven this morning I'll be on a Delta flight home. By the time they find your dead body, I'll be safely back in the States."

In turn, Emma moved closer to the door for her escape.

Swiftly, Diana lunged toward Emma with the knife ready to strike. But Emma was quick too—out of the room with a sharp turn to the left within seconds. Diana followed, screaming, but she halted and froze as Courage stepped in her path from the right with his rifle aimed dead center at her chest.

"Stand still, drop the knife, and follow my instructions. I'm a sniper and I won't miss."

Diana's face fell. The game was up.

BEFORE DAWN, EMMA, Courage, and Boateng watched Christopher and Gertrude Cortland march into the CID charge room looking very angry. Christopher began to shout in fury at the charge officer.

"Where is my wife?" he demanded. "What the *fuck* do you think you're doing arresting her under false pretenses?"

Boateng approached. "Sir?"

Christopher whirled around. "And who are *you?* Are you part of this charade?" He caught sight of Emma. "*You!* You bitch . . ."

He launched himself at Emma, but reversed his course as he met Courage with a palm outstretched, pressed to his chest.

"Chris," Gertrude said quietly but sharply from behind him, "knock it off."

He shut up and stood in place, wretched and breathless.

"May we speak to Diana Cortland?" Gertrude asked Boateng, firmly avoiding Emma's gaze.

"You may say hello and ask of her welfare," Boateng said, "but you can't discuss the allegations."

Boateng signaled to the commanding officer, who ordered a female jailer to bring Mrs. Cortland out.

Emma had already spotted Diana, a pale face standing out against the black skin of the other prisoners. Her makeup long washed off by the rain, she appeared bland, even dazed, as she approached the desk. Christopher broke down. Though Gertrude had turned pale, she kept her composure.

"Honey," Christopher cried out tearfully, "what happened? What did they do to you?"

Boateng shook his head and wagged a scolding finger. "No chat like that."

"I'm fine, Chris," Diana said calmly. "Hi, Gerty."

Her serene tone sent a shiver through Emma.

"We'll bail you out, sweetie," Gertrude said. "Don't worry your little head."

"It's because of you and my husband that I'm here," Diana said with cold clarity.

Emma's ears pricked up and she exchanged a curious glance with Courage.

"What?" Gertrude said, startled.

"Wait, what are you saying, honey?" Christopher stammered.

"I'm the stupid one, huh?" Diana said to him icily. "I'm the one who can't get things done, right? You can slap me around and rape me because you think I'm a dumb blond with no ideas, no initiative. Well, look how ineffectual you and Gerty really are. Speeches, speeches, speeches. You think that makes any damn difference to these Ghanaians?" She swept her hand in a wide arc over the staff and prisoners, who had now gone silent.

"Ghanaians aren't listening to any of your bullshit, Christopher," Diana continued. "Words mean nothing around here. The only thing that matters is *action*. That's what Africans understand. You and Gertrude think you're the wise guys, but you haven't done anything that useful. What you've been able to achieve is nothing compared to what *I've* gotten done. I've had three of these LGBTQ sinners murdered. I masterminded every detail, including using a dating app to lure Marcelo to the Trade Fair Site and Abraham to a deserted spot in Weija." She tossed a filthy look Emma's way.

"Jesus, Diana," Gertrude whispered, but her brother was speechless.

"Oh, you poor siblings"—Diana taunted—"abused by your bisexual piece of shit dad—"

"Stop, Diana, stop," Christopher pleaded. "Don't say anything now. Wait for the lawyer—"

"I'd planned to wait till we got back the States before I told you everything I'd achieved," Diana said. "You might sit at the helm of the ICF, but it's me who commanded George and Kwabena to actually *do* something. Three of these LGBT are gone, so, even if the anti-gay bill doesn't pass, I've made my mark. So now you see who you were dealing with. Oh, sure, I played dumb, but all this time I was working behind the scenes." She gave a short laugh. "You look shocked, as you should, but all I regret is this liar getting ahold of Kwabena's phone. Otherwise I would have been in the clear."

"Are you done, madam?" the commanding officer asked, "because we are ready to charge you."

THE TRIO, EMMA, Courage, and Boateng, sat in the unenclosed waiting area on the ground floor of the Ghana Police Headquarters and watched the dawn creep in.

"There's one thing I still don't understand," Boateng said to Emma. "How did Kwabena and George know where Abraham had run to?"

"When Manu and I went to Ego's," Emma said, "Festus mentioned a relative had called to ask about Abraham. It was George or Kwabena faking it."

"Aha," Boateng said. "Makes sense."

"Besides justice," Courage said thoughtfully, "what good can we hope to come out of this?"

Emma released a deep sigh. "I'm not sure. It depends whether we learn to love one another."

CHAPTER FORTY-TWO

"So," Akosua said on the phone, "how did your case go?"

"It went well, Mama. Thank you for helping out. It was the first break in the clouds that let in a ray of sunshine."

"Thank you, dear. I'm so happy to have been of help. How's Courage?"

"He's fine, thanks. He's actually right here, and he wants to say hello."

Emma handed the phone to him, and he turned into a kid, answering Akosua's questions with a soft, "Yes please, madam," or "No please, madam." It was extraordinary to watch.

The conversation over, Emma snuggled back against Courage. "You don't work this weekend, do you?"

"No, love. I took the weekend off to be with you."

"Good boy."

Courage picked up his head. "I was expecting something a little bit more along the lines of gratitude."

Emma snorted, and then Courage did the same, and they laughed. All was back to normal, and the world was good.

Emma held a get-together that afternoon for Jojo and his roommates, Ofori, and friends. With appetizers, drinks, music in the background, and jokes and laughter rippling through the room, it was a happy time, even if only temporary. Courage, serving up drinks, made it a safe place because an attempted police raid would never succeed as long as he was there. Emma smiled at him, and he smiled back with a wink and a thumbs-up.

GLOSSARY

Abeg (ah-BEG): please (from "I beg.")

Agoo (ah-goh): requesting permission to enter, e.g., a home

Akpeteshie (ahk-PEH-teh-shee): strong, locally produced alcohol

Ashawo (ah-sha-WOH): sex worker, prostitute

Awurade (eh-woo-rah-DAY): God, usually exclamation (Twi)

Batakari (ba-tah-ka-REE): smock originating in Northern Ghana and other areas of West Africa

Bola (BO-lah): trash

Chaley (cha-LAY): bro, dude, pal, buddy

Chinchinga (chih-cheeng-GAH): Ghanaian shish kebab

Cedi (SEE-dee): Ghanaian monetary unit

Ei (Ay): exclamation of surprise or alarm

Ete sen? (eh-tay-SEN): how are you? (Twi)

Fufu (foo-FOO): soft, glutinous food item made from pounding starchy foods such as yam, plantain, or cassava, typically eaten with palm nut and other soups

Gari (ga-REE): granular flour of varying texture made from cassava roots

Kenkey (keng-kay): fermented corn wrapped in a ball with dried corn leaves

Kojo besia (koh-JOH bay-see-ah): gay man considered effeminate by observers (derogatory)

Kontomire (kone-toe-m'RAY): stew made from cocoyam leaves

Kwasea (kwa-see-AH): fool, idiot (insult)

Mantse (man-cheh): chief or king

Mi fie (mee fee-ay): my house (Twi)

Nyass (nee-YASS): variation of "ass"

Oburoni (oh-boo-roe-NEE): foreigner or white person

otsiame (oh-chee-AH-me): chief's spokesperson

Paddy (pa-DEE): friend

Tro-tro (traw-traw): mass-transit minivans common in Ghana and throughout Africa

Trumu trumu (troo-MOO): gay man (derogatory)

Waakye (wah-chay): rice and red beans (or black-eyed peas) cooked with millet leaves

Wahala (wa-HA-la): trouble

ACKNOWLEDGMENTS

I WANT TO EXPRESS my sincere thanks to all who have contributed to the creation of *The Whitewashed Tombs*. Soho Press has always been incredibly supportive throughout my writing process, and I'm grateful for their commitment. Their dedication to diverse and meaningful stories is genuinely appreciated.

As always, I am eternally grateful to Rachel Kowal, my editor, whose expertise and guidance have been invaluable. Her insights significantly improved this manuscript, and I'm thankful for her patience and support. In that vein, thank you to the freelance copyeditors and proofreaders for their careful work and attention to detail. Your efforts have been essential in refining this book, and I appreciate your hard work. An author isn't much without their editors.

Special thanks go to Yahya Azure and Solomon Mensah, private detectives in Ghana whose knowledge and insights have added a layer of authenticity to the story. Your contributions have been invaluable, and I thank you for your input.

Your support and hard work have been indispensable to everyone involved in this project. Thank you for helping bring *The Whitewashed Tombs* to readers.